It's two a.m., ten below zero, one hundred yards on the wrong side of the Iron Curtain.

"Move!" I screamed.

The silence had gone now. The night was raucous with panic. A brassy bell jangled. An electric hooter yowled. Suddenly it was the brightest, noisiest place on earth.

Yokel and I slid down the tank trap and threw the girl up to the top. Kit grabbed her and as we scrabbled up the sheer side of the pit, he was leaping ahead of her through the minefield.

Footsteps clattered. The door at the back of the tower opened. Two soldiers, their thick grey jackets unfastened, ran out with rifles in their hands. By now Kit was safely in the wood with the girl and we weren't far behind when I saw a third German coming straight at us . . .

ABOUT THE AUTHOR

Colin Dunne has been a journalist in Fleet Street for the past fifteen years. He has written regularly for national newspapers and magazines. His first novel, *The Landsbird*, was a finalist for the Yorkshire Post Prize.

RETRIEVAL

Colin Dunne

BANTAM BOOKS
TORONTO · NEW YORK · LONDON · SYDNEY · AUCKLAND

RETRIEVAL
A Bantam Book

PRINTING HISTORY
First published in England in 1984 by
Martin Secker & Warburg Limited
Bantam edition / July 1985

ISBN 0-553-25074-4

Published simultaneously in the United States and Canada

Bantam Books are published by Bantam Books, Inc. Its trade-
mark, consisting of the words "Bantam Books" and the por-
trayal of a rooster, is Registered in U.S. Patent and Trademark
Office and in other countries. Marca Registrada. Bantam
Books, Inc., 666 Fifth Avenue, New York, New York 10103.

PRINTED IN THE UNITED STATES OF AMERICA

O   0 9 8 7 6 5 4 3 2 1

To Sarah, Becky, and Matthew

1

One thing about Kit—you need never be stuck for any time-passing conversation with him. All you had to do was push his patriotism button and he started chirping away like a red, white, and blue parakeet.

He always rose to it, even that night we were holed up in the Harz Mountains waiting to lift a girl over the border.

In the valley below, silent in the snow, we could see the concrete watchtower where we had to cross, and the three *Grenztruppen* inside.

All our last minute checks were completed and we still had half an hour to go, so I decided to set Kit up. It wasn't quite as silly as it sounds: the four of us were perfectly safe, tucked away in a small wood overlooking the border, and we needed something to keep us alert.

So I asked him what he was looking forward to most of all back home.

He surprised me. I'd half-expected him to say the Duchess of Bigbum's ball, or salmon fishing in the upper reaches of the Teachers. Instead, he nominated showing little Luke how to play rugby.

"God, not the playing field," I said, trying to fire him up.

"Not necessarily," he said. "I thought one of those cheerful little clubs down in Sussex where all the old hands show the kids the ropes on a Sunday morning. Maybe near the Downs."

As he said Downs, I could've sworn his voice trembled. On the other hand, things do tremble a bit when it's ten below freezing.

1

RETRIEVAL

By way of widening the debate, I asked Yokel what he was fighting for, too. Good old Yokel. He went straight for the abstract noun without a second's embarrassment.

"Freedom," he hissed, "the freedom of old England. Best bloomin' place around. I love her, I do. Die for her any day."

(He did, too, although maybe not the way he would have hoped.)

And me? I couldn't match Yokel's Wiltshire innocence or Kit's twill-and-tweeds line.

"The England I fight for," I said, "is a place where a man still feels at liberty to tell a traffic warden exactly where he can put his parking tickets."

Then I asked the Chimp why he did it. He was surprised. He wasn't really one of us and wasn't often included in our talk.

But none of us could ever forget his answer. He looked up from cleaning the terrifying pump-action shotgun he'd brought along and said, "Why? Because I like killing people, I suppose."

All of it came back to me eight months later when I was refereeing a Sunday morning game and looked up and saw Kit making his way down the touchline. I could hear his walking stick smacking against his raincoat.

Mid-October, trees burning with yellows and oranges, but just enough heat left in the sun to bring the damp off the grass in wisps of moisture. The boys' breath pumped out in plumes, and with knees and faces red in the raw air, they fought with the sort of passion you lose once you know the cost.

It was exactly the sort of scene he'd had in mind that night in Germany.

"Well, was it worth fighting for?" I asked him, as he came alongside. "Come on you load of pansies, get your heads down and shove."

He knew what I meant right away. "Oh absolutely," he

2

said. That's another thing about Kit. In fifteen years I'd never once heard him answer with a simple "yes."

I was usually glad to see him at these coaching sessions because Luke always tried his hardest when he had both his uncles in attendance.

But this morning I'd had to give him instructions in the basics of natural justice, and I wasn't at all sure that Kit would go along with it.

It worked out just as I'd planned. The ball came whistling out to Luke and, about five seconds after he'd passed it on, a stocky little lad called White crashed into him, late and dirty.

They both fell. As Luke rose, he slipped so that one bony knee jabbed White a few inches south of the navel. White doubled up on the ground, howling.

"He did that deliberately, sir," he moaned.

"Nonsense," I said. "Don't be a bad sport. It was an accident."

"It wasn't sir, he—"

"Look at poor old Luke," I said. I pointed to the front of his shinbone. It was stripped pink where White had been grating his boot with every tackle. "Now, how did that happen?"

"It wasn't me. . . ."

"'Course not, White. Now, how's your tummy? Okay? Good. Watch that late tackling, won't you? Okay boys, all off for a shower. See you next week."

As they slouched off, Kit stooped to examine Luke's leg.

"I say, did he really do that?"

"Yes, he was doing it all morning and it's not fair." Pain and outrage wobbled his lower lip.

"Even so—" Kit began.

"It was my idea," I chipped in, before he could get warmed up, "and next time we'll get our retaliation in first won't we, young Luke?"

3

He was hanging on to my good arm and when he looked up and grinned he almost forgot to limp.

"Even so," Kit repeated, with emphasis, "I can't say I approve of taking the law into your own hands."

"Best place for it," I said.

"And you're supposed to be teaching them the ethics of sport," Kit protested.

"So I am. Twister White will think twice before he cheats again."

We swung Luke between us as we crossed the trampled pitch. Across the field, a herd of sheepskin was retreating into the clubhouse for booze, backslaps, and lies about old triumphs.

To the south, the mist was clearing and you could see the South Downs. They were probably in Kit's dream of England too: along with the clump of boots in the clubhouse and the dawdling boys lobbing sticks at the last, high chestnuts.

"Uncle Pete?" said Luke, hopping and swinging between us.

"Yes?"

"You knew my dad, didn't you? Or was it you, Uncle Kit?"

"Why, Luke?" I asked, sidestepping the first question.

"Nothing. Only I was wondering if he was good at rugby."

"I believe he was, wasn't he, Kit?" I passed it to him, in mild panic. I'd no idea how to handle this one.

"Absolutely. Standoff like you, Luke. Very useful chap in his day. Should have made the county side, so they say."

Then, realizing he might have gone too far, he added, "But you must check that with your mother, of course. She'll know much better than we do."

For two old warhorses—one who couldn't have kids and one who daren't—that was a tricky moment.

2

I should've known something was wrong when, within minutes, Kit broke two of his favorite rules. A great one for the rule book, was Kit.

Between us, we played at being fathers so enthusiastically that poor little Luke must have prayed for one sleepy old dad who only wanted to read the paper, instead of two frustrated old superstars forever inflicting their fantasies on him.

What usually happened after the game was that I'd ask Kit in for a drink, and he would look at his watch and politely decline. That was the rule.

"Gladly," he said this time, and, removing his cap, walked in.

At first I thought he wanted another wrestling match over Luke's education, because no sooner had we taken our drinks through to the kitchen to talk to my sister Jenny than he began to suggest prep schools again.

Jenny was tending pans among clouds of steam. "Oh dear, I hope you two aren't going to squabble again."

"Not at all," he said. "But it is time we were looking around."

"The village school's fine," I said.

Jenny groaned. Ever since we met, Kit and I had been sniping away at each other over the class barriers. She was usually in the middle, ducking the bullets.

"Let's look at the pluses," Kit said, addressing himself to her. "Public school will make him independent, teach him to stand on his own feet, and instill some of the good old virtues in him."

5

"Don't forget the minuses," I said, "like teaching him fun with whips, excessive fondness for his own gender, and that quality is something you buy, not work for. . . ."

"All that flagellation ended years ago," he snapped.

"They still don't produce their rapists' quota."

"Pete!" Jenny said.

"Anyway," I said, "we don't want the poor kid going around using slang like 'yaroo' and 'leggo.'"

Kit's features registered patient irritation with persons of limited intelligence. "I don't see that as a serious possibility," he said.

Sometimes it's so easy to annoy him that I feel ashamed. Well, nearly.

"I suppose," he said, lifting an eyebrow to signal imminent irony, "you'd like to see him educated as you were, in the university of life."

"Me? I went to the polytechnic of the gutter."

"Now boys," Jenny said, "don't fight in here. Take your drinks through to the sitting room and squabble in there, will you."

It was times like this when I suspected Kit of being Luke's father. He was caught in a loveless and childless marriage with a professional invalid—Jenny always said Diana had a real agoraphobia, like many British housewives. Kit never complained, of course. He was too much the gent to do that.

He and Jenny had what he would call "a thing" together about ten years ago. When she'd announced she was having a child just over eight years ago, I'd assumed it was Kit's.

Then one day when I'd said something about it being a shame his wife couldn't have children, he'd said it was his fault. "If fertility is a matter for blame," he said.

Now we'd both adopted Luke. And Jenny never did say who the father was.

We tacitly dropped the schools subject when we went through into the other room. We stood by the window looking down the garden where a tire swung by a rope from a tree.

"Arm okay?" he inquired, probably remembering the FFE tests where we had to shinny up ropes to test our arms.

"No problem," I said. "Not a twinge."

"Really?" He gazed at me, then shook his head. "Jenny says some days you're quite white with the pain, and that you can't move it an inch."

"So I've got a Jewish sister," I said, doing Golders Green with my hands. I nodded down to the left one. "That's moving okay, isn't it?"

I could move it, but it still had very little strength in it.

"Good," he said, without conviction. "I often think about that. Yokel could have been court-martialed, you know."

They were my two best friends. One of them had saved my life and the other wanted to court-martial him for it.

I was about to point this out to him, when, to my amazement, Kit broke the second rule.

"Do you see much of him these days?" he asked.

When we were in the regiment together, we had no secrets. Since we'd left, all three of us, we stepped carefully around the blank spots in each other's lives. The reason was that we'd all been involved, in different ways, with the Operations Unit. It was a government security agency whose existence was recorded nowhere and whose activities never happened.

And whose employees didn't have office get-togethers.

"That's a bit of a direct question for you, isn't it?" I said.

He put his glass down and pinged the top of it with his fingernail while he thought.

"I do have good reasons for asking."

"And authority?"

"Do I need authority with you, Peter?"

"No. Tell me the reasons, though."

He played some more music on the glass rim, and watched the motionless tire. Trouble clouded his pale brown eyes.

"I'm not doing this lightly. You know that. Strictly speaking, we shouldn't be having this chat. But for God's sake, Peter, we were like triplets the three of us. Surely we can trust each other, can't we?"

"Go ahead."

"Well. Right." Even then, he found it hard. "The truth is that Yokel's in trouble."

"What sort of trouble?"

"Big trouble."

"Why?"

"Talked to a newspaper. He was wanting publicity for a fish café or some such enterprise he's taken on. Gave an interview to the local rag and said things he shouldn't have said."

"Okay, so he gets a slap on the wrist. The papers are full of stuff about our old lot these days."

We'd been with a regiment that didn't do a lot of saluting, and whose idea of drill was to swing through windows in black balaclavas, shooting. We'd had a lot of cosmetic press treatment.

Kit made an exasperated noise. "You know as well as I do that all that stuff is cleared. Apparently this wasn't and there's hell to pay."

"How do you know all this?"

I was under the impression that Kit had left to work for "funnies abroad," the "educated" police. I thought he ran security for a sheikh, to show our democratic support for the inalienable right of man to have thirty-two wives and more Rolls-Royces.

"I'm still plugged in to some of the old circuits. . . ."

"He's in trouble. But he's not in danger?"

He didn't answer. He shifted his head from side to side to show his uncertainty.

8

"Look," I added. "Shall I go over and have a word with him. I haven't seen him for a while anyway."

"Why not?" Kit brightened. "He'd listen to you. I think he might have had an official call, as you might term it, but you know how stubborn old Yokel could be. He was always so bloody personal about everything—Down!"

As he screamed and dropped his glass, I'd already hit the carpet and was rolling behind the sofa.

What we'd both seen in the window was brown-and-green camouflage. It was all it took to trigger such long-tuned reflexes.

Then I heard him.

"Brrrrp, brrrrp, come on out you cowards. Brrrrp. Got you, Uncle Kit."

Slowly I hauled myself up. So did Kit. Standing there on the edge of the lawn was Luke in his boy's commando outfit—the one I'd bought him for his birthday.

"These terrorists get smaller every year," said Kit.

"Yep," I said. "You know you're getting old when the PLO start to look young."

"Come on, you lot, lunch is . . ." Jenny, in the doorway, cracked out laughing. "Don't say Luke's put the wind up the two big, tough men."

"Just testing, Jenny," Kit said. "That's all."

Over lunch, Kit just happened to mention that his old school, Wellington, was an excellent background for service life. So I just happened to mention that no nephew of mine was going to a school named after an unfashionable form of footwear.

"Might as well go to a school called Clog," I said.

Luke giggled. Kit frowned. That put me one ahead.

Afterwards, I had to go back to London. Most weekends I visited Jenny, and Kit usually came over from his home near Croydon, but my home was still a basement room in Wandsworth where the cockroaches scampered to the door to greet me. Although I hadn't tested the theory for a while now, there was just room enough to squeeze in a willing model or two.

"What's that flower, Uncle Pete?" Luke pointed to a crimson thing under the hedge, as I got in my car.

"There are only two sorts of flowers, Luke. Daffodils, and non-daffodils. That's a non-daffodil."

"You'll never make a country boy," Kit said.

I looked back at Jenny's cottage—mellow tiles sinking into a lush sea of creepers and bushes and trees. Beyond it, rounded fields dipped and rose. Everything was either green or gold. It was a restricted color scheme, but it seemed to work here.

"Oh, I like it all right," I said. "But I miss London. I like the challenge of negotiating the two-hundred-yard overland trek to the pub without being caught by bandits. Anyway, I'm working tonight."

This time he kept to the rules and didn't ask me what I was doing.

It was a typical job. I was doing a watch for the police, which meant spending a lot of time in a club called Tracy's in South London. I was keeping an eye on some thick-necked men who kept drawing money out of banks where they didn't have accounts.

I was supposed to make friends with them. That was why it was designated a high-risk job, which the police were prepared to sacrifice to me.

I blew a kiss to Jenny and shook my fist at Luke.

"Do have a word with Yokel," Kit said, through the car window. "It's rather serious. All he has to do is to say he's sorry and stay away from trouble."

"That's all any of us has to do," I said, "But we don't always manage it."

He ignored my morsel of homespun philosophy and clapped me on the shoulder. "Good man," he said. "You'll put him on the right track."

I drove back to London wondering what he meant by

"rather serious." In Kit-speak, Armageddon was only "quite serious."

There was another thing, too. Kit shouldn't know any of this if he'd quit the Unit. If he was telling the truth, that is.

And if he was, that made him the only person in our line of work who did.

Our line of work? If it was a department store, you'd go straight through Military, turn left at Espionage, and you'd find us on the right, just past Crime.

3

It wasn't the best night I ever had. The czars of the underworld, far from walking into my trap, didn't even walk into the club. They were probably having a wine-and-cheese party in the vaults of the Bank of England.

I spent two profitless hours leaning on the bar. A young man in black leather and blue eyeshadow told me in a fresh-into-Euston accent that he was so hard-up he'd do owt for a few quid: it was the way he pursed his lips over "hard-up" that made you think there might be two levels of meaning.

An old girl did an impersonation of Gracie Fields. What she didn't say was that it was an impersonation of Gracie Fields having her toenails pulled out without anesthetic. Then she took a collection, presumably for a set of false teeth.

A drunk with rubbery legs spent an hour explaining to two cheery, young blacks why they all should be sent home, then got upset when they asked him for their fares to Antigua.

All in all, an average London evening.

At closing time, I rang Tamara, a mettlesome King's Road girl who referred to sex as "jollies." She'd always been grateful to me since I said she disproved the old saying, "Tamara never comes." Occasionally she shared a hot-water bottle with me, mainly, I suspected, so she could brag to her friends that she was the only one who'd been to bed with someone who wasn't a member of Lloyds. As it happened, the person who answered her phone sounded very much like a member of Lloyds.

RETRIEVAL

So I got an Indian takeout and went home to "Squalor Towers." I played Jelly Roll Morton on the stereo and kept rerunning that bit of "Smokehouse Blues" where he cries out "Oh, Mister Jelly!"

Then I called Yokel. The moment he answered I knew Kit wasn't joking when he said it was "rather serious."

"Yes," he said. A flat, lifeless voice.

"Pete here, how's things?"

"They've told you?"

"Who and what?"

"Crumbs, Pete, don't give me that. Fifteen years in the regiment and they treat me like this."

Yokel was unique. He was the only old sweat who didn't swear and didn't drink. He drank tea and said "crumbs" and "bloomin'."

"Give you what?"

In the silence that followed, I could detect a muffled puffing sound. It took me a few seconds to realize what it was—Yokel was crying. He wasn't as tough as the Chimp, or maybe even Kit, but he was braver than either of them, and certainly more honorable. If he believed he was right, he'd take on the world without even considering the odds. And he was crying.

When he began to speak again, anger drove the sobs away.

"All I did was have a chat with the local paper. It was our last chance, this place, for me and Rosemary and the girls. She'd more or less said if this didn't work out she was off. So I thought a bit of publicity might help. A few photos of me with my souvenirs. Do you remember my souvenirs, Pete?"

Did I remember? Everyone else had booze and cigarettes and he came back loaded with native spears and decorated shields, shrunken heads and the lot.

"I remember."

"Well, I talked a bit about some of the stunts we'd been on, and I mentioned the retrieval last winter."

"Was that wise?"

"No details, naturally, no names, no places."

He was quiet again. I could hear someone shouting in the background. That would be Rosemary. I heard him say, "We can try again, sunshine," and then her Victorian villain's laugh.

"They came around. From the Unit. Well, I suppose they were, they never say, those boys, do they? You're not with them on this are you, Pete? You're not just calling to put the boot in, are you?"

"No. You know better than that."

"But you are with them. Working for them, aren't you?"

"Sort of. But not on this. You can talk to me."

"It just makes you so you can't believe in anything any more. They came round, two of them."

"Professors?"

"One professor, one chimp. They gave it to me good and hard, Pete. A lot of talking, disgrace to the regiment, dishonorable conduct, persona non grata with the rest of the lads. A bit of muscle, too. And you wouldn't believe what they done to Roly."

Roly? He had two daughters, I knew, but I couldn't think of a son. Then I remembered: Roly was his sheepdog.

"So that's what you get. Fifteen years I was a good soldier, a bloomin' good soldier, and that's what you get. Well, I'm not taking it, Pete. I'm going to find out what's at the bottom of this mess, and I don't care what it costs."

He started crying again. Twice he tried to talk, but he couldn't.

Slowly, I said, "Are you listening, Yokel? I'll come around. I'll be with you inside an hour. Okay?"

We'd called him Yokel right from the first day. He was the son of a Wiltshire farmer and through it all he remained the same.

I met him on the third day of the qualifying tests in the Black Mountains of South Wales. I was there from the

Marines and he was with some West Country regiment. So were another hundred-and-thirty volunteers when they told us to climb a bleak, rugged peak and report back inside of two hours. It meant jogging at least half the distance.

When we got back the examining officer asked how we felt. "Fine," we both said.

"Good," he replied. "Do it again."

He sent us back four times. The last time I blew up on the way down. Night had fallen, rain was blasting across, and the rucksack on my back felt like the Hammersmith Odeon. I dropped to my knees and slipped into a coma of exhaustion.

The next thing I heard was singing and whistling. I looked behind, and I could just make out Yokel coming toward me. He was rocking on his legs, but he was singing "Pack Up Your Troubles."

We'd been told it was a solo effort, without teamwork, and that was his way of giving me a nudge in the ribs. I struggled up, and fell in behind him.

When we got off the moorland and onto the road, we saw a three-tonner parked. The driver started the engine and said, "Hop up the back, boys, I'll give you a ride for the last mile."

Yokel had started to run, he was so pleased, but I soon stopped him.

"Piss off," I said, with a burst of vehemence. "We're walking every sodding step."

The country boy was better on his legs. But it took a streetwise city kid like me to see the con trick. We were among the eleven who passed the test.

The driver, a young lieutenant, knew the two of us were helping each other, but he couldn't prove it. He said later that he admired the way we bonded together under pressure. It showed character. That was why he asked to be put with us when they broke us up into groups later. The driver was Kit.

By the end, we three were closer than brothers or

lovers. We'd shared the fear you feel when you hang over the edge of the grave, and we'd shared the hope you need to pull back again. We'd all been touched by terror in our time. There was nothing in our characters the other two hadn't seen. We had, quite literally, killed for each other.

We had respect and we had love for each other, and that's more than most marriages could boast after fifteen years.

London's streets were cold canyons, shiny from the rain, and there were only a few of the night's diners and drinkers making their way home. As I drove up to Hendon, I cursed myself for not having brought some booze. Yokel wouldn't have any, of course, and it looked like a long night.

He'd seen more bodies than an undertaker, and he'd helped to make quite a few himself. I wondered what they'd had to do to him to make him cry.

4

Even in the better days of our relationship, Rosemary and I had always been highly separable. We never did light fires for each other, and time hadn't improved things.

"Oh, it's you," she said, emerging from the doorway of the shop. She was definitely this side of rapture.

"I try to deny it but no one believes me," I said, silly-smart.

The shop hadn't been hard to find. It was the only light in a road running alongside the railway and it smelt of oil and cold steam. The other shops in the row were either boarded up, or they were those shops which, because they sell nothing, try to sell everything.

Yokel's establishment bore the marks of someone else's hopes, now long dead. Still clinging to the window were the flaking remains of a picture: a patch of sea, clumsily-painted mermaids and flying fish, and the jaunty slogan, "From Neptune's Larder." It looked more like Davy Jones' Locker now.

Night after night he'd told us about the market garden he planned to open. He had the countryman's touch with plants and animals. That was what he did with his pay-off when he left the regiment, but he had no flair for bookkeeping, and Rosemary didn't rhapsodize about living in a few acres of radishes while watching the overdraft mount.

So, much as he hated cities and indoor work, he took the fish shop and small café in the hope of earning enough money to make Rosemary stick around. She said it was his

17

last chance. What everyone knew, except Yokel, was that his last chance was exactly no chance.

Even in the poor light from the window, I could see that she hadn't lost her looks. She had that sort of prettiness that comes with built-in vanity. There wasn't a room she'd left without a flick of that sheaf of brown hair and twitch of her pert behind. There was nothing about her that suggested life with a penniless squaddy.

"I'm leaving," she said.

"So I see." I nodded at the suitcase in her hand.

She threw a half-smoked cigarette up the street. It died with a fizz in the gutter.

"So you can have him back, the regiment, the Unit or whatever you call it, the whole damned lot of you."

"Thanks."

She glanced at me and the contempt came out of the other side.

"Wasted years! When I think of those wasted years . . . All that time, waiting at home, worrying, the bills and the kids to sort out. . . ."

There was a school of thought that said she'd done most of her waiting in cocktail bars, and not for long, but I let that pass.

". . . And where was he? Off in some bloody jungle or desert somewhere. All we heard was the occasional post-card for the girls, thank you very much, and then he'd come waltzing home with a stuffed alligator or something and expect us all to have the red carpet out."

She wanted to start a fight and I wasn't going to help her. "It's tough on wives," I said.

"Tough? You don't know what he's like. Or maybe you do. Maybe you know better than me. All boys together, eh? At least you got somewhere. He went in a trooper and he wasn't much more when he came out. He hasn't got a scrap of ambition in him."

She leaned forward and peered up the street. "Come

on, girls," she called over her shoulder. "The car'll be here in a minute."

"And how are the girls? They must be . . . what?"

"Fifteen and sixteen. Old enough to want better than this. But don't worry, I'm going to build a new life for them, and we shan't need him. Or this place. Neptune's Larder! Well, it's all over now."

The two girls, wrapped against the night and also carrying cases, shuffled up behind their mother. They didn't know whether to acknowledge me or not. I could see that they both had their father's sandy hair and bright blue eyes. Pretty girls, just like he'd said.

"I should've gone that last time. When you took him off to Germany or wherever it was to get that youngster. When he left the regiment he said that was it, but the first nod from you and he goes flying back."

"Perhaps he thought it was a matter of loyalty."

"Loyalty!" That enraged her again. "What about loyalty to me? Then this business now." She shuddered. "Those men. Friends of yours I suppose. They're monsters. All of you are."

One of the girls began to sob. "Tell him what they did to Roly, Mum."

"He'll see. He'll soon see for himself. Anyway, it's nothing to do with us anymore. We're off."

She leaned past me to look up the street again and I touched her on the arm to get her attention. "There's something I'd like to tell you about your husband, something you perhaps don't know."

"I'm not staying!" she snapped, fearful for a moment that her plans were threatened.

"No, no, of course not. He used to talk about you a lot, you know. He had pictures of you by the dozen. He was always handing them around—to be quite honest, we used to moan when old Yokel got his pictures of Rosemary out again. I saw them so often I can remember some of them.

RETRIEVAL

There was one with your hair up, holding a towel to your mouth, bare-shouldered."

"Well," she said. "What if there was?"

"I'm just saying, just explaining. He showed me that picture once when we were up to the waist in a Malayan river with leeches all over us. He didn't notice them, he was so busy talking about you."

"Oh, where's that car?" Rosemary muttered.

"After each job, we were offered R. and R., rest and recuperation—you know, a bit of a break, plenty of swimming and exercise. We never took it. We always drew our money and headed for the bright lights, the booze, the bar girls. He was the only one who took the clean-living holiday. Every time. I just thought you'd like to know that he was the only soldier I ever met who loved his wife so much he was faithful to her. I hope your next bloke's half as good."

She looked everywhere but my eyes. She could stand anything except the knowledge of his worth.

"I'll tell you something, too. He's a murderer, a killer. He's a butcher and you're no better. Ugh, those butcher's paws touching me!"

She shuddered as she spoke, and when she looked at me it was with a queer triumph in her eyes. "That's why she left you, isn't it? Liz. Was it Liz? I bet she couldn't stand you touching her with your bloodstained hands either. I bet that was why she walked out on you."

It wasn't, but that didn't mean I hadn't worried about it often enough. For a moment I contemplated the pleasure of slapping her silly, empty face and knocking the victory out of her eyes. But that would only prove her right.

"I expect so, Rosemary," I said.

She pushed past me and hurried the girls into a car that had pulled up a few yards along the road.

Liz. I flexed my hands as I remembered her. They'd caused a lot of pleasure as well as pain. Rosemary had stirred some ashes that had never quite cooled down.

RETRIEVAL

I walked down the carpetless hall to a back kitchen. Yokel was working furiously at something on the draining board. It was his black-and-white sheepdog, Roly. But it wasn't black and white any more. It was sludge colored, and its coat was stiff and spikey. It was plainly dead.

Without looking up, he began to talk.

"That's what they done. Well, I say 'they,' but it was him. On the way out. After the warning. 'This isn't some sort of joke,' he said. 'You do realize that, don't you?' I said I did. It was true. He said a lot more, too. Then he bent down and scooped up old Roly here—you know how placid he was, go with anyone—anyway, he threw him into the bloomin' deep-fryer. Crumbs, Pete. They fried my bloomin' dog."

So that was what it took to make a brave man cry.

As I helped him to clean the dog, he filled in the details. Two men had called. One professor, one chimp. Those were the terms we used for the different types in the regiment. "Professors" were mostly officers, men with qualifications in things like languages or psychology. Like Kit. "Chimp" was the name we chose for the heavy-duty men, the ones who specialized in every form of death, whether it came from their fingertips or a knife or a gun. They were men who could tear your head off three different ways, and frying a dog was just the sort of thing they'd do to underline a point.

The third category was "tommies." Yokel was a tommy, a straightforward soldier who'd march all day and fight a rhino if he was ordered. A simple, loyal, trusting, courageous old-fashioned back-to-the-wall soldier.

Which was I? I'd often wondered. A bit of each maybe, and a bit of something else, too.

There was a patch of rough ground at the back of the building, and we buried the dog there. Then I took Yokel back inside and found some cream for his hands. He'd burned them trying to get the dog out of the pan.

"The screaming was unbelievable," he kept saying. "Poor old Roly sounded more like a seagull than a dog."

Holding his hands in the air, he nodded to a plastic carrier bag under the table. "Maybe that'll help," he said. After all that had happened it was a fine sight: a bonny bottle of Scotch. "I was going to drink it myself, so you can help me. It wouldn't do any harm, just this once, would it, Pete?"

"Not just this once," I said. And we raised chipped teacups and Yokel, as only he would, said, "Happy Days."

The newspaper cutting was the lead item in the diary column of some North London weekly. It was accompanied by a picture of Yokel standing beneath a native shield and crossed eight-foot spears which I remember he'd brought back from Borneo. He'd used all his souvenirs to decorate the small café at the side of the shop.

"You didn't collect souvenirs, did you?"

"Only the ones that needed three weeks' penicillin treatment," I said.

"Bloomin' daft game," he said.

The headline said: "Fish Café Is Fighting Man's Haven." The report outlined his service with one or two safely vague stories about individual actions. The only reference to the retrieval was a paragraph which said: "Since his retirement, he has been recalled once to help bring a refugee girl to safety from an Iron Curtain country, a cloak-and-dagger operation which is still very hush-hush."

I read it through a few times, puzzled over it, had a drink, and was none the wiser. It was utterly harmless. There was nothing there that would hand World War Three to Russia on a plate. I couldn't understand it.

"But this was the bit that upset them?"

"Yes, that was it, without a doubt. They gave me hell over it."

"What did they say exactly?"

"Well, I kept asking but they didn't say in detail like. Just that I'd opened my mouth too much, and the Official

Secrets Act and all that, of course. I said, what about all these films and books and what-not, and they said it wasn't the same. Blow me if I can see any difference."

"Me too."

We were perched on two plastic café chairs before a paraffin heater. Yokel was clearly shocked. The whisky lifted him a little, but confused his line of reasoning so he skipped from one point to another.

He wanted to know if Rosemary had gone. I told him she had. How? In a cab? Yes, I assured him, without saying that most cab drivers were not in the habit of greeting their fares with a kiss.

Then he wanted to talk about Kit: what was he doing, and so on. I told him he was making a million pounds keeping sheikhs safe.

And me? What was I doing? Was I one of the funnies now? I said I was, in a way. He wanted to know what we did. I told him. Retrievals. If someone in London wanted to talk to someone who was in Rumania, we might retrieve him. Tidy-ups. If, say, a cabinet minister's mistress tried to rearrange his features in a way that might undermine public confidence, we might try to sort things out quietly.

Watches, like the one I was doing now for the police; publicly it would never be any more than that phrase in the newspaper: "acting on information received, the police . . ." And postman jobs, picking up and dropping off.

"Maybe I should've gone in for that," he said.

"Maybe," I said.

Tommies were never asked. When you left the regiment, there were certain skills they were reluctant to lose. Some people were asked if they'd like to do government security work. That meant the Unit.

They took some professors like Kit, and they also took some chimps in case they wanted any doors kicked down. And people like me, whatever that was. But they never took tommies. The one thing they didn't need was honesty.

23

He saw me kneading my shoulder—it was going numb again—and that reminded him of how he'd hauled me to the helicopter. The whisky had turned his Wiltshire accent into a soft drone, like bees.

"I'll never forget that day, I really won't, Pete. I don't know where all those blinkin' Ay-rabs come from. We'd been on that ridge all day hadn't we? Melt into the rocks, they said, same as usual, and we lay up there watching their movements and bringing the strike planes in, and it must have been 120 up there. I thought all hell had broken loose when that lot came up behind us, thirty or more, and they were pretty useful, them Ay-rabs. They got so close that our mortar man took it off the bipod and held it between his thighs so he could narrow the angle. Do you remember, Pete? I saw you go down with your shoulder shot up and Kit had us all rushing for the chopper when I decided to go back for you. Well, you were a good mate to me. Your shoulder was a bloomin' mess. I thought you'd end up selling matches outside Paddington Station. I upped you over my back and scampered fast as I could. Old Kit was furious. Said I'd gone against orders. Who cares about orders when it's your mate, eh? He'd do the same himself. Our mortar man said any woman was bound to be a disappointment after he'd had an 81 mm mortar going off between his thighs! Laugh! We had some laughs right enough. Do you know who he was, Pete? Our mortar man out on the ridge that day?"

"Chimp Three."

Me and Kit and Yokel always worked together. Sometimes they wanted us in groups of four, and since they thought we might be a bit light on muscle, they usually gave us a chimp. We numbered them. It was easier than remembering their names.

I could remember Chimp Three all right though. He was short, but wide and deep too; with brass handles he could have been a wardrobe. He had long hair tied in a bandanna and a quiet, light voice that echoed with dispassionate death. He was the one who said he liked killing people. I hadn't seen him since the night of the retrieval.

"That's right, Pete," Yokel said. He was slurring badly now, crashed back on his chair and squinting up into the light bulb as he had into the desert sun. "Chimp Three. He was the man who threw old Roly into the deep-fryer today."

"Him? He was on the retrieval." I was too surprised to manage anything more intelligent.

"He was, wasn't he?" Yokel's light blue eyes were fixed on me. "Do you remember what he did to that dog there?"

"Yeah. I won't forget that too quickly."

"Seems to have a thing against dogs."

We were both quiet for a minute or two then. I poured out some more whisky.

"What did he say when he knew it was you?"

Yokel gave a grim smile. "He knew all along. I could tell when he walked in. 'You've been a naughty boy then,' he said, or something of the sort. He looked pleased about it. 'Course, I had words with him about the dog on the border. You wouldn't remember."

I did. Yokel was nuts about animals. When we were doing our jungle stuff, he always used to dismantle his terrorist boobytraps before we left an area in case any wild animals strayed into them.

The professor, he said, was a youngish man called Brocklehurst. I didn't know him. He'd done most of the talking while the Chimp had padded about, picking things up and inspecting them. Yokel had told his wife and daughters to stay upstairs, out of the way.

It wasn't until they were leaving that the Chimp had joined in. Quite suddenly, he seemed to go mad. "People like you make me sick," he suddenly screamed. "Flapping your bloody loose mouths off all over the place. Putting your old mates' lives in danger." Then he'd thrown the dog in the deep-fryer. And he threw Yokel into the street to stop him rescuing it. For the first time I noticed the grazes on his arms.

"The professor seemed annoyed with him for going over the top," Yokel added. "He told him to get himself under control."

I nodded. It wasn't worth explaining that it was all a standard procedure. Besides the official warning, they wanted Yokel to know that there was personal anger involved, too, and that they might not be able to control it. In the business, they call it a double-decker frightener.

"Crumbs, it was too much for poor old Rosemary. Natural enough. What woman'd want that?"

I grunted.

"I mean, no one would. So she's gone." He drained his glass and held it out for more. "She's not coming back, is she?"

"I'd say not."

"No. Well. At least there's one good thing, there's not another man involved."

"No. That's something."

"So all I got to do now is find out what all the fuss was about."

I sawed at a broken thumbnail with my teeth. I could feel his eyes on me. "Why do that, Yokel?" I said, eventually.

"I want to know why. That's all. If a feller loses his family and gets told his life's work has been a farce, he wants to know why. You must see that."

I remembered Kit's message. Tell him to say "sorry" and stay away.

"Leave it."

"What do you mean, leave it?"

"Leave it. Forget it. Put it behind you. There's no point in going back into it all. You won't get anywhere. You know that. It's over. Done with. *Finito*."

Noisily he staggered to his feet. He had to put his hand on the chair back behind him to steady himself. His face was wild and red, and he was shouting and crying at the same time.

"You bloomin' bastard," he yelled, down onto my face, and he hurled the remains of his whisky into my face. "You're one of 'em, aren't you. You're all in on it together. All you funnies. You think you can just come in and kick a man's life to pieces and then tell him to forget it. I saved your life once and all you can say is 'forget it.' Who are you? What are you? I don't know. What's going on? Will someone tell me what's going on?"

He dragged at the collar of my jacket and tried to hit me around the head, but he was too drunk to make it work. This was what he'd been working toward, and now he'd got there he couldn't stand the feeling of being blind and powerless.

I didn't know what to do with him, wrestling and slamming out at me as I stood and tried to take hold of him. So I chinned him. Once, neatly.

I caught him as he dropped, and carried him upstairs on my good shoulder. There were twin beds in the front room and I laid him on the one with bedside photographs of the two girls, and one of a younger, happier Rosemary, signed "All my love, forever, darling." The wardrobe doors were still open where she'd emptied it when "forever" ran out.

Downstairs, I poured out the last of the whisky. I sat scraping off the bits of congealed fat on my clothes from cleaning up the dog. He was right. Two men walk into your life, tell you everything you believe in is untrue, kill your pet, and your whole family walks out on you. Even in my sort of life, that's a full evening.

And there was no explanation. He talked a bit too much, but what did it matter? Who had he offended? And how? I felt blind and powerless, too.

Most of the jobs I do I don't know why or who for. It doesn't matter. It's not my job to understand. It's my job to do. A missile doesn't know where it's heading or why either. That's me, a missile. Point me and bang the button and I'm on my way.

"Why" was a troublemaking word, like "love."

5

The next morning the distance between us was a mile wide and Yokel wasn't building any bridges. Somewhere at the bottom of that chasm was the corpse of our old friendship.

He was out when I got up. I couldn't find any tea, so I had to have coffee, which made my mouth taste even worse. Out of the window I could see the fresh soil where we'd buried the dog, and there was a slight discoloration on one of my knuckles where I'd clipped Yokel. Outside the rain shone on the slanting roofs. The shops that weren't boarded up opened their doors and got about as many customers as the ones that were boarded up.

He came bouncing through the door in a gray track suit. Sweat mingled with the rain on his face. He said he felt terrible. He couldn't understand why anyone wanted to drink that stuff, and I could see his point of view. But when he'd had a shower, he looked sharp and fit.

"Don't you train at all?" he asked, eyeing my waistline.

"No. I decided I'd lost my schoolgirl figure."

"You haven't lost the rest." He rubbed his chin where I'd punched him. He was smiling, but it was a smile that didn't encourage anyone else to join in.

He poured the coffee out for me as I had the Scotch for him the night before, and he asked the questions. He wanted to know what I remembered of the retrieval. He wanted to check tiny details; some I could remember, some I couldn't. All the time he was watching me, and I was painfully aware that he thought I might be lying. It wasn't like Yokel to be tricky.

"Are you opening the café today?" I asked, to try to move him on to safer ground.

He shook his head. "No point now, is there? Now there's only me."

I nodded. "Liz went," I said.

"So I heard."

He didn't ask why, but I told him. If I showed him my failures perhaps he wouldn't feel so lonely with his own.

"She wanted kids. She always used to say she didn't, then quite suddenly she changed her mind. I told her it was me and no kids, or kids and someone else, and she said that she'd rather have me, and give up the idea of having a family."

I was sitting on one of the chairs. Yokel was standing by the window looking down the garden, but he was listening.

"I thought that would be fine, but it was ridiculous. Every time we walked past a baby carriage I thought she was peeping in. Every time I looked at her I thought I was depriving her of the wonders of motherhood, or whatever they call it. So it was good-bye, and now it's baked-beans-and-bachelor-fun time again."

"Sorry about that. She was a smasher."

Only Yokel could use a word like that, "smasher."

"In the end I chose for her. Between me—a snip—and one lady owner—only used at weekends, and a child unborn and unseen. I awarded her the child."

"Why didn't you want kids? I love my two girls."

I thought about that. I'd thought about it a lot, and I knew the answer. I wasn't sure if he'd want to hear it, but I gave it to him anyway.

"For the same reason midwives would find it hard to kill someone. You're either at one end of life or the other. I've always been nearer the coffin end of the business. Me with a baby? It'd be like having an undertaker at a christening party. You're either a life man or a death man, and I'm a death man."

He stood by the window shaking his head and blowing

on his mug of coffee, and I wondered where his mind was taking him. He was far too buoyant after all that had happened. When he began talking again, it was more questions about the retrieval. Who'd given the orders? Were they from the Unit? What had happened to the girl? I didn't know most of the answers. I don't with most of my jobs.

With as near to a sneer as he could ever get, Yokel said, "And I suppose you'll be telling me you don't know the name of the bloomin' agency that looked after the girl."

"I don't," I said, without a second's hesitation. I didn't.

For a moment then, I thought about telling him about the face I'd recognized in the hotel foyer, the day after the hand-over. I only saw the man for a second, and he was wearing one of those big fur hats that you don't see much in this country. I realized that I knew him, then his face vanished from sight as he embraced the girl. A month later I saw the same face on television. Then I remembered. It was male, handsome, fortyish, and quite famous. And it was nothing to do with me, so I kept quiet.

"You won't stop me," Yokel said. "You nor none of 'em. I'll get to the bottom of this, you see."

That was where his buoyancy came from. He was tense with the urgency of it. He'd turned the tragedies of the past twenty-four hours into a mission and that was where he was getting his drive. Nothing would stop him. He was an honest man with a grievance; a deadly combination.

I told him it was his business. "But you'll make a lot of enemies," I said.

"That's what the Chimp said yesterday," he said. From the look in his eyes, I wasn't benefiting from this comparison. "In fact, you might be able to tell me what he meant, you being in a similar line of work. . . ."

I tried to interrupt but he silenced me with his hand.

"He said he'd know where to find me if I made any more trouble, and he told me that I'd know what to expect. So I says to him, I says, 'this is a free country' and he could get into a lot of trouble if there were reprisals like that, and do you know what he says? I'll tell you, Pete, though I suppose you know. He laughed. Then he said, and I can almost remember his words, he said, 'Nobody'll know except you. What if you get mugged in the street? It happens to hundreds of people every day, so what's so special about it happening to you? You could be in a road accident or a couple of drunks could pick on you in a bar. These things happen all the time, and it might not be for a year. But when it does,'—he says—'you'll know, Yokel, you'll know.'"

It was almost word for word from the training lecture. I could have recited it with him.

"What do you think he meant by that, Pete?" He was laughing at my discomfort. I said something about it being a warning, but he wasn't interested. He knew what it meant as well as I did. And he didn't care.

"I'll have to do what I think's right, won't I?" he said, as I left. "That's all anyone can do. After all, it's a bloomin' free country."

There was nothing left to stay for. Our friendship was dead. Six weeks later, so was Yokel.

6

That saying about the early bird catching the worm is just a story they put out to fool the gamblers. So they get up at six o'clock and rush out there, and all they catch is the first bus to a production line or a building site. Then, when they're all safely out of the way, the fat birds get up, munch their health-food breakfasts over the share prices, drink coffee made by lovely, loving wives, coast off to the office for coffee made by lovely, loving secretaries, and settle in for another day's worm catching.

Or perhaps I was only thinking like this because Kit and his talk about public school had brought me out in a rash of Rousseau. Anyway, I pushed my unwashed Morris Minor—the only exercise I get is folding my six-foot-one through its door—through the Volvos and Porsches of the midmorning traffic, and wondered if any of them knew about the secret world which existed beneath their own. Like the foundations. Or maybe more like the sewers.

I still felt soiled from the way Yokel had looked at me. I thought it through. I'd done my duty, if that's what it's still called. I'd tried to help him. I'd tried to advise him. I'd even forfeited his trust in doing so.

But I didn't know if I was a participant or a spectator. Kit had sent me, certainly. Had he done that as an act of friendship, so that I could help Yokel, as another act of friendship? Or was I the cat's paw, a dumb, unknowing agent at the sharp end of a subtle and complex machine? Was I a postscript to the official warning? Perhaps this one was a triple-decker, with me as the third layer?

I didn't know.

RETRIEVAL

By the time I got home I'd almost completely laundered my conscience. Yokel wasn't a brains man. He'd ask a few questions and knock on a few doors, and he wouldn't get anywhere.

It wasn't that the Unit was impregnable. It was amorphous. You couldn't fight it any more than you could wrestle with clouds. Weariness would get him in the end, and he'd give up and go away.

That made me feel better. But then, I'm good at conscience washing.

I threw some water on myself, changed, shaved, shook eggs about in a pan, and rang Tamara. I'd had a great idea. I wasn't having a lot of luck. My part of London seemed to be teeming with unbusted gangsters and untended women, so I thought I'd try to get them all together so I could have all my failures in one room.

Also, she was useful for getting people talking. Tamara was not easily ignored.

"Fancy a trip to South London, razors optional?"

"Ooooooo!" I held the telephone away from my ear. Surprise affected her the way tunnels used to get the Flying Scotsman. She would have made a great girl for a train enthusiast.

"*Quelle* excitement!" she whooped. "Are you going out burgling people? Can I carry your bag and does it have "Swag" written on it like they do in the Beano?"

I'd once told her I was a burglar. Sometimes I regretted it.

"No, just to have a nice drink with some lovely people."

"Wonderful! Will they be terribly common?"

"As muck."

"Super." Then her voice shrank. "But won't little Tamara have her jollies then?"

"Later."

Her voice lifted again. "Really? Lots of jollies?"

34

"An adequate amount." Where do these girls get it from? I think it must be having ponies when they're young.

"Scrumptious," she said.

I arranged to pick her up later on, and lay on my sofa and listened to "Smokehouse Blues" again. I decided that Jelly Roll shouted out because he was so transported by his own talent. I wondered if I was similarly transported by my own talent at the moment. I decided I wasn't. I didn't shout out "Oh, Mr. Pete!" I saved it for a better day.

When we walked into the pub, we got people talking all right, and it wasn't about me.

Tamara is pretty, very pretty. Tiny, slim, one of the few women who really justifies the word "petite."

What you see first of all is a mass of lustrous black curls. Beneath, eyes that could light home stormbound mariners, a wrap-around smile, and a face that fizzes with life. She was wearing something short, shiny, and pink, suspended—I'd swear—only by her nipples. If the breeze dropped, I was sure it would fall off.

One of the men I was hoping to chat with was playing cribbage at a table near the bar. He was Gus Miller, a solid citizen, middle aged, wearing a heavy coat and carrying a briefcase.

The more successful gangsters are, the more they look like bankers, which must prove something.

I got her a glass of bitter and a packet of crispy pork bits.

"Will I like it?" she said, uncertainly.

"Yes," I whispered. "It's terribly working class."

"Ooooo," she whooped again, touched by a frisson of delight. "*Quelle* joy. It's exactly like Coronation Street."

I felt her standing there, like a rabbit in a field of greyhounds, while I went off to talk to a chap who'd just finished a working holiday on the Isle of Wight, and it wasn't sailing.

When I got back, she was encircled with admirers and having a fine time.

RETRIEVAL

"This lovely man has just bought me another drink," she said, fluttering at Miller. "He said ladies shouldn't drink beer."

She had something with a cherry in it. She took the stick out of the drink and studied the cherry for a moment. Then she engulfed it with her mouth and pulled the empty stick out.

"Mmmmmm, scrumptious," she said, looking around a circle of faces rapt, dazed, and damp with sweat.

"Charming lady," Miller said to me. "You want to keep your eye on her, friend."

"I try," I said. "Not easy."

He gave a wheezy laugh. "I can see that." As she turned to speak to the barman, her dress pulled over her thighs, and he sighed. It was a sigh of pure nostalgia. "Beautiful aris, friend. Beautiful aris."

He tapped his colleague's arm. Together they nodded in wonderment.

"What's that?" Tamara asked, spinning around, face alight with pleasure. "What's an 'aris'? I hope it isn't something terribly rude."

"Aris," I began, tapping the stages of development off on my fingers, "Aristotle. Rhymes with bottle. Bottle and glass. Rhymes with . . ."

"Rude!" she shrieked, "*Quelle* sauciness!"

She had them all beside themselves by this time, and half an hour later we were all pals together. The drinks were coming faster, the laughter was getting louder, and then I looked up, and saw across the bar a face like an open grave.

He was younger than me, but his eyes were a hundred years old. His face had been handsome once; it still was, beneath the hoofprints and tiremarks. He was a couple of inches taller than me and his black leather jacket only just managed to make it from one shoulder to the other.

"Evenin' Big John," said Miller. He spoke with some respect.

"Evenin'," he said, but he was looking at me. "Getting to be your local, this place?"

"Nice place. Nice people." We raised our glasses across the bar and drank to that. As soon as I could, I asked my new friends who he was. The name was Big John Dodd. I was told that he helped people out.

"You know the sort of thing, if someone was botherin' you and gettin' you really upset, Big John would pop along and have a word with them for you. For a price. Naturally. Show him your knuckles, Big John," he called out from his seat.

The big man smiled a soft smile and held out a clenched fist that would have covered a manhole. The knuckles were almost completely flat.

"You've damaged those a bit," I said.

He shook his head, still smiling. "You should've seen their faces," he said. "You want a job doing?"

"No thanks. I do my own tidying up. I'm just the same about the housework. I don't think it's been done properly unless you do it yourself."

He winked. "That's my philosophy, too, pal."

Soon after that I thought we'd won all the hearts and minds we needed for one night. Anyway, I wasn't sure they could stand any more excitement, so I took Tamara home, where jollies ensued.

Two hours later, the bedsprings were white hot, the clothes were all over the floor, a headmistress in the flat upstairs was threatening to call the police unless the screaming stopped, and I felt as though I'd done fifteen rounds with a sabre-toothed tiger.

Tamara perched on the edge of the bed like a very small hunter over quite a large kill. Her pink dress hung behind the door. There wasn't anything else to hang.

"Wasn't that wonderful?" she cooed. "It was so scrumptiously working class, my sweet. My little chums from Lloyds simply wouldn't believe it."

"I'm not sure I do," I said, wondering where the

37

nearest intensive-care unit was. "I'm not a young man, you know."

"Don't be silly, darling. Have a little rest, then we'll have the other half."

I had to think of some way to keep her busy. So I sent her out for fish-and-chips and four cans of light ale. She loved it. It was the commonest thing she'd ever done.

I was just wondering if I'd ever walk again when the telephone rang. It was Kit. Could I be sure to be at Jenny's at the weekend? Luke's headmaster wanted to talk to me. I said I would.

He must have heard her voice in the background.

"If I've interrupted something, I'll be off," he said.

"No. Don't go. Talk for a bit. About anything."

7

Most of the scratches had healed up by the time Friday came and I was trundling down into the Sussex country-side.

I hadn't done much the rest of the week. I limped along to a pub in Battersea to see my Scotland Yard contact. I told him all about my social success with the men who kept going into banking unofficially. He was happy enough with that.

I asked him about Big John Dodd. His face went very serious. "Hard man, our John. Don't tangle, son."

"Free lance, isn't he?"

"That's right. Hires out. Very pricey. Very discreet, though. Runs a reliable business, I'm told. He's had some very respectable clients over the years. You'd be surprised who uses Big John."

Kit was waiting for me at the gate when I got to Jenny's. Slim, straight-backed, he looked every inch the squire in his soft tweeds and polished wing tips.

"Been otter hunting, Kit?"

He gave me a sideways look as we set off to walk to the village school. "All this inverted snobbery only exposes your social inadequacies, you know. Talking of inadequacies, whatever was going on at your place the other night?"

"I was in a tight corner."

"I don't doubt."

We walked through the village. The ground rustled and cracked with heaps of dried dead leaves. Among them, chestnuts and acorns gleamed like treasure.

"That's the trouble with the country," I said, kicking up a cloud of golden leaves. "It's jerry-built."

"What do you mean, jerry-built?"

"Falling to pieces. Look. Bits falling off everywhere. They'd never put up with workmanship like that in town. If they can't make trees that last, call in another firm of contractors. Some of these leaves are only months old. They've hardly been worn."

"You don't improve, Peter."

The school was a single-story wooden building and its immaculate white paint shone pink in the setting sun. Kit opened the door and waved me through. The lights were on in the corridor, and I could see they were also on in one room at the end. It was Luke's form room.

I walked past the empty pegs and the walls covered with bright pictures of big square houses and people with round, moon faces and legs at the corners. Our footsteps clumped with a hollow sound on the wooden floor. I opened the classroom door.

Sitting, facing me, at the teacher's desk was Mr. Blanchland. He had recruited me to the Unit. Mr. Blanchland was big in our trade, whatever that was.

"Sorry," I said. "I forgot to bring an apple."

"Peter!" he said, rising to his feet and shaking my hand. "What a real pleasure to see you. Sorry about all this." He waved at the small, wooden desks scratched with the initials of the generations.

"Yes, sorry Peter," Kit said, leaning on one of the pupil's desks. "But we did need a bit of cover."

"Fine," I said. I stepped back and sat at one of the desks. "Just so long as you don't make me sit for my CSEs again."

Mr. Blanchland laughed. It was a rich and civilized laugh, like everything else about him—white hair, pink face, plump jowls, tubby figure with a cardigan under his worn, quality sports jacket.

RETRIEVAL

"Reminds me of my old prep school, that smell of polish and humbugs," he said.

"Mine smelt of mouse droppings and terror," I said.

He sat down again behind the desk. "Same old cynic, eh?" he said. "Now what have we had you doing lately? Doing a little listening job for our friends at the Yard, at the moment, aren't you? I believe it's going well. So they tell me."

I didn't say anything. There was nothing I could tell him that he wouldn't know.

"That's all well and good then. Really . . . do you smoke? Do go ahead if you want to. I don't myself. Filthy habit, I think."

He flapped at the air in front of him, at imaginary smoke. I didn't suppose many people took him up on his offer.

"No, it's this business about Makins that brings us all here. As I'm sure we all realize."

Makins. It was a few seconds before I realized he meant Yokel. I hadn't heard his surname for years.

"I'm afraid," and he pursed his lips and shook his head, "I'm very much afraid our friend Makins has got into hot water. You've had a word with him, I understand. Something of an old friend. I wanted to hear all about it firsthand. Off you go."

He lowered his pink blancmange of a face onto cupped hands, his elbows on the desk, and leaned forward. We were the schoolchildren, me and Kit and the absent Yokel, and he was the stern, but not unkind master. I thought Yokel would probably get a hundred lines.

After I'd told him, as best I could, he sat back and his eyes roved around the ceiling. Then they came to rest on me again, blue, babyish, intelligent.

"And how would you describe his . . . errr, let's say his *mood*?"

"Hurt, confused, angry."

"Tell me, why hurt?"

"They killed his dog."

"I did hear about that. A shade extreme, I thought."

Kit coughed into his hand. "It does happen. Slight misjudgment, someone goes too far. . . ."

"Quite so."

Yokel deserved a better advocate than me, but I tried again. "He was a loyal soldier. He meant it when he took the oath of allegiance. He's probably the only man in Britain who stands up when he hears the national anthem. He believes in all the institutions, in British fair play and British justice. He's exactly the sort of man you like best. So he's hurt when he's treated like a piece of filth."

Blanchland sat looking at me for a long still moment. He tapped his nails on the desk. When he spoke, his voice was sharper without being any louder.

"Cut that out immediately. We don't need instructions in the philosophy of patriotism from you, nor for that matter do we need any of your bumbling amateur psychology. Makins has made a fool of himself, a dangerous fool, and now he's got to pay. . . . What on earth are you doing?"

"Going." I had the door half open and I was talking to him over my shoulder. "You obviously don't need me."

"For heaven's sake, Peter . . ." Kit said, and I saw the anxiety on his face.

Blanchland was on his feet. "I'm sorry," he said, with a gesture of resignation. "He's your friend. I should have realized." He walked around the desk and up the aisle and leaned against the wall next to me. Kit gave him a look as he passed: it said, *he's an awkward customer, handle him with care*.

A little tentatively, he put his hand on my arm. "We do need your help. Makins needs it, too. He's putting himself in a . . . in a . . . well, a vulnerable position."

I didn't say anything.

"Did he say anything to you about making any inquiries?"

"No." It was the first direct lie I ever told the regiment

or the Unit. In many ways, behind my cynicism, I shared Yokel's sentimental sort of patriotism. Now he'd slipped, and I had a vision of many unseen, dark forces storming around him. Suddenly he seemed small and defenseless. That was why I lied.

"I see. We were hoping . . . never mind. Apparently he has been making inquiries into the circumstances surrounding the retrieval job you did in Germany. Would you have anything you could usefully tell us about that, perhaps?"

I shrugged. "It went a bit wrong, a lot of metal flying, but you know all that. We managed to pull it off."

"Yes, of course, and a brilliant job it was, too. I was thinking more of any oblique information. Side issues, that sort of thing. Did you see anyone after the retrieval, anyone you recognized? Did Makins? Did you hear about any agency that was concerned in this business? Has Makins said anything along these lines?"

Kit cut in then. "We're trying to see what his next moves might be. He's been making a nuisance of himself, pestering people."

"I don't know anything that might help you. I'm sorry but that's it."

They exchanged glances. They both knew they'd made a mess of it. If they'd coaxed me along, they might have got something. But Blanchland had misread me.

"One last thing," he said, "and I can't stress how important this is."

"Absolutely," said Kit, nodding his lean face.

"What do we have to offer Makins to get him to stop? What is it he wants? What have we got for him?"

"Nothing," I said, and I opened the door. "Or rather he wants the only thing you can't give him. The truth."

"That's not so simple."

"It is for him. He's a very simple fellow."

I went then. I left Kit to talk to him. I walked back through a blue, country evening. The last of the light was draining from the vast bowl of the sky, but there was still enough silver up there to make black, scraggy scarecrows out of the trees.

When I got back I played the sleeping giant with Luke. It was a game I'd invented. I held him a prisoner in my—the giant's—arms, then I pretended to nod off. He had to escape without waking me up. Whenever he was almost free, the giant would suddenly wake up and retake him.

It did occur to me that was how Yokel must feel about the regiment and the Unit. He thought he'd got away, but he hadn't really.

Half an hour later Kit came in. Jenny gave me one of her significant looks and went to put Luke to bed.

Kit braced his well-bred calves in front of the fire for a while.

"That's it now," he said. "The whole thing is over as far as we're concerned. We've done our best for Yokel, and it's out of our hands. Right?"

"Right."

"I have your word."

"Scout's honor."

"Excellent."

He seemed quite happy with that. He believed me because he saw me as a man of honor, like himself. What he didn't know was that my honor's bespoken: it's made specially for me and it doesn't fit anyone else.

The writer chap was right, though, about the way you start with small sins and slowly move on to bigger ones. I'd begun with murder and here I was telling lies already. Next, careless parking.

8

With a series of minor triumphs, the next six weeks slipped quietly past.

My new friends in South London were simmering nicely. I called in now and again, taking Tamara with me in what she calls her thermal clothes—"they make men go hot all over, tee hee."

About a year earlier I'd spent three months in Brixton Prison on remand for a wage snatch, for which I was acquitted on a technical, legal point. I would have been very cross if I hadn't been. The wage snatch was phoney and the trial was a dummy, but it did give me credentials for jobs where they don't want to see your "O" levels.

Miller had obviously been asking questions. He mentioned it one night, and said he might be able to put a little work my way. So that was progressing satisfactorily.

My blithe charm did go awry one night when I asked Big John what he would do if another manual mercenary came along and rolled him over. It was half a joke and half curiosity, but I realized it was a mistake, wholly and entirely, when the packed bar fell silent and people began to edge toward the door.

John sat at the bar looking down into his pint. When he looked up he wasn't smiling.

"If some geezer done me over?" he rephrased it.

"Something like that." It was too late to move into reverse. He held out his vast, flat-knuckled hand. He flexed it. Then he opened it. He looked up at me and said, "I fink I might sulk."

RETRIEVAL

Everyone roared at his joke. I laughed so loudly I had a sore throat for a week.

Some nights I took Tamara in her glamorous rags back to Squalor Towers for a writhe and a shriek.

When I told her I thought I might have to call in reinforcements, she said. "Triple jollies—*quelle* sauciness!"

"Not triple," I said, panting. "I was thinking of the Gurkhas."

Each weekend I got down to Sussex to work on Luke's imminent debut as the English standoff, which should make him the first under-eight to have that honor. As briefed and coached by Kit and me, Luke tackled White so hard, bony shoulder ramming into stomach, that he nearly sawed him in half. Kit and I exchanged winks as we sympathized with him.

The trees stripped and looked naked against cold skies, and the wind began to bite again.

Luke thrashed me at soldiers. At the end of one game, all I had left was a one-armed crusader and a lariat-whirling cowboy to defend Fort Laramie. He had me surrounded with a scratch force drawn from dozens of different countries and centuries. Roman legionaries fought side-by-side with Rommel's desert troops, Sioux Indians beside their brothers from the Household Cavalry bodyguards.

He sprawled on the carpet, advancing them inch by inch.

"I resign," I said. "I'm a bit outnumbered."

"You can't," he said. "It's against the rules." A matchstick from his mortar hit my crusader on the left shoulder. He spun around and dropped, exactly as I had when the Arab shot me. Only that was a Kalashnikov, not a Bryant and May.

"I think he's outmaneuvered you," Kit said, sipping a gin over the Sunday papers.

"Bloody armchair generals," I growled.

"Bam bam!" Luke suddenly shouted. An Indian he'd

been worming up the palisade knocked my cowboy off his horse.

"Hey, that's not fair," I protested.

"He was just the same in uniform," Kit told Luke. "Always complaining. Frightful whiner he was."

Luke began to heap all his soldiers into the fort. It was one I'd made for him, with a special heavy, wooden base. He marched them in. He was providing the martial music as he pushed them along, and even shouted out orders.

"If you could be any of these soldiers, which would you choose?" he asked.

I let Kit go first on that one. "Oh, Scots Guards without a doubt," he said.

"Are they really good?"

"Absolutely. First-class bodyguards. And British, of course, which makes all the difference."

"Which would you be, Uncle Pete?"

"The crusader."

"Why?"

"He seems to manage okay with one arm, and I quite fancy the idea of plenty of distressed damsel duty."

Jenny smiled to herself, and Kit fixed his eyes on the newsprint. Earlier I'd had the pleasure of coming into a room and shouting, "Caught you at it!" It wasn't quite as good as it sounds. They were standing in an eye-locked stance and I thought I caught a whiff of nuance in the atmosphere. Jenny giggled, of course, and Kit brushed it off with indignant denials and complaints about my school-room behavior.

For me, it was wishful thinking. If I could choose a father for Luke and a husband for Jenny, Kit would be the man. I still hoped their old romance might heat up.

When I wasn't on uncle duty, watch duty, or jollies duty, I stayed in my room—more of a *toe*-à-terre than a whole *pied*—and baked a few bachelor's beans and listened to Jelly Roll, particularly George Mitchell's opening cornet break on "The Chant." If Beethoven could have played a few bars of that, he wouldn't have bothered about all that other stuff.

And all the time I thought about Yokel. He never telephoned. I didn't expect him to. He'd obviously lined me up with the rest of the enemy. I felt uneasy about him, mainly because I wasn't sure he was wrong. Friends and enemies—that was a gray area. I knew now that I'd been part of the treatment he'd been given, and I wasn't happy about that. Then I thought of him living in that closed-down café, without Rosemary or his beloved girls, and I wondered what was going to happen to him.

So a couple of nights I drove up to Hendon and past the shop to see if there was any sign of him. What I would have done about it, I don't know. There was nothing: no light, no movement. In a way I was relieved.

The third time I called I knew everything was wrong. It was well after midnight—I'd decided to drive up there after a session in Tracy's—and as I drove down the forlorn street I felt my skin prickle and my stomach hollow.

In the violent professions, you don't last long without intuition.

I slowed the Minor down to walking speed and craned forward to see what had reached my instinct before it reached my brain. It was raining. It was one of those streets where it always would be raining. Domed bubbles sprouted in black puddles. A couple of battered streetlamps threw dull yellow paths across the oily black street. There were lights in a few of the terraced houses and I could distantly hear a tinny radio somewhere, but it was a street where life had wound down, given up, and resigned.

I opened the car window. The smell was still there. It was a smell of rain and cold and old railways. It was a smell of defeat in a poor street where the sun never shone. Suddenly I knew it was a smell of fear. I'd seen only a deserted street, but then I saw a figure standing in front of Yokel's closed shop. It was a man, a small, lightly-built man, but it was his stance that had touched a warning in my senses. He was still, leaning forward, listening and watching, too, but afraid to step any nearer.

I stopped the car beside him. When he turned I saw he was an Indian, and he looked relieved that someone else was there. He didn't wait for me to ask.

"I heard a lot of noises," he said, pointing at Yokel's door. He was about two yards away from it.

"What sorts of noises?" I was whispering. So was he. The whole of the silent street seemed to be eavesdropping.

He gave a little shudder. He was thin, stooping, and frightened. "Nasty noises. Horrible noises."

"Voices?" I got out of the car. I closed the door. I didn't slam it. I bent nearer his mouth so he could lower his voice even more.

He nodded. "Some voices," he croaked into my ear. "Shouting, and some nasty, crying noises, and sort of grunting." He wrapped his arms around himself and looked up at me. "Something very wicked is happening in there, mister."

I could not see the flicker of a light behind the shop window, with its banal sea-creatures, or in the black patches of the upstairs rooms. The front of the building was as serene and peaceful as a sea full of sharks. Then I saw the front door move. It was only a fraction, but it moved.

Stepping nearer, I could see that the door wasn't locked as I'd thought. It was open. Only about an inch, but open.

This was the moment I lived for. When fear and courage fight in your heart to see who owns you. When the nerve endings creep outside your skin to pick up the signals. When you can feel every sinew move and each muscle in its place, when you can even feel the blood moving around your body. When you begin to live at a higher, rarer level of consciousness and for a few seconds, you know what it's like to be one of the gods. Once you've tasted high-risk nectar you never want to drink anything else.

I charged the door. I hit it with my good shoulder. As I burst in, the shape of the shop registered but I saw—really saw—only one thing. And I saw that too late. A man was standing on the counter inside the door. I didn't see him immediately because he was above the usual field of vision. Which was why he was there.

All I really saw were two legs, in jeans, and two ragged track shoes.

One of them was swinging toward me so slowly that I could have loosened and retied the laces three times before it reached me. But my head was even slower. It waited for the shoe to come. It turned slightly, again so slowly, and the shoe smashed me half-an-inch behind the ear. The sky lit up bright yellow and I dreamed my head was soaring high in the air and through the posts at Twickenham.

He damn near kicked my head off.

When I came around, I could hear the Asian outside.

"Are you all right?" He'd come a little nearer, but not much.

"I don't think I'll ever be all right again." I struggled to my feet, holding onto the counter. I touched behind my ear. It was swelling by the second and there were fireworks going off behind my eyes.

"I heard some banging," he said, now in the open doorway, "and then I heard someone running off through the back. Did he hit you?"

"Either that or I slipped on the step. Bang that light on, will you?"

He knocked down the switch next to the door. Two overhead striplights came on forcing me to close my eyes against the pain. But only for a moment. When I heard the Indian scream, I opened them pretty quick.

Yokel was flattened against a pine-clad wall at the far side of the shop. He was facing the wall, and his arms were flopped against his sides. You might have thought he was trying to listen in on next door's conversation.

"Police, quick," I said, pushing the Indian back through the door. He went. He was glad to get out.

I went around the counter to see if he was still alive, although I knew he wouldn't be. If you have a four-foot Borneo spear driven so hard through your back that it can pin you to the wall, it is fairly final.

But he was still warm. Blood was bubbling out, soaking his shirt where it was nipped into the wound by the spear shaft.

The spear was made from some strange jungle wood. It was almost black, and the shaft was carved with pictures of hunters and their prey. I didn't need to look. He'd showed it to me many times.

Yokel was very proud of it. He'd spent six months living with a tribe picking up bits and pieces about terrorists' movements. He loved them. Not many years before they'd been headhunters, yet he said they were the most placid people he'd ever met. In six months he never heard one argument. He lived with them, ate with them, and hunted with them barefoot through the jungle. They must have loved him, too. They'd seen the clear light of candor in his eyes.

He had saved my life. If only I'd been a few minutes earlier perhaps I could have saved his. If I'd had one less drink in the pub. If I'd got up earlier that morning. If I'd had a faster car. If all the traffic lights had been green. All the ifs in the world couldn't light his honest face up again for me.

He was the best of us. The bravest and the best. And he'd died believing his friends had betrayed him.

Disgraced and deserted, he'd died, pinned like a scarred, old butterfly to a cheap shop wall.

I remembered then that I'd been warned to stay clear of whatever happened to him. But then he'd been warned, too, and he'd ignored it.

It was a long late night and it never stopped raining. The police came with a lot of questions and a lot of headshaking. They rang some numbers in Whitehall I gave them, and I answered their questions as best I could. Well, some of them.

They unpinned him and put him on a stretcher and carried him out and they put a label on the spear and took that, too. They stepped around me with some care. They avoided my eye. They get unsettled when the funnies are around. Men schooled in obedience to every printed word of their masters, from dog crap on the footpath to eating live babies, can't adjust to men who swing through the jungle of regulations like criminal Tarzans.

"Okay," said the detective inspector, with a sigh of resignation. "You don't want to make a statement except to say you called to see the deceased and found him?"

"That's about it."

"There won't be any prints on the spear or anywhere else for that matter?" He glanced around at his two colleagues dusting a door handle, but the question was for me.

"How would I know?"

"How indeed. And you've been cleared at the highest possible level, so I'm told."

"Thank goodness someone still likes me."

He gave me a long steady look without too much effort to conceal his contempt. He scratched his short mustache.

"In that case I suppose you might as well go. Thank you for all your help, sir." The "sir" had a built-in sneer. Then he dropped his head and spoke quickly to me. "Please go, sir. I don't like you people on my patch. I'm an honest old policeman who lives by the law and tries to see that other people do the same. I don't have any time for you cowboys. Move it."

I could have tried to explain, but what was the use. He was probably a good honest cop.

As I walked out, I heard him say to one of the others, "You know these buggers. This is probably their idea of an interdepartmental row. It'll go down as 'killed by an unknown intruder.'"

RETRIEVAL

I would have felt angrier about that remark if I didn't suspect it might be true. The thought lay like bile in my gut all the way home. I've been hated by a lot of people, and a meeting of all those who wish me dead would need the Albert Hall and then some, but I still find the contempt of an honest man hard to bear.

It was nearly three o'clock when I got home. The first thing I did was to ring Kit. He said, "Christ!" He asked for some details, time, weapon, that sort of thing.

Then I asked him the question I had to ask. "Did you know this was going to happen?"

The pause lasted so long I thought he'd gone. "No. No, I didn't." He was silent again. In a careful voice, he said, "Peter, there's not much trust in this business, but we must try to keep ours. Yokel upset some dangerous people."

I didn't say anything because I didn't know what to believe. Kit continued a minute later.

"Do you remember when we first met? You two were coming down off the mountain and I was in that truck. I thought I'd got Yokel when I offered him a lift. His face lit up with really genuine gratitude. That was Yokel. He was too honest for this world. Then you chipped in, of course, and I knew we'd got someone who was pretty sharp, and I thought what a hell of a combination we'd all make. And we did, didn't we, Peter?"

I still didn't speak.

"Didn't we?" he asked again.

"Yes. A great team." Then I put the phone down.

I lit the gas fire and curled up around an Olympic-sized whisky. There was a lot of hard thinking to be done. It all went back to the retrieval. Everything stemmed from that. That was why he'd been warned off. That was what he'd set out to investigate. I'd no idea how far he'd got, or in what direction.

All I knew was that the reason for his death lay in that operation in the Harz Mountains, the last time the three of us worked together.

9

The first hint I'd had of an operation was the previous November when Kit suggested one Saturday that we take Luke up on the Ashdown Forest for some passing practice. It registered with me as something more than a suggestion.

We consulted Jenny's Winnie the Pooh map of the forest which she kept on the kitchen pinboard, and decided on Gill's Lap, as it's known on the map, and the Enchanted Place in the books. To me it was just a place with plenty of open country for running.

Up there it was a perfect day: iced air and a hard, blue sky, and the bracken crisp with frost.

I kicked my foot through it. "There you are," I said to Kit. "That's the country for you. Get a load of green bracken delivered in the spring and it's faded by winter."

We ran over the forest, Luke in the middle, passing the ball to and fro. I stayed on the right wing so I could shoot the ball off my weaker hand.

I was neither sorry nor surprised to see Mr. Blanchland. By then I was puffing a bit and it had struck me that a few thousand acres of open countryside was ideal for a discreet briefing.

From a bench beneath five scraggy pines, he watched kites dance against the sky.

"Lovely things," he said. "I could never make mine work as a boy."

I could imagine it. He'd be the fat boy who couldn't climb trees and got his homework in on time.

"Ah, you've brought the young man. Rather thought you might. May he have these?" He handed over a bag of sweets and Luke went to practice his kicking over a low oak branch.

The job was a retrieval. We had to bring a girl over the border from East Germany.

"It's not like crossing the road," I said, on the general theory that it's always a good idea to remind your boss how tough your job is.

But it was true, too. I'd done a lot of work over that border and it got harder every year. It was a fifty-yard strip that stretched a thousand miles right up to the Baltic in the north, containing every device that human ingenuity could contrive to slay, maim, or terrify.

All we had was a contact on the other side who could offer limited help. That was Kit's province. He had to go through to East Berlin to meet the contact and make the arrangements. Facilities were provided for that. The crossing itself was handed down to me. I had to get us over and get us back.

"Two things," I said, ticking them off on my cold-reddened fingers. "First, can we get the girl as near as possible to the border? Second, we've got to have markers out for the minefield."

From his seat, Mr. Blanchland blinked up at Kit. He was supposed to be the fixer.

"Is our contact that plumbing chap?" he asked. Blanchland nodded.

"We should be okay for the markers then. I agree with you on that, Peter. That's an absolute necessity. And he should be able to help us get the girl up to the border. He's got a brother in the border troops, if I remember correctly, so we'll have to go wherever he's on duty."

Blanchland added more. We were to carry nothing to identify us as British. If anything went wrong we were one of the gangs who smuggle people over the border for money. It was a job of the utmost importance and—here he wagged his fat little finger at us—delicacy. He couldn't stress that too much—delicacy.

"Capital, young chap, well done," he called out suddenly, and I turned and saw Luke had managed to clear the branch with the ball.

"Absolutely," said Kit, and they both began applauding. That's one of the ways you can tell ex-public schoolboys: if you blow your nose successfully they react as though it's the end of a symphony concert.

After some thought, Blanchland said that he'd allocated Chimp Three to our group.

I grunted a bit over that. I wasn't too keen on him. They asked why. I said he wasn't a good teamman.

"Hmmm," Blanchland said. "But a first-class, small-arms man."

"Too damn quick to prove it," I snapped.

In the end I compromised. I'd take him if we could have Yokel, too. I stifled their protest. Yes, I knew he'd packed it in four years ago and that he wasn't considered suitable for Unit work. But he was totally reliable. If I was taking them over, that was what I wanted. There was no room for the unpredictable.

"Also," I said, "he's magic with dogs."

That swung it. They gave in.

When I told Yokel, he was delighted. He was in his market garden then, near Salisbury. It was after ten at night and he was still working in a shed at the back.

"I'm still bloomin' fit," he said, his eyes shining like a boy's. "I go out for a run every morning and I do twenty minutes with the weights, too."

"Good, you might have to carry me home."

Rosemary was furious. "You can't make this job work and now you're going back to that stupid, secret soldiering again."

"Old Pete here was saying it'll be worth a few bob," he said, as you would to a sulky child. "If your mother'll have the girls we might get away to the Canaries for a few days afterwards."

But she'd gone, nearly ripping the shed door off its rusty hinges.

"She'll be all right. She doesn't mind, really. It's just that she's used to having me at home now. Crumbs, it'll be great to be back in harness again."

Immediately after Christmas, Kit went to East Berlin for two days. He traveled as a Mr. Duncan Houghton, buying manager for a firm of wholesale plumbing suppliers based near Reading. They were interested in downspout and guttering systems being produced at a factory in East Berlin. He was welcomed by a government trade official, who was astonished and delighted at the opportunity to sell anything to the decadent West, and he was fêted as well as a man can be there. It's a bit like a night out in isolated Skelmersdale.

"Was there a naked blonde in your room with a gun in her hand saying, 'Give me zer plans, professor'?" I asked him, later.

"You wouldn't have been interested anyway, would you Kit?" said Yokel. "We're not all bloomin' girl mad like you."

We reckoned he'd got the soft end of the job. It was certainly well set up. He'd visited the factory, he'd examined the products, he'd spoken to the factory managers. He'd talked prices and delivery dates. He put a substantial order through and—in case that route was ever needed again—the delivery was made, the systems were sold, and there are still people in Berkshire complaining about a cut-rate load of leaking guttering.

There was, he said, one anxious moment. In the moldings shed he'd asked to use the lavatory. The trade official was all for taking him back to the offices. The workmen's lavatories, he explained, were . . . only adequate. Great achievements had been made in correcting social injustices and guaranteeing health treatment and education and jobs for all the workers, but in some areas they were slightly behind the times. . . .

Kit mimed desperation, which did not come easily to

him. The official relented. Kit raced into a thin shack. Inside it was black and stinking and the facilities were a hole in the ground.

But behind the door, tucked into the corrugated eaves, was a crude map with a few instructions. He read it once, dropped it down the hole, and insured that it could never be rescued in the only appropriate way.

"It's here," he said, pointing it out on the map. It was in the middle of the Harz Mountains. "We cross ten posts up from the border watchtower, going east. The girl will be in the old watchtower, a wooden building about a hundred yards from the new concrete one. She'll be alone."

"The markers?" I asked.

"They'll be there. Cigarette packets."

"Weighted?" I wouldn't want to follow a trail of cigarette packets in a high wind.

"Weighted," he reassured me.

"Great," I said. "It's years since I had a winter holiday."

10

"And that," I said, counting ten posts along, "is the front door."

The steel fence was just visible, this side of a concrete watchtower, which stood like a lighthouse among seas of smooth and glistening snow.

We were in a patch of pine wood two hundred yards away from the tower, which lay in the bottom of a valley. We were safe enough for both watching and talking, but we still talked in whispers. Sometimes, after a job that's gone on for a few hours, it's difficult to adapt to normal conversation.

For the past ten nights I'd lain out in this wood, watching, monitoring, timing. This was my winter holiday. At the skiing hotel where I stayed, near Braunlage, they knew me as the quiet chap who spent the days walking and doing a little gentle skiing and went to bed at ten o'clock when the serious schnapping was beginning.

What they didn't see was me slipping out of my cabin an hour later to keep watch on the border post.

When the other three joined me the previous day, I showed them a map I'd drawn of the layout of the fifty-yard strip of land between the two fences.

This was where the East German defenses were thinnest. They reckoned that their residents wouldn't wish to add the threat of freezing to death to those of being shot, blown up, or torn to pieces. They were right. It was one of the quietest parts of the border. There were none of the black crosses and wreaths which mark the bids for freedom in Berlin.

Here the only memorial was a shot in the night or an unexplained explosion, and the next day, perhaps blood on the snow.

The tower was manned by three men. That was their system. One to watch the border, one to watch the watcher, and one to watch the other two to see they didn't make any deals. They were shuffled around at frequent and irregular intervals so they don't get too friendly.

The Germans have a bitter joke about the three-men squads. One can write, they say, one can read, and the other is there to guard the two intellectuals.

But tonight, if everything went well, one of them was our man.

I passed the night glasses to Kit. "One of them's reading a paper," he said. "It all looks very relaxed."

"The other two should be sleeping by now. Or at least resting. They don't get much passing trade up here."

It wasn't surprising. It was ten below and a Russian-trained wind whipped powder off the top of the hard-frozen snow. Warm as we were in our top-to-toe snowsuits—courtesy of the Norwegian Arctic patrols and almost as thermal as Tamara's clothes—the sight of the forest beyond this clearing, rising to the hulking Brocken, was enough to start a shiver. That was the East, half lit beneath a clouded moon.

I was glad about those clouds though. The less light the better.

"Why don't we just roll them over?" said the Chimp, after his turn with the glasses. He'd questioned my strategy earlier. He wanted to storm the place, shoot it up, and very likely kidnap the Moscow State Circus, too.

I left it to Kit.

"This is Peter's job," he said. "This is how he's calling it. It's also supposed to be a discreet undercover job, not a bloody fireworks display."

"And one of them fellers in there is on our side," said Yokel.

RETRIEVAL

All you could see of the Chimp was his eyes but he still managed a sardonic look. He knew he wasn't one of us.

Quietly he added, "Too kid glove," and turned away.

"Where's the old tower?" Kit asked. I pointed him at the new one, a bit to the right, up a bit. "Ah yes, that's no distance."

We had half an hour to wait then. We kept moving, changing position to stop the cold reaching our bones. We checked our gear for the last time.

Me, a screwdriver and bulldog clips; Kit, heavy-duty metal cutters; and Yokel, half-a-dozen prime steaks we'd swiped from the hotel's kitchen.

I had my Browning Hi-power, and so did Kit. People say they're heavy and they are. But with thirteen to a clip, a Browning has still got a bellyful when the others run out. Who cares about weight then?

The Chimp had managed to find the weapon that was the perfect reflection of his character: undersized and murderous. It was a Mossberg Slugster, a pump-action shotgun with a pistol grip.

You could have stood off Genghis Khan's first team with it.

He was slotting twelve-bore slugs in as we talked about our ideas of England. Kit had his provincial rugby ground, Yokel his freedom, me my traffic wardens, and the Chimp his cheerful philosophy of killing for fun. Odd conversation, odd place.

"I don't mind killing if it's him or me," Yokel said. "But I couldn't kill just anyone."

With a glance that was colder than the weather, the Chimp said, "When you're working, a human being is just a slab of meat."

He was right. He was the perfect warrior. One way or another, we'd all hung on to some romantic ideals or scraps of sentiment, or invented woolly moralities to justify our lives. He hadn't. He didn't need to. He was death on two legs. And that was what the job required.

61

RETRIEVAL

"Any minute now," I said, checking my watch.

At two in the morning, the one on duty was supposed to come out to check the snow for footprints. In the cities and towns and in the lowland where there was no snow, there was always an area of raked sand.

However futile it was here, he'd still do it in case the others reported him for failing.

Sure enough, the door at the back of the tower opened. Yellow light spilled across the snow. He didn't bother to check the snow. He bent down by the dog run, then, after a minute, went back inside and closed the door. Time to go. I moved down the hill with my men behind me.

The first fence was twelve feet high and made of thick steel mesh. When some of the escapees see it and realize that's all that stands between them and the West, they rush at it.

Some of them get their legs blasted, some have their stomachs ripped out, and some have their heads blown off. Every twenty yards along its one-thousand-mile journey, the fence had three claymore mines fitted at different heights from the ground. Thoughtfully, they'd fitted each one with a small trumpet to direct the blast. To set them off, all you have to do is to touch the trigger wire which feeds in at either side. They call them *Selbstschussanlagen*—self-shooting devices.

I knew an East German who escaped and who took a mischievous delight in irritating his former landlords. He used to steal the mines, and sell them to tourists. He made a handsome living at it.

He showed me how to do it. That was a fortnight before one blew up on him, and he made a handsome death at it, too. That was also when I had two good arms. But I was the only one who knew how. Or who thought he knew how.

I looked around. Silence. Whiteness. Nothing. At a nod from me, Yokel and Kit bent down and raised me, one knee on each of their shoulders. I held on to their hoods until they found a steady footing, then I took my hands off their heads and took hold of the steel post. There was no explosion. This was the only way I could do it: my left arm wouldn't raise high enough to do it from the ground.

All I had to do now was to work my hands through the mesh, find the trigger wire, and secure it. Preferably without setting it off.

Over the last few days, I'd done it dozens of times in my hotel bedroom, with a model of the claymore. I'd done it in the light, in the dark, with my snowsuit on; I'd even done it lying on the floor and reaching up onto the bed. There was only one element missing in my practice sessions—imminent death.

I took off my mitten and rubbed my fingers together to dry them. Within seconds the cold was getting at them.

With my right hand, I hoisted my left up. It couldn't make it by itself. But although the arm was weak, the sensitivity in the fingers was perfect. I couldn't see what was happening on the other side of the mesh. Blindly my fingers moved and touched. Then I felt the cold, thin line of the wire.

Holding it with my left hand, I fished a clip out of my pocket with the right. I slipped the clip through and fastened it securely to the mesh.

Without pausing to think, I did the same with the other side. The more quickly and the more firmly I did it, the less chance there was of a twitch or a shake. The less chance of blood on the snow.

"Okay?" I heard Kit whisper. I didn't reply. If it wasn't, he'd be among the first to know.

Then I took out the screwdriver, worked my fingers through, and disconnected the two wires. That was one rendered harmless.

The other two I could reach from the ground, so I jumped down. I had to move quickly now because my fingers were prickling with cold and as soon as they lost their feeling I wouldn't be able to work.

Suddenly a torrent of light flooded me and I looked up

expecting to see a searchlight. It was, in a way. The wind had whisked away the clouds and there was the moon lighting up the whole mountain range with a deadly silver clarity. I carried on with the stomach-high trap. It was like picking a lock on the stage of the London Palladium. But with the security of my own feet under me, it was much easier.

My fingers were deadening at the ends. I slipped them through to find the last wire. I was rushing trying to find it too quickly and with a clumsy wriggling movement I hit the wire hard with two fingers. Every muscle in my body tightened. The silence was undisturbed. Quickly I clipped it safely. I don't know why. It must have been rusted solid not to have gone off.

The Chimp hadn't given it a glance. He was keeping his gun trained on the tower. But I felt Yokel and Kit watching me, and I stepped back and took a couple of deep breaths to get the tension down.

No air ever tasted as sweet as that did then. That's how life tastes when you've come close to losing it.

When I looked back, Kit had cut a two-foot wide door in the fence and Yokel had peeled it open. I looked through.

In the day-clear light it was easy to see the markers our friend on the other side had placed for us. There were three Club cigarette packets, four feet apart, their blue stripes clear in the snow. With a similar stride at either end, that covered sixteen feet, the usual width of the minefield on the border.

Or that was what my information said. And, since it was my information, I went first. There was no point in delaying. And at least the bright moonlight showed the way clearly. One stride, two, three, four, and I was clear.

I turned and looked up at the tower. It was only about twenty feet away now. There was no one to be seen at the window, but I thought I could hear a radio playing inside.

I beckoned Kit. One, two, three, four, he hit my

footsteps, and caught my arm as he landed. Then Yokel. He took one stride, checked to hold his balance, looked up at the tower, and dropped into a quivering crouch.

I spun and followed his appalled gaze. A soldier was standing at the window. He was young, about eighteen by the look of him, with high-shorn black hair and a plump face. In that moonlight he couldn't fail to see all four of us. We waited. The Chimp by the fence with his gun raised, Yokel crouching in the middle of the minefield, Kit and I shoulder to shoulder.

Slowly the soldier held out one raised thumb, then moved away from the window.

Yokel and the Chimp came through quickly. These defenses, so the East German government says, are necessary to stop starving Westerners breaking in to enjoy the fruits of Communism. I'm sure that's true, but I've never understood why the tank traps face east.

But they do. We jumped down the steep side and climbed up the slope.

At the top, behind a six-foot fence, a dog like a chow was braced back on its haunches, growling low, its teeth as white as the snow.

"Tchk, tchk, tchk," Yokel said, making those funny noises in his teeth that country men do with animals. It could have been a poodle in the park for all the fuss he made. "There's a good fellow, now who's a bonny old dog then. . . ."

As he talked, he pulled one of the steaks out of a bag and forced it through the mesh. Still talking, holding another one, he scrambled over the fence. Then he bent down with his arm around the dog's neck, patting it and talking to it.

We followed. Twice when the dog tensed up and began to growl again as we climbed over, Yokel calmed it down.

We left him there, and the Chimp inside the last fence, covering the back door of the tower. Kit and I were over the last fence in a minute, another twelve-footer, but this time without fireworks.

It was a few minutes' walk up to the old tower, which was halfway up the other side of the valley. It was a wooden construction, so badly deteriorated that the bright light of the sky shone through its black boards and roof in many places.

Kit pushed the door. It swung open loosely and stayed there. We both had Brownings in hand by this time. He stepped through the door before switching on a pencil flashlight. At first the beam found only muddy straw, and a second's doubt clicked in my mind. What if Kit's arrangements had gone wrong? What if the girl wasn't here? Then the beam hit a sheaf of lovely, long, blonde German hair, and she looked up from where she was sitting in the corner.

Seen suddenly like that, a picture created for your eyes in a twinkling, she looked magically lovely. She had a long gentle face, large, frightened brown eyes, and this hair, the only gold in a night of black and silver. And she looked defenseless, an animal caught in the light.

Without a word she rose and went down the hill between us.

We hoisted her over the fence. The Chimp caught her, and although she was quite a tall girl—she looked about twelve or thirteen—he caught her in one arm, without his gun once wavering from the door of the tower.

From there it should have been straight back along the path we'd traveled. And it would have been, but for the Chimp and the dog.

He'd said earlier we should slit the dog's throat. I decided against it. Before we knew the man on watch was prepared to cover for us, there was the danger that one of them might come and call the dog; lonely soldiers often make pets of them. And I knew Yokel could handle it this way.

The plan was for Kit to lead the way back, Yokel and I

with the girl between us, and the Chimp had to be last to cover us with the shotgun.

And everything went to plan until Yokel helped the girl over the six-foot fence out of the dog run, and followed himself. Once he left the dog's side it began to circle the Chimp. It growled and flattened its head down. In that light, against the snow, it looked as frightening as any wolf.

He could have come then—it wasn't making much noise—but when I looked back as we slid down the tank traps I knew he wasn't going to. He dropped down on his haunches facing the dog and he'd put his shotgun down beside him. The dog charged at him, low, fast and roaring in its throat. He had his hands together on the ground and—whatever I thought of him personally—it took courage to do what he did. He waited until the dog's breath must have been in his face and its fangs inches from his throat, then he smashed his linked hands upward in a double uppercut.

The crack of the dog's neck breaking was high and clear. So too was the roar of a bark as he hit the dog's throat, and it turned into a terrible haunting howl that rang the length and breadth of the valley.

For a moment we were all transfixed. The dog's body, which had spun backward through the air, was slumped in the snow. We could hear noises from the tower. There was a face—not the one I'd seen earlier—at the window, holding a telephone. Then he saw us.

"Move!" I screamed.

The silence had gone now. The stillness, too. The night was raucous with panic. A brassy bell jangled. An electric hooter yowled. Suddenly it was the brightest, noisiest place on earth.

Yokel and I slid down the tank trap and threw the girl up to the top. Kit grabbed her as we scrabbled up the sheer side of the pit. He was leaping ahead of her through the minefield.

Footsteps clattered. The door at the back of the tower

opened. Two soldiers, their thick, gray jackets unfastened, ran out with rifles in their hands.

The Mossberg boomed. The noise filled the valley. Then I heard the rattle of another shell being pumped up, and another deafening boom.

The first soldier clapped his hands to his middle, folded, and dropped. The slug would have blown a hole in him. The Chimp was firing from the hip at no more than twenty-five yards range. He must have snatched at the second shot because this time I saw half the soldier's head disappear before he rose in the air, spun, and finally sank to his knees like a man at prayer. Without any rush, the Chimp came after us.

We were five white-suited ghosts fleeing through the night. Kit was through the first and last fence, pulling the girl behind him, and Yokel and I got through as he began to climb the slope to the wood. We were back in the West.

Over the top of the hill on the eastern side, two headlights appeared. They rose and sank as it hammered down the incline. Kit was safely in the wood with the girl and we weren't far behind when I saw the third German. He'd come out of the tower and was following us. I looked for his gun, then saw his hands above his head.

"Please," his voice echoed over the snow. "Please I come. Please. Thank you."

The ear flaps on his fur-lined hat bobbed as he came on.

"Quick! Run!" I shouted.

The headlights had turned on sideways. I could see soldiers swarming over the side of a truck.

"*Schnell!*" I yelled again.

The soldiers were milling around all over the place. An officer raced into the tower after briefly examining the two bodies.

Two of the soldiers stepped outside their own headlights, which were blinding them, and craned their heads toward our side of the valley.

RETRIEVAL

One of them shouted and the officer came running out of the tower.

Then I saw the Chimp. He was below me on the hill. The two of us were watching the East German. He was tottering in our footsteps through the minefield. He reached one foot forward, wobbled, then quickly brought the other up. He did it again. One more step and he would be through.

Then I heard that heavy boom again. He was balanced on one foot when it hit him in the chest. His hands flew up. He sloughed sideways and fell.

He seemed to fall into an orange and yellow pit. The ground shook. He'd landed on one of the mines.

The soldiers beyond the border stood and watched as we climbed up the hill to safety. In our white snowsuits we were invisible to them. They didn't even fire a shot. Someone knocked off the two alarms.

All I could hear then was the girl sobbing. Apart from that, the valley was silent. Much more silent than it had been before the noises and the deaths.

11

Back at the hotel, Kit sent me to hand the girl over to two officials from the refugee agency while he took the Chimp to his room for a one-man court-martial.

Apart from crying, the girl hadn't said a word. She'd taken off her snowsuit now and was wearing some badly fitting jeans and a soiled sweater. Most of the time she kept her face down and kept brushing her long, fair hair with her hands. She must have been very nervous.

It was a motel-style layout. Kit gave me the cabin number—until then he hadn't said anything about them staying there—and we marched on soft carpets through warm air along the corridors.

Outside the snow glittered. But somehow it didn't look the same snow as that where we left the bodies lying. That was another country, in every way.

I knocked on the door, gave the girl a reassuring grin that immediately had her retreating behind her hair, and then found a stooping, old bird of a man standing in front of me after nearly ripping the door off its hinges.

"Yes?" he shouted. "What's gone wrong?"

"Nothing, nothing." He was wild with panic, but he calmed down when he saw the girl. He grabbed her and inspected her for bullet holes.

"Is the child safe?"

"See for yourself. Yes, she's quite unharmed."

"Thank the good Lord for that." About then I arrived on the edge of his consciousness. "Oh, I do apologize. You must think me so rude."

"I can see you've been worried."

70

"Worried? I've been out of my mind. It's such a . . . well, such a desperate escapade."

"Not for us. And I would have thought you'd be used to it by now."

He gave me a canny look there. "Not really. We don't usually operate in this manner. We're a perfectly reputable agency."

"And you hand out hymn books for good attendance."

From inside the room I heard a short laugh. It was a coarse laugh. Well, a coarse laugh for someone on gratitude terms with the good Lord.

It was followed by a voice that was even coarser. Even for a white slaver.

"For Christ's sake stop pissing around, Algan. The fellow says the kid's all right."

The accent was East London. With more time I could probably have named the street. That was where I learned to duck.

"Just one thing."

"Yes?"

Somehow I didn't want the door to close. For no specific reason, I was trying to string the conversation.

"Do you have any identification?"

"Oh, I don't think there's any need for that. All's well that ends well, as they say, so . . ."

"I'd like to see some ID. How do I know you don't run a brothel in Beirut?"

His eyes popped at that. The voice inside, chuckling, said, "Show the geezer some papers for God's sake, Algan."

"Yes, yes, of course. There."

From his wallet he handed over a card which identified him as Arthur Algan from the WAIFS agency in Earls Court.

Trying to look thoughtful, I scratched my jaw with the card. It scraped. The last shave was a long time ago.

"Why did you want this girl particularly?" I asked.

"What?" His head flicked about in alarm.

"Why her? Millions of people over there would like to cross the border. I wondered why this one."

"Err, policy. It's our policy to . . . errr, help young people. . . ."

"She must be very important to be worth all this trouble."

The door swung fully open. It was the voice. He was small and stocky and his hair was bright ginger and permed in a million curls. The accent was East London, the tone was rough, but the face was pure Dartmoor Prison. His nose had been smeared across his face, and he hadn't got that fastening bibs.

"Look, son," he said, taking the girl by the arm and dragging her in. "You don't need to know nothing, right, so scram."

"Three people died out there tonight. For her."

Algan's fingers fluttered to his lips to catch a small scream. He looked white and frightened. His colleague looked interested.

"Three dead? Busy night. Now move it before there's any more."

"Three dead," Algan repeated, bubbling with panic. His fingers were all over, knotting in front of him, wriggling in the air, smoothing the front of his suit. "Merciful heaven, I'd no idea it was going to be like this. Whatever will happen to us?"

He was still speaking when Ginger Curls grabbed him, too, and flung him back into the room, stabbed one finger at me, and then slammed the door.

I stood there for a minute. I could hear Algan twittering and the other man telling him to shut up. There were a few things I wanted to ask and a few more I wanted to say, but I studied the door, remembered the rules, and backed off.

Passing through the foyer on the way back, I met the Chimp. He was looking for the ice machine. We both stopped, facing each other in the warm, deserted darkness.

"How'd it go?"

He shrugged his vast shoulders. "That had better come from Kit."

He was right. That was the protocol. But there was also a matter of personal feeling.

"Fine," I said, in an even and pleasant manner. "Whatever he says, I'd like you to know, from me, that I'll never work with you again."

He stood there, solid, calm, with about as much emotion as a mountainside. "That's your judgment," he said.

It was an acknowledgment, and only just that. He didn't care what I said or thought. It didn't interest him. It didn't annoy him. I had nothing that would touch him.

Yokel had gone to bed. But Kit, who was sharing a room with me, handed me a toothbrushing glass of Scotch and motioned me to sit on the next bed. He was wearing a worn terry cloth robe. Outside, dawn was coloring up the snow and the sky.

"You'll want to know how it is, Peter, so here goes. I asked him what he thought he was playing at killing the dog, waking everyone up, and then starting a shooting match. He said he had no choice because the dog went for him. He says he tried to do it quietly, with his hands, and it wasn't his fault that it made such a damned noise. Then, he says, he had no choice but to take the men out."

"Okay, and what about the last one? He was trying to escape. He wanted to come through with us."

Kit shrugged. He was unhappy about this. "His answer to that is that he couldn't be sure."

"Oh c'mon, we all heard him calling out. He was your contact's brother. We saw him giving the thumbs-up at the window earlier."

This time Kit pulled a face and made a doubting noise. "Again, our friend says if it had been a trick, or a trap even, and the last man had produced a gun when he got through, the whole operation would have been wrecked."

73

RETRIEVAL

"He was genuine, that soldier. Running out like that, calling out, risking his life . . . everything about it says he was the real thing."

Kit took a drink from his glass and presented me with an unsympathetic face. "I'm afraid I don't agree. He acted quite correctly. He took the only course that was totally safe, however unpleasant that course might have been. That is the one he's trained to take. All of us, for that matter."

That was a dig in the chops for me. I finished my drink and took my anger off to bed. It was a futile anger that wasn't going anywhere. First there was the killing, then Ginger Curls pushing me around, and now I'd had my wrist slapped.

What hurt most of all was knowing they were right. The plan you have in your head never works out: what makes a good man is the speed with which he reacts to the changing circumstances. That's in the handbook. The Chimp had been swift and decisive. That's in the handbook, too.

I was angry with myself. I was softening up. People who point gunbarrels for a living shouldn't think too much.

We'd paid our bill the next morning and we were setting off for Hanover airport when I saw them again. Algan and the other fellow had emerged in the foyer and the girl was looking around, obviously meeting someone.

Then she ran to this figure in the Russian hat. I caught a glimpse of his face, felt a hundred memories stir, then he took her in his arms and buried his face in her hair. It was weeks before I realized who it was.

So that was the retrieval. I've been on worse, and I've been on better. At least we did what we went to do, and at least our party came back complete.

Mr. Blanchland awarded us eight out of ten for it, I heard later. But then, the only thing he'd ever fired was a shorthand typist—and even then I bet he needed help.

12

Yokel's cremation wasn't a sellout. We just managed to reach double figures. At least the ticket peddlers failed to clean up for once.

His mother came up from Salisbury, a tubby woman with a handkerchief to her face, and two elderly farmers—uncles, I think—in suits that appeared to be made from buffalo hide. I picked them up at Paddington.

"He wouldn't hurt a fly, our Phil," she kept on saying.

"Them's the ones as always gets it," said one of the farmers.

Rosemary was there, in a dainty pillbox hat. She must have got up at 6 A.M. to get the angle exactly right. The younger daughter was red-eyed, and mouthed a silent hello to me. The older one hung onto her mother's arm and sought out safe middle distances with her gaze. They were even taking sides at a funeral. Sometimes I'm not sorry I haven't got a family.

Rosemary had got in touch with me after reading about his death in the newspapers and talking to the police. She was staying in Nottingham with—as she put it—"a friend in need."

Any other time I would have said he wouldn't stay "in need" for long with her around. But I didn't, just this once.

She had asked me to make the funeral arrangements. Kit suggested having a word with the regiment to see if he could be buried in the quiet corner of a graveyard reserved for their dead. I thought about it and said "no." Yokel had finished with all that. Quite possibly "all that" had finished with him, too.

RETRIEVAL

So I fixed it up at the local crematorium.

Jenny came, on Kit's arm. She was quite distressed. She'd met him a few times over the years. "He was one of those men who get eaten alive by women," she said. "He didn't have enough of the bastard ingredient."

I wasn't going to let it turn into one of those sob jobs, so I brought Tamara along. She helped to keep the numbers up, too. I did warn her about not wearing gold lamé or anything silly, but she did me proud.

She swept in in something high-necked, long, dark blue, and beautifully cut, and wore a dip-brimmed hat. She was all elegance and restraint. I told her so, in a whisper, as the organ music began.

"But no drawers, darling," she whispered back. "*Quelle* turn-on?"

I couldn't expect her to step completely out of character.

The business only lasted a few minutes. I did warn the vicar we were a bit light on conviction, but we put lots of punch into "He Who Would Valiant Be." I chose that for Yokel. It was his sort of tune. The vicar said something about soldiers and the army of the Lord, but abandoned it before it became too painful.

As the coffin slid away, I found myself thinking that it was a soldier's death after all: that's the way you go if you get a grenade in a centurion.

Afterwards, we all hovered uncertainly on the lawn, not knowing what to do or say. Tamara was dabbing her eyes. "It seems so sad," she said. "All the fun and jollies in the world, and now he's out of it, poor lamb." To her it was like the end of a party.

I was pointing out to Kit that the evergreens in North London, solid slabs of impenetrable greenery which ringed the grounds, didn't start losing their upholstery like the inferior, rustic product, when I heard a small voice next to me say, "Excuse me."

It was the younger girl. I looked down into Yokel's eyes again. It was a shaking sensation.

"Mum says you chose the hymn," she said. I nodded. "I wondered why you picked that one?"

I could have said that it's one of the few that heathens like us know, but there was a reason, a genuine one, and I wasn't ashamed of it.

"There's no discouragement shall make him once repent his first avowed intent. . . . That was your father."

"The three of us were very close," Kit said to her. "Peter's right. It was exactly the sort of hymn he would have loved."

"I know," she said, her face puffed up pink with crying. "He used to talk about you two such a lot. Kit and Pete, my mates, he used to say."

She was on the edge of tears again, so I led her back to her mother. On the way I said something I'd been hoping to say to her if I got the chance.

"Look at it this way, love. Perhaps you didn't see much of him and perhaps it all ended up in sadness, but for fifteen years you had a dad who was ten feet tall, a real man, a hero. Well, fifteen years of that is better than half a century with some boring little sod in a blue suit who flies a ballpoint for a living."

It wasn't entirely guileless. I'd seen mother's friend waiting outside the iron gates in a firm's Cortina.

She spun around and stared up at me, quite breathless. "I didn't know what to think," she said. "But I do now. Oh, thank you."

I switched from her gratitude to her mother's icy suspicion. "And what is Becky supposed to think?" she asked.

"That her dad was a good man," I said.

For a moment I thought she was going to contest that. Then she abandoned her chin-jutting stance and slumped a little.

"I suppose he was," she said. "But not for me." She

lifted her face and in a steady tone she asked, "It wasn't an accident, was it?"

"Who knows?"

To my surprise, she asked me if I would arrange to have the house cleared and the contents sold. She wanted to sell it as quickly as possible. I asked her if there were things she wanted. She shook her head.

"Not even the souvenirs? They must be collectors' items."

"Spears? Weapons? Don't you ever get sick of killing?"

People were going. I could see Kit loading the Wiltshire trio into his car to take them to the station. Jenny was standing with Tamara beside my Minor. I was talking about my questionable profession with a pretty widow in a pillbox hat.

"Killing," I said, "is a reputable trade if it's kept in the right hands."

"Like yours," she said, and turned and walked away.

"I'll keep his souvenirs," I called after her. "If the girls want them when they're older, they'll know where to find them."

After we'd been to Paddington, the four of us went for a drink. We needed one. With the lamentations over, Kit and I had an unfinished conversation.

Since I talked to him on the telephone after Yokel's death, we hadn't discussed any of the ramifications. Neither of us asked about the cause of his death, or its possible effects. That was why he'd said we mustn't lose each other's trust. But we also knew, both of us, that it had already been eroded.

"Have you spoken to the police?" Kit said, pocketing his change. We'd found one of those depressing old Victorian pubs with a modernized back bar that's always empty. I think it's the tropical sunset on the carpet that frightens the customers off.

"Just routine stuff."

Out of the corner of my eyes, I saw Jenny had turned

Tamara away and they were searching for the common ground between motherhood and mistressdom.

"I don't suppose you got a decent look at the chap who kicked you?" he asked.

"No. Except his training shoes. Police believe the wanted man is one of the twenty million who wear training shoes. Do you think he gets boot money from Adidas?"

Kit ignored that, and coughed to clear his awkwardness. "And you've no idea why?"

"He disturbed a burglar, didn't he?"

"Do you believe that, Peter?"

"No. But you're going to ask me to."

His eyes blanked for a moment, as he thought. "I don't know. I'm not sure. I think he'd got into some funny areas."

"Is that the chat around the Unit?" I leaned forward. I wanted every word of this. "Is that what you've picked up?"

He became diffident. "The odd word, you know how it is. Nothing firm. Nothing to get one's teeth into."

Jenny called over, "How's your head, Pete?" I mimed huge swollen heads and turned back to Kit.

"Don't pussyfoot with me, Kit. We know each other too well. He hit a nerve somewhere. Someone wanted him silenced."

He gave the table a sharp rap with his closed fist. "Oh no, I'm not saying that for a moment. What you don't understand is that there are plenty of other . . . errr, rough people around, apart from people in our business. There's no saying what he found or whose toes he might have trodden on."

I spoke quietly and softly then. Kit always found it hard to swim against the current. It's not his fault. It's all that public-school stuff: it's a team game, chaps, and rally around the school.

"Before, you warned me off, too. Now you're saying he wasn't killed by a burglar."

"Absolutely. Well, no, not absolutely. But it is possible."

He was coming to it very slowly.

"Do you think I ought to ask a few questions perhaps? Is that what you think, Kit?"

Confusion rampaged over his thin, handsome face. "Oh, God! No. No. I can't say that, can I? I think we'd better see what the authorities can come up with first."

He put his glass down sharply. Nothing in the world would make him go that far. Not yet. So I sat back and smiled at him.

"We've already seen what they can come up with, haven't we?"

"Pete!" Jenny waved at me across the table, smiling sweetly. "I think Kit and I had better be going. Tamara was just telling me that she finds funerals have a fiercely aphrodisiac affect."

13

You have to start somewhere. I'd no idea what Yokel had done, where he'd been, or who he'd seen. All I could think of was one man who might know something.

The next morning I made some toast and tea and opened the back door so I could stretch my legs and got on the telephone. I rang the Workers' Democratic Alliance.

"I wonder if you could help me. I want to come along to one of Walter Starburn's meetings."

"You'll be lucky, mate," the man on the other end said. "You couldn't get hold of a ticket for one of Walter's meetings for love nor money."

"Oh." I should have thought of that. "Has he got any meetings coming up?"

"Tonight. Islington. But don't waste your time going without a ticket. You won't get in. It'll be packed."

I wasn't surprised when I thought about it. Since he first sprang to fame in that area where industrial relations and politics overlap, Walter had moved from being a terror figure of the left to something very close to a folk hero.

No one had ever heard of him until he led a dockers' strike when London had some docks left to strike in. They didn't have any public sympathy, and not much interest either, until Starburn popped up on television. I remember it. He was standing in the street with the traffic crawling past and the interviewer asked him if it was true that he and his friends had used gangster tactics. "You don't get where I am by kissing babies," he said, and laughed hugely.

He'd got that quality they call charisma now. When he went into a room the temperature rose ten degrees, and when he left it was as though they'd put the lights out. He gave off a personal warmth that came right out of the television screen at you.

He'd got looks—his face was used and trustworthy, like a handsome but battered satchel—and there was something about the way he didn't worry about the locks of uncombed hair flopping across his face that ruled out vanity.

He preached romantic Marxism, supported with quotes from the Bible and Shakespeare. His style was forgiving, tolerant, and amused, as though he saw a joke we were all blind to.

Naturally the unions were pleased to have a star in their ranks—a spokesman who could speak. They soon had him on every committee in the country. In no time at all he was standing outside No. 10 talking about what had happened inside.

That was all ten years ago or more. Since then he had taken on stature, dignity, and a load of money. He made it by the bucketful, opening employment agencies and print shops. You might have thought it would count against him, but he turned even that to his advantage.

"All these years," he said on television, "I've been thinking how wonderful all these businessmen are. They're so clever, aren't they? That's why they're entitled to live in big houses with flashy cars. But when I've got a few bob, I can do just as well as them. And if I can do it, believe me, anyone can. All you need is the cash and a chance. They're not clever at all. They conned us again!"

And somehow that made it all right.

The left-wing intellectuals loved him. They tried to cart him around the Hampstead drawing rooms like the Noble Savage sprung to life. He wouldn't have that. In the docks and pits and factory towns they loved him because he was proving they were as good as their masters. Even his targets, the rich and the influential, were obliged to say through gritted teeth that the man was clever.

He could court disaster and escape. At his first public

meeting, he began by taking his mother on the platform. She was a thin, little old creature, completely blind, and his enemies were onto that fast. "A vulgar plucking of the heartstrings," someone said.

At his next meeting he stood at the microphone with his arm around her.

"Know what?" he said. "They're telling me I've got to be ashamed of my old mum. You know what sort of people they are, don't you. Them narrow-gutted people who are frightened to cry at funerals in case people laugh at them, and scared to belch after a meal in case they look badly brought up. Well I am badly brought up. I'm so badly brought up that I love my ma and I don't mind saying so. You know what they're really scared of, don't you? They're frightened to show what's in their hearts—because they're empty."

They took the roof off.

Next time I saw him on television was when he'd been elected MP for one of the East End constituencies. He was driving around the back streets in a white, open Rolls.

Then there was his marriage. It was like something out of a soap opera. On a trade delegation to Thailand, he met a lovely young Thai girl, fell in love, and brought her back and married her. He even brought her brother, too, and the suggestion was that he'd saved the two of them from the brothels of Bangkok. He adopted her brother. All the magazines were full of pictures of him and his new family, arms around the pair of them.

He stayed in the East End, although by now he was living in a vast and luxurious flat above the warehouse overlooking the Thames.

That was Walter Starburn, the man I was going to see. He was the man I'd seen hugging the girl in the hotel foyer, after the retrieval.

Everyone in Britain knew his face, and me better than most. But I couldn't place it then, out of context and seen so quickly. It wasn't until I'd been back a few weeks that he popped up on television again and I realized who it was.

I put it on one side. In my trade you often stumble across things it's better not to know, or that it pays you to forget.

Now he was the only link I'd got with the retrieval that had led to Yokel's death.

They were right about the crowds. I had to park half a mile away and walk. I'd left it late so that I'd just catch the end of the meeting. At the door I showed a Press pass that must have fallen out of someone's pocket some time.

"Trying to dig the dirt up again on Walter?" the man sneered. "You won't find any. He's clean."

I stood at the back and watched. Even then people turned and glared at me for making a noise. They were like kids watching a conjuror. He had them mesmerized. He was a big, heavy man and he used his hands a lot when he talked. There was a table of officials on the stage, trying to catch his reflected glory, and sitting with them was his mother.

I turned back to Starburn. He spoke slowly, loving every second of it. In one hand he had a drink and in the other a cigar, and that's what he was talking about. . . .

". . . a Labour man who held high office, and do you know he used to buy fifty-quid suits and fill the pockets so they looked all cheap and baggy. And he used to drink beer and smoke a horrible, great pipe whenever he was in public. But in private, well, would you believe it, he was a different man. He drank brandy, expensive, fancy brandy, and smoked cigars that would cost you a week's wage."

He stopped, took a deep lungful of smoke from the cigar, and tossed back the drink.

"That's champagne, that is. The best. That cigar's the same as he used to smoke. I got a Rolls outside the front door and the cops said I shouldn't leave it around here because the wheels'll get ripped off because you lot are a load of thieves. Really. That's what they said. But they don't get stolen. I don't lock the door of my flat neither, and that don't get done, and I got things in there worth thousands."

I looked around. They were craning forward to see where he was leading them. They'd have followed him anywhere, I think.

"And I'll tell you for why. Because I tell you the truth and you know it. Because you're not thugs and I know that. Because we're made from the same stuff, all of us."

He bent forward, suddenly an odd figure in the spotlight, and his right arm pointed off into the wings.

"There was a Yank preacher, Martin Luther King, who used to say he'd been to the Promised Land. Well, I been there, too. I seen the big houses out in Surrey and holidays in the West Indies and I like it. This suit"—he plucked at a lapel—"this suit cost four hundred pounds. What I say is that if it's good enough for the chairman of Marks and Spencer, then it's good enough for me. And I say that if all those bank managers and lawyers are content to live out in Surrey and go to the Bahamas, then we should be, too. Like I say, I been there, and you lot are going to follow me. That's where we're going, bruvvers—the Promised Land. It's ours."

Released from his spell, the audience leapt to its feet. I couldn't see a thing for the people on their seats and others jumping up to get a glimpse of him. Then I saw him through the crowd, one arm around his mother, the other held out wide.

He might have learned his politics from Marx, but he'd learned his psychology from Gracie Fields, the singer, or Max Bygraves, the loud comedian. He plugged straight into the most powerful emotion among ordinary working people: sentiment.

Most politicians went for the wage packet. Starburn went straight for the emotions, and he hit the nerve every time.

I pushed my way down the aisle, showed my pass at the stage door, and went through. I found his room backstage. It was easy to recognize. All the people who wanted a bit of his magic were thronging through the door to try to get near him.

Good shoulder first, I prized a way through until I was inside the door and I could see his face, full of good humor, at the far side of the room. He was asking for a bit of air for his old mum.

As he glanced around the room, flicking back his hair, his eyes caught mine. His head stopped turning. His smile died.

"Well, look who's here," he said, and he said it with a softness that commanded more than any shout. The room fell silent. Everyone turned to see who he was looking at.

Suddenly he was thrusting his way through the crowd. He almost climbed over the top of them, pushing people to one side as he drove through. When he reached me, they'd pulled back so that the two of us were in a small clearing.

Then he put up his fists, big hard fists, dropped into a fighting crouch, and moved in on me. He swung a hook that nearly took the buttons off my shirt and hit my chin . . . like a feather. Then he flung the same arm around me and roared out, "Christ everybody, this is my mate, Pete! Know something? He was the only kid in the whole of Stepney that I never beat in a fight. He was the gov'nor, was Pete. And I ain't seen him for twenty bleedin' years."

"Twenty-four," I said.

"There you are, what did I say, he can bleedin' count, too!"

14

We went back to his flat in the white Rolls-Royce. Along the way, he made his chauffeur turn off down the side streets to see our old haunts, and everywhere the kids crowded around to see the silky machine slink through the shabby streets. It was as ridiculous as touring high-class Mayfair on a mule, but Starburn didn't seem to notice.

"Remember that place, Pete?" he yelled, pointing out of the window and hammering me on the knee.

It was teeming with memories for both of us. I sat quietly, feeling them come alive inside me. Starburn shouted them out.

"That's the old gym, remember? What about that night we done fifteen rounds in there and I never got a glove on you and my face looked like a piece of steak? Here, and that's where they used to have the old Shiny Garter Club. It's derelict now. Remember how I used to help the bouncer out for a couple of quid? Threw Chancer Brown down the stairs and give him a bunch of cracked ribs. . . ."

He was like a kid, he was so excited.

But first, when he'd tipped everyone out of his back room at the hall, he'd led me up to his mother. She was sitting in the corner, as fleshless and dry as an old stick, her silver hair piled in a bun and dark glasses over her eyes. Around her was that aura of silence that all blind people have.

"Ma, you remember young Pete, don't you?"

She held out a handful of bones. "Course I do. He was the smart one, was Pete."

"Not smart enough to be in the House of Commons."

Glancing from her to me, Starburn was plainly elated.

"Oh, you know Walter," she said. "He'd be king if the hours were better."

"And the salary, don't forget the salary," he said. "Seriously, Pete, don't you think she's looking great? Live to be a hundred, won't you, Ma?"

"I'm ready when the Lord is," she said.

"Go on, you'll live forever. Won't she, Pete? Lives like a queen, don't you darling? Best of everything, that's what you get."

She started to chuckle. "I know," she said. "I'm a lucky old biddy, and who'd ever have thought it. Your ma died, then, Pete?"

"A few years back now."

"I heard. And your dad never did come back, did he? Still, I dare say she was better off without him. Men never brought nothing but grief. Except this one."

She grabbed his arm and rubbed her cheek against it.

She'd had six children, and no two to the same man. I remembered her as a sparkling little thing who had such a fast throughput of men that she used to call each one her "new friend." None of them ever stayed long enough to be "old" friends. To her children, they were all uncles.

Walter's dad—or so everyone said—was a Greek Cypriot who stayed around for a few months. It seemed likely when you looked at his oiled, black curls and long Mediterranean face.

In a place where we were all poor, they set new lows. Furnished rooms, eviction, furnished rooms—that was the pattern. Once, I remember, they had to live in a disused railway tunnel for a whole winter. Later, in the good times, they had two rooms just off the Whitechapel Road. The kids shared a bed, and the mother slept on a pile of old clothes in the corner.

We were class: three rooms for a family of four. Once I even had a toothbrush of my own.

Like most of us, they hung onto the driftwood of life,

waiting for the next wave. No one around there did a lot of forward planning. The life reflected in the glossies could have been a travel brochure for the moon for all we knew.

In the car, Starburn sat between us and kept up his Memory-Lane stuff.

"And what about your Jenny?" his mother said. "She was a really pretty girl, Jenny was."

"Lives out in the country, no feller, but a little boy called Luke. What they used to call an unmarried mother."

She gave a sympathetic laugh. "Got caught, eh?"

"No. That was how she wanted things. You know what girls are like these days."

She gave a soft laugh. "When I think of all the times we tried not to get caught, now they do it on purpose."

"We're not so bad now we're here," her son said, patting her on the hand. "Here, Pete, look at this. Remember hanging around the door there?"

We were going down the Whitechapel Road, passing The Grave Maurice. We used to peep around the door to see the Kray Brothers, sitting over their light ales while they discussed who to build the next motorway over. They were our heroes. We didn't know then what real villains they were. If we had, we'd probably have admired them even more.

It was hard country. You got by with your fists or your wits, nothing else. Starburn had both. So did I, I suppose.

Those tight terraces spawned friendships and loyalties that were so close they were almost incest. From them sprang the gangs, and from the gangs the crimes and violence that so fascinated sociologists with 2.3 children and four bedrooms in suburbia. They had problems understanding it.

It didn't matter how often you walked around or who you talked to, the only way to know it was to be born there.

I wound down the window and felt it. It's somewhere between a smell and a sound, a knowledge that's deep in your bones. It's people making deals in order to live. A guy'll fix you up with a market stand if you can give him a hand to shift some hot cars at the auction tomorrow for a mate who's got a load of comforters, brand new, to push in the parking lots quick, before the police catch on. Everywhere in those half-lit streets humanity was scrabbling to make a couple of quid. It was people going about their daily task of staying alive.

It's changed a bit since I left. The straight trading, once handled by the Jews, is now left to the Asians. The planners have stacked the hardness on its end in blocks of flats now. There was a warmth to the terraces that went when they demolished them.

Now the cruelty is more anonymous. Mugging hardly needs a motive. In my day you always knew who you were hitting. Sometimes you even knew why. Gentlemen of the old school, we were.

It was amateur stuff when we were young. Joyriding in cars, lifting things from shops and helping things fall off trucks. Starburn ran a gang—he had the mouth for it even then—and I was his number two. When we left school we had to think about moving into the senior league of serious crime.

I got out. Instead I joined the biggest gang in the country, the one with the unfashionable haircuts: the army.

"Why?" I remember Starburn going on at me. "You of all people. The bleedin' army, Pete. You got to be off your trolley. Why?"

"Because they've got better guns," I said. And it was true.

I hadn't seen him since then. He hadn't changed much. He'd thickened around the neck and waist, but he still had the same tumultuous energy, and the same hot emotions that could turn a slap on the back into a knife in your throat.

That's why I always beat him in a fight. If I'd lost, I was afraid he might kill me.

RETRIEVAL

"Isn't it great to be back?" Starburn asked me, and I could see he wanted to inflame me with his excitement.

I didn't have to answer. We were stopped at traffic lights and some young boys tapped on the window. "Mr. Starburn, Mr. Starburn, can we have a ride? Can we, go on Mr. Starburn?"

With a smiling shake of the head, he pushed a button so the window came down. "Wait around here, I'll send Harry back in ten minutes, you cheeky little beggars."

The window hummed up again. We moved off. It obviously wasn't the first time he'd let the local kids run around in his car.

A few minutes later we swished over damp flagstones at the back of a blank-walled warehouse.

Starburn tapped me on the knee. "You're staying the night, right? Dinner, a few nice drinks, chat. Right?"

I didn't argue. I could always catch up with the housework another night.

I got out. There was an echo in the air that meant we were near the river. Then I heard the soft slap of the water somewhere in the darkness.

A short corridor took us into a wood-panelled elevator, and we stepped out onto a few dozen acres of off-white carpet. Scattered around on it were soft leather chairs so big and baggy you could be dropped in by air without a bruise.

His mother had gone off somewhere down a long corridor. Starburn took me over to the window. It was the whole of the riverside wall.

"Look at that. My city. I love this damned place, Pete, I really do."

From here the buildings were small and dark and insignificant against the broad, black curve of the river. They looked as temporary as sandcastles against that historic flow.

"What do you think?" He saw me looking around the room. There was an antique desk in the corner that could

91

have been rosewood or, for all I knew, plywood. On the olive-green walls were paintings which even I could see weren't just paintings—they were Art. They were old battle scenes: wild-eyed horses plunging around and generals dying gallant deaths amidst the fray.

"In my experience of war," I said, "generals usually die gallant deaths in Knightsbridge. Of gout."

Starburn roared. Anything I said would be wise or funny for him that night. He gave me the world's largest whisky in the world's largest glass.

"Scotch?" he asked, after he'd delivered it. "We was both on pints of bitter last time we had a drink-up and we was under age then. But I knew you'd be a Scotch man now. Scotch drinkers are the royalty of boozers. You were talking about war just then—I hear you're working with the funnies?"

It was a question but it didn't carry a lot of doubt. I wondered what Blanchland would think of this after all the fuss he made about security.

"Packed all that in years ago," I said casually. "How good's the rest of your information on me?"

He was grinning at my denial. "Let's see . . . grotty flat in Wandsworth in a road full of blacks, visits sister near the coast most weekends, lost his woman a while back, Liz, wasn't it. . . . Knocks off the odd doll, mostly a Chelsea piece at the moment. . . . How am I doing?"

"Half right," I said, but I knew from his face that he knew damn well he was right. "How'd you keep tabs on me? And why?"

"Cos you're an old pal and I want to know what my old pals are up to. I've got a big organization here. I've got a lot of useful people. I can find things out if I want to."

He looked up. A maid in real maid's clothes was standing in the doorway arch.

"Let's eat," he said, again laughing at my surprise.

We ate steaks that must have been takeouts from the

Connaught and a red wine that my gourmet tastebuds told me was definitely not from Algeria.

"Excuse me, sir," the maid said, as though she'd been up all night practicing. "Harry says is he to put the car away?"

"Did he give those kids a ride out?"

"I believe so, sir."

"Right then, we won't need it. My guest here is staying the night. Put some stuff out for him, will you?"

Suddenly I remembered all I'd read about his family. I asked him, but he brushed it aside. "We got too much to talk about," he said.

We had coffee in eggshell cups as we capsized in the leather chairs, then another bottle of whisky decanted into crystal. Starburn excused himself while he went to say goodnight to his mother. I was standing watching the river down below when I became conscious of a figure reflected in the window. I spun around. It was a young Chinese man. He laughed. Then suddenly I remembered he must be the adopted son, the Thai boy.

He was wearing a brilliant blue silk shirt with a black scarf knotted under one ear, black trousers, and soft black boots with a heel most women would have had trouble managing. From what I remembered I put him at about 14.

I was about to introduce myself when he suddenly said, "Where is my daddy? My daddy! You are his friend? You are quite old. You are not German. No, I know you are not German."

I didn't know what any of it meant, except that the way it was delivered it wasn't meant to cheer anyone up. There was more sneer than cheer in that laugh.

"I'm quite old, I'll give you that," I said.

"That's the only crime, getting old," he said.

"I wouldn't say it's the only crime, but it's quite widespread," I said, to keep things ticking over.

Suddenly a second figure appeared beside him. She'd come from the long corridor which emerged by the elevator, I realized. This was where Starburn had gone to see his mother. Obviously it led into the rest of the flat.

She was Starburn's wife. She was as small and soft and beautifully fashioned as a petal. She was wearing a white sheath and her black hair was trimmed to the perfect roundness of her head.

She gave me a glance of despair and clutched her brother's arm and began talking to him in whatever it is Thais talk in. He kept his flat black metallic eyes on me, but spoke to her once, curtly, out of the corner of his mouth.

Whatever it was he said, it worked. She slapped him hard across the face. His head jerked, but the smile stayed put.

She took one step back and said what could only have been "sorry." Then she half-turned and faced me without raising her eyes.

"Please forgive us. This is very stupid. My brother and I are having a silly fight. Walter will be so cross. I am his wife. I am pleased to meet you."

I was moving across the carpet to try to get the social niceties on the move when her brother said, "You wanna buy my sister, mister?"

She stood there, her head down, as he gave a high hysterical laugh that stopped as though it had been axed.

Starburn's hand was on his shoulder. He must have walked as silently down the corridor as they had. The young Thai boy began shaking as soon as the hand landed on him.

"What's he doing here?" Starburn said to his wife.

"I'm sorry," she said.

Catching my eye, Starburn pulled a troubled face. "My son. Problems. You met my wife?" He waved his hand between the two of us, and we each attempted a courteous smile. They were both quick and they were both strained.

"Anyway," he said, with a heavy sigh, and I saw him turn the boy with his one hand, "you get along back to your room now and have an early night. Kim will come along with you. All right?"

"Won't you put me to bed?" He gave that high screech of a laugh again.

"Kim'll see you off to bed," Starburn repeated, working him toward the corridor.

"Because I'm a big boy now," the Thai said, again with the sneer in his voice. "Too big, aren't I?"

"Off you go, son," Starburn said, in a kindly tone. "We don't want you to have any more of those nasty nightmares, do we?"

His wife led the boy away, with one last effort at a hostess's smile for me. The newspaper reports had said she was about twenty, but she looked quite a lot older than her brother to me.

I wondered why he'd pronounced the slogan of all juvenile pimps in the third world. If he came from Bangkok I supposed he must have heard it often enough. And I wondered what sort of pills he'd been taking to knock him crazy enough to do it.

Starburn was full of apologies. I was as full of the right responses. He said they were having a lot of trouble with the boy. He hadn't settled in properly and he'd made some dangerous friends. I asked him if he thought he was perhaps on some pills, and Starburn was startled, then thoughtful, and said he'd look into it.

"Your wife is gorgeous," I said.

"Who? Oh, Kim. Yes, of course."

I had to work hard to get the conversation back on course. Starburn was upset, understandably enough, by the scene with his adopted son. But eventually he settled, had a drink, and became his old self again.

"Why didn't you come and see me?" he said, once his quietness had lifted. "I was really put out about that. My old mate never coming around. You'd know where I was from the papers."

"Success changes people."

He leveled a finger at me. "Not me. You can't say that, Pete. I'm just the same, ain't I? 'Course I am. That's why I sent Harry back to give those kids a ride."

"The Starburn I used to know didn't have a chauffeur to send anywhere."

"That don't make me different."

"No. Maybe that was unfair. Perhaps it makes me different. Maybe I find it hard to handle a rich friend."

He sat up in his chair then. "I get you, Pete. Don't worry about it. That'll wear off. Come and work for me, Pete. I want you, boy."

"Nice of you, Starburn, but no thanks."

"You don't want to work for those bleedin' fascists you're in with now. I didn't blame you for going in the army, plenty of good boys do that. And I can see why you went for all that adventure-playground stuff. But pack this lot in, Pete. I know about them. Bully boys for the bosses, that's all they are."

"I don't know what story you've got hold of," I said. "I do security for private firms. It's okay, it pays, I get by."

"I know what you do, son, and I don't like to think about it. Come and work for me."

"Carrying your briefcase?"

He waved his hand to brush that aside. "Look at the way you spotted that with the boy tonight. Maybe he is taking pills. You've been around; you know things."

He'd got up and was standing over me now. "What I need is one person I can trust. You're right about success. I never know if people are really with me or if they've hopped on board for the ride. I want someone I can trust. I want you, Pete."

"It's a long time since we were together."

"Okay, so we haven't set eyes on each other for twenty-four years . . ."

His voice faded away as he saw the look on my face. I shook my head. "Wrong. We saw each other a few months ago. In the foyer of an hotel in the Harz Mountains in Germany."

I watched that one sink home. Slowly. Then he put back his head and gave a great howl of laughter.

"You secretive bastard," he said, between guffaws. "And you let me think you hadn't recognized me."

15

That was my ace, and when I'd played it he didn't raise an eyebrow. If anything, he seemed relieved to have it out in the open. I was relieved, too; his candor swept away any idea of furtive guilt. I hadn't much enjoyed the sensation of trying to catch out an old friend.

He dragged the chairs up to the window and turned down the lights so we could see the river catch the last flickers of life from the city. Another day's fight for survival was over down there.

He put the decanter of whisky down between us. Then he collapsed into his soft-bellied chair and began the explanation I'd waited all those months to hear.

"First, you got to remember I'm not just a political animal. Christ, you should know that if anyone does, Pete. But once you're into politics, the way I am, everyone sees you all the time in political terms. Stupid, but that's how it works. Anyway, remember that while I tell you the rest. Right?

"About a year ago, I'm in East Germany. Trade mission thing, unions and governments and international socialism—the lot. I was heading it, to be honest. I meets this feller, gets pally with him. It turns out his wife took off to the West a couple of years ago and he's left with this youngster. Girl, of course. The kid wants to join her mum the way they do. Natural thing. Anyway, top and bottom is can I help him to get the girl out."

In the half-light, he looked like a Greek. His features looked heavy and sensual, his black curls draped over his forehead. But the talk was old-fashioned Cockney corn.

"Me, I'm only human, like I said. So I talks to a few fellers who know about these things, an agency was involved at some stage, and lo and behold, I'm told it can be done."

I saw the profile of his head as he threw it back and gave a strong confident laugh.

"What I couldn't possibly know, my old son, was that it was going to be you doing the job. Talk about small world, eh?"

"Who did you ask about it?"

"About what?" He sounded puzzled.

"About doing the retrieval. Getting the girl out. Where did you start making inquiries?"

I was trying to work out the line of connections that had brought the two of us together that day. He didn't find that important.

"Oh, I think it was the army first of all. That's right, some brigadier geezer. He said to leave it to him. I don't know what happened after that. Except it worked, of course. All I know is that I go along to have a look and there's old Pete, large as life and twice as bloody devious."

That was another thing that had been bothering me. "Why were you there?"

"Ah." He sat forward and I saw the decanter glint as he swung it up. He splashed whisky into both glasses. It sounded like half a bathful, but in those glasses it barely covered the bottom. "Good question. I'd got some business over there about that time. I realized that if I bent schedules a bit I could see the last act, so to speak. I thought it'd be nice. If it's your baby, you want to see it born, don't you?"

"You knew the girl well then?"

"I wouldn't say that."

"But in the hotel she went running to you, flung her arms around you." I didn't like to say he'd gathered her up in his arms, too.

He laughed again. "Gawd, like the bleedin' inquisition this is. I see what you mean, though. I was a bit surprised myself. I saw her face light up when she saw me and she came rushing at me and I bent down to catch her. Instinct, I suppose. I think seeing a familiar face like mine suddenly made her realize she was free."

I nodded. Perhaps he didn't think I was convinced, because he added, "And I dare say she thought she had me to thank for it, too. She was a bit hysterical. Nice kid, though."

If he minded these questions, he didn't say so. So then I asked him why he had ignored me if he recognized me. That made him chuckle. A second later I understood why.

"For the same reason you ignored me, I suppose. I didn't know what you was doing there, and it was the same for you, I expect."

"I suppose."

"In fact, I'd got a better reason than you. I knew you were mixed up in all this dirty work—sorry, Pete, that's how I feel about it—and you wouldn't expect me to walk over, and say 'hiya kid, how's things,' would you?"

He hauled himself out of his chair and leaned by the window. For the first time I realized there was a balcony outside. He sat out there, he said, when it was warmer. It used to be an old tea warehouse, he went on. Clippers raced here from the other side of the world to unload in the dock below. The rest of the building was offices now, some of them his.

"Over that balcony it's a straight drop into the Thames. Splash. That's the way for a Londoner to go, eh? Look at it. This city. The people. Salt of the earth. You know that."

"What was the name of the agency you mentioned?"

"What?" He'd lost the thread of our talk. "Oh, back on that are we? Gawd, you are bleedin' remorseless, you are. I dunno. I don't know if I ever did, now I think about it. I think the army put me on to them."

He turned with his back to the window, a faint silhouette. "Any more questions? I know you boys, it'll be the bright lights and the rubber truncheons next."

"One more."

"Shoot."

"Why so secretive?"

"What?" He gave a gale of a laugh and went on, "Why so secretive? Bloody 'ell son, where you been? I thought you was a man of the world. I'll need another drink to give me strength for this one."

He poured one. Then he crouched beside me, holding the glass yet somehow tapping off the points on his fingers at the same time.

"Right? It goes like this. Starburn, socialist and man of the people and proud of it, helps out a mucker by getting his daughter exported. Don't matter from where and to where. Not to me, anyway.

"But I'm a politician, right? I got enemies. And they clap their dirty little hands together and say Starburn is helping people to escape from the yoke of Communist oppression, and what a fine bloody socialist he is, right? What does that mean?"

He drew his finger across his throat. "Starburn's politically dead. And a lot of people on your side of the fence—nothing personal—pray for that every night of their lives."

"Wouldn't they be right?" I asked. "Isn't that hypocrisy?"

He chuckled again. He was loving every second of it. He could talk all night and never miss a trick or put a foot wrong. No wonder he'd done well in politics.

"I'll tell you honest. No, I don't think the Eastern bloc is paradise on earth. In a lot of ways they've made a mess of the whole thing. There's a lot of elitism left, a lot of privilege. I don't even think it is Communism. But at least they're pointing the right way. That's how I see it. But in the end it's human happiness that matters most, and if that kid would be happier over here with someone she loves, to hell with international politics."

There was a lot to admire in what he'd said. He put his

personal principles before his political principles, without sacrificing his belief in either. He wasn't afraid to show the faults of his argument, and that took a strong man.

"And I don't suppose it would do your cause too much good to be seen using people like me?"

"Special forces? Sneakies? Crack troops of capitalism, you lot. I'd get hanged for it, wouldn't I?"

"And there you are, pouring out a Scotch for a workers' oppressor."

The decanter chinked on the glass. His teeth were suddenly white in the dark. "You know me. Hate the sin and love the sinner. There's only one question left now, and that's mine. Why are you going to all this trouble to unravel that bit of an escapade?"

It was fair enough. I'd plenty to ask him. Once or twice I'd almost accused him of lying. He'd taken it. He hadn't held back. I owed him an explanation.

So I told him. I told him all about Yokel and what had happened, and how he'd said he was going to find out about the retrieval.

He whistled. "Speared to the wall? That's hard. You boys don't hang about when you want to make a point, do you?"

I protested that we didn't know who'd done it, but he only laughed. "Admire your loyalty, Pete, but you know as well as I do. Speared to the wall? The Kray twins, who chopped up a woman and fed her to chickens, would've been proud of that."

He made it sound like casual chat, but I knew the point he was making. There was no difference between us and common murderers. For the moment, I had to swallow it.

"He was a good mate of yours, this Yokel?"

"He was. He was an innocent really."

"In that class of work? All right, I'll take your word for it. Look. Tell you what. I know a few people in this town. I'll put some feelers out about that German girl. Don't worry. I'll find her for you within twenty-four hours. No problem."

A drink haze settled on me after that. I relaxed and let the fumes steam up my mind. It had done enough work for one night. All the questions had been asked. All the questions had been answered. I was back with an old friend.

I remember asking Starburn about his wife. He talked a bit about Bangkok. I'd been there as a soldier, but I didn't mention it. He was talking about the corruption and the degradation. Then somehow he was talking about his mother again, and with such passion that he burned away the drink mist for a few minutes.

"Those kids out there. It's degrading, dehumanizing. That's what exploitation really is. But it was just the same here for my old mum. All those uncles she had, it didn't fool us kids. That was the only way she could feed and clothe us all. Lucky for her she was pretty. She'd get a feller and for a few weeks or months we'd be all right. Get the rent paid and regular meals. Then he'd up and away and we'd be in *schtuk* again. She was whoring just like those kids were in Bangkok."

It all merged then: heated up memories of the East End, Bangkok brothels, and the blood in the snow of the German mountains.

I remember turning down a long, long corridor to a room the size of a tennis court where I fell into bed, and a whisky-fired coma. I dreamed I heard laughter and a high, thin scream. And I dreamed that Starburn's petal-faced wife was the whore I'd bought with my soldier's pay in a Bangkok brothel.

16

In the morning, when I was still half asleep, I was vaguely conscious of Starburn standing beside my bed asking some questions. I gave him some answers and hoped they matched.

It must have been a couple of hours later, just before nine, when I awoke properly. I lay with one eye open waiting for the hangover to drop on me; it didn't. I was already one ahead of fate and I hadn't even got up yet.

Although heavy drapes kept the daylight out, I could see that everything in the room was colored cream: carpet, bed, paintwork, apart from some modernistic paintings on the walls that looked like multi-colored geometry.

I found a robe at the end of the bed, and after a long trek overland I found a bathroom off the main room. I wondered why it is that rich people always need five empty acres around them before they can sleep.

The bath was filled and steaming. Hot, thick towels were on the rail, a razor and soap on the basin. My usual after-shave comes in two flavors: hot or cold. This one came from a Frenchman whose main work is making ladies' frocks.

As I came back into the bedroom, a pile of stainless steel next to the bed emitted a stifled buzzing sound, just enough to awaken an old soldier with a small hangover. The next minute the room was filled with Mr. Ory's trombone, Messrs. Bigard and Howard on clarinets, and Jelly Roll Morton's boys were in full swing.

Before I had time to get over the bewilderment, the door opened and a maid—not last night's, a brand new one—came in pushing a trolley. On it I saw tea, scrambled eggs, bacon, and toast.

"I can manage that," I said. "And tea, too. Most places you get coffee automatically these days."

"Mr. Starburn always says he likes to get the details correct, sir," she said. She was a middle-aged woman with a local accent.

"Mr. Starburn seems to get everything right."

She pulled a sash and the drapes swung back. Rain blurred the window. Below, London lay under weeping skies, soaking it all up like a big sponge.

"But even he can't do anything about the weather," I added, reaching for the teapot.

"That's not to say he couldn't if he wanted to," she said. "He's like God around here, is Mr. Starburn."

With that tribute she left the room. I had to admit that he'd made a good show of omniscience so far. I remembered him coming in earlier—about seven I suppose—and he'd asked then what time I wanted a call.

But I hadn't told him I only drank tea. And I hadn't told him about Jelly Roll.

At that point, his voice, full of chuckles, came at me from all around the room.

"Mornin', Pete, hope you feel as bad as you deserve, you naughty boy," he said.

I crossed to the unit by the bed. I could see a tape revolving.

"Sorry I can't be here to see you off. As I told you this morning, I got a meeting early. Whatever you want, ring the bell next to the bed. The driver'll be hanging around to run you home. Hope we cleared up all your questions last night, and don't worry about that German girl; I've got people working on it already. . . . We'll dig her out. And think about what I said. I need you, Pete. We live well, as you can see. Why don't you come and have a slice? See you."

He went with a click, and Jelly Roll came back. I

realized what they were playing. It was "Dead Man Blues." Starburn liked his little joke.

Yet at the same time he'd given me a glimpse of his power.

He knew all about me. He'd had me turned over. Now it's not hard if you know what you're doing. All you have to do is to ask the right questions and maybe slip the odd window catch, but what interested me was which way he'd done it.

The MP's way—a discreet word with the Special Branch, pulling strings, official but backstage. Or was it someone quite unofficial who'd jumped that tired, old lock on my Wandsworth box?

It could be either. Starburn walked both sides of the street—the one in the sunlight where you raised your hat to ladies, and the one in the shade where you kept your collar turned up.

I ate the breakfast and drank the tea. He did live well, that was for sure.

The flat was silent. I couldn't even hear the rattling of a distant kitchen. I walked back down the long corridor and as proof of my good breeding I resisted the temptation to open the numerous paneled, brass-handled doors.

Then I was back in the sitting room where we'd talked and drunk the night away. I walked over to the window. On the balcony, trailing plants sagged under the misty rain. In daylight the river had shrunk and the buildings had grown.

"Did you sleep well?"

A surprise voice got me for the second time. This time it was his mother. I had to cast around the room to find her. She was half swallowed up in one of the capacious soft chairs. Her hands were folded in her lap. Her dark glasses faced out across the city she'd never see again.

"I did, Mrs. S. Bit too much of the old Scottish wine last night. Your son is too generous."

"That's Walter. Anything in the world I can have, just by asking. He's a wonderful son. He's been on at me to go to

America for an operation. He says they might be able to get me a bit of sight back. He don't care what it costs."

"That would be great."

She shook her head. "I won't go."

"Why not?"

"I can hear what the world's like now. It's not my sort of place any more. I'd rather remember it the way it was, the way your ma and me saw it. I could understand that."

"But your life's a lot easier now."

"What's hardness if you're brought up to it? It wasn't anything to us. You know that. We knew when our luck was good. If I got a good man for a while, I was lucky and I knew it."

Her son might see her life as a whore's, but she obviously didn't. She pushed back a few stray white hairs, and turned her scrawny neck so the black glasses were directed at me.

"And Jenny's got a boy then? She was a nice girl, Jenny. Pretty. And sensible. And ordinary. You could understand her. Not like this foreigner."

That was where my good breeding deserted me; I thought I'd kick a few doors open.

"Walter's wife?"

"That Chinese piece."

"I thought he was very fond of her."

"Fond?" Her fingers picked at each other in her lap like little animals. "What's fondness mean? She sleeps in a different room. She always has. Is that fondness?"

"It doesn't mean . . ." awkwardly, I realized I didn't share a vocabulary with this old woman. "It doesn't mean they're not close," I said, glad no one was there to hear it.

"I never did that to no man. Always saw they got their greens. It's not as though he has anyone else."

"Maybe they've got a different system."

"Did you hear the noises last night?" She wrapped her scraggy arms around herself and shivered. "I'm glad I ain't got my sight. That was him, her brother. He steals, he's

107

always in trouble. I heard him and them talking. And the way he speaks to them. Says whatever he wants. I'd like to get my hands on him."

She was talking to herself really, and I was eavesdropping. It didn't bother me. Starburn had done plenty of peeping into my life.

"She's nice as pie to me, to my face. I suppose you'd say she was very kind. But I can hear things in voices; it's with being blind. I can hear all the things they aren't saying, not in words anyway. There's no love in her for him. Not a drop. She thinks more of that brother of hers than she does of my son. And he doesn't love a soul, that boy."

"You never know what goes on in families, Mrs. S."

I was only throwing a bit of fuel on in case the fire died down. It kept her going nicely.

"No, but you know what's normal and what isn't. It breaks my heart. There's only one thing I want before I die and that's to be a grandma. I've told Walter. 'Don't ask what I can't give,' he says, but it's not him, it's her. That Chinese bitch. He'd love a kiddie, would Walter."

I was surprised to see tears working their way down her dry cheeks. She didn't try to rub them away. She sat there, an old blind lady, crying into the unseen daylight. I left.

I found the lift and went down. At the bottom, Starburn's wife was standing in the corridor. I said the usual morning things and stepped out to hold the door open for her. Then I saw she had her finger on the elevator button.

She glanced theatrically over her shoulder. "Please, I want to talk to you," she said.

"Go ahead."

She looked tiny in a bulky sweater and white jeans, and it was clear she'd been waiting there to catch me on the way out. It was also clear, from one glance at those usually emotionless features, that she was terrified.

"I am in such trouble," she said. "I hear Walter say you

are a man who deals in dangerous things and I thought perhaps you can help me."

"Certainly if Walter thinks I can. . . ."

A hand so delicate you could almost see through it shot out and clutched mine. She pushed her petal face up to me and I remembered my dream: that she was the Bangkok whore I'd had all those years ago.

"No. Please, Walter must not know. Never. He must not even know I have spoken to you like this."

She looked over her shoulder again. There was nothing to see. Only the twenty yards of the corridor to the door which led outside.

"There's nothing to worry about," I said. "And Walter doesn't have to know anything. I'm not on his payroll."

"My brother, he is so foolish, he doesn't know what he is doing."

"Is he on some sort of dope?" I mimed smoking. "Or pills?"

She nodded. "Yes, yes. He has foolish friends. But he doesn't realize how dangerous everything is for him now. Everything has changed. It is dangerous for me, too."

Then I remembered what he'd said and wondered what it meant. "Why does he think he's too old?"

Her eyes flashed with understanding. "That is it, he is too old." She paused.

"So thank you very much for your kind hospitality, and I'll be in touch with Walter soon. All right?"

She got into the elevator and gave a fearful little nod. "Good-bye," she said.

"Good-bye, and once again thank you for a delightful evening."

"Are we ready to get off, sir?" said the driver, who'd been standing in the doorway at the end of the corridor when I saw him. I didn't know how much he'd heard. But I was sure he hadn't seen me slip my card into her hand.

"I think we are," I said. "I think we are."

17

I was sitting listening to a record by the late, only marginally great, Count John McCormack when the telephone rang. I don't know why I was playing it. Everyone else seemed to be giving me surprises so maybe I thought I'd join in.

It was Starburn. He sounded rushed and went straight into it.

"Pete? The German girl. I got her traced and she's escaped. She found her mum over here all right, and then ran off to the great U.S. of A., land of the free. Six months of that and she'll volunteer for a gulag."

"Anyway, she's gone?"

"Yep. So that's that. Sorry. It doesn't get you anywhere, does it?"

"Not really."

"Do you have any other lines to follow? Any I can help you with?"

"I don't think so. One blind alley and that was that."

"Sorry I had to run this morning. Did you like the tape?"

I should have mentioned that first. He obviously was proud of his technical wizardry. "Fantastic. I wondered what the hell was going on when you started rabbiting away at me."

"And the music? Was that the right stuff? Jelly Roll or something."

"Right on. But the thing that gets me is how did you know I'd turn up to hear it."

He laughed. I thought I heard a nervous echo in it.

"I've got a room put aside for all my pals with their favorite music on tape by the bedside."

"I'm beginning to wonder what you are, Starburn. You're not hiding behind the oven taking pictures of me right now are you?"

"Could be. Someone's got to watch your back. Did you have a word with my little Eastern rose before you left?"

Again, there was something in his voice that shouldn't have been there. I tumbled out a casual reply. "Saw her as I was leaving. Quick good-bye and thank you. Lovely lady you've got there."

"Yeah. And you think about what I said. You could do worse than chuck in with me. Hello, I'm wanted. See you."

Could do worse. I studied the remains of my gourmet meal on the table. Only the black bits of my frozen chicken pie were left in the delicate tinfoil tray in which it had been cremated. Those and the mushy green peas which had set so hard that it would take a power drill to shift them now. My seat afforded a clear view of the shirts drying over the bath, and the bed was not so much unmade as ploughed. Although the television was on, without sound, I couldn't see it properly because I couldn't seem to get my head more than a yard away from it without moving next door.

Could do worse. Have done worse. Am doing worse. And if he thought he could buy me simply with such obvious bribes as unlimited Scotch and rides in Rollses, he could very well be right. Every man has his price and I could be bargain of the week. He didn't know how close he was to winning a convert.

It was a couple of days since I'd seen him. I'd spent them quietly in my squalid little rathole.

I'd been going to ring Tamara for some whooping and shrieking therapy when I saw a ball of cotton behind the radiator. I fished it out and unrolled it. It was a pair of Liz's pants.

Christ, a year later and her things still kept turning up. Sometimes I thought she'd hidden them around the place like old mines. So I put on Count John—she liked him in a mocking sort of way—and sat looking at the telephone. I knew her number in Exeter by heart, although I'd never dialed it.

"Ring, tell me it's over and I'll be there," she said. That was all I had to do. Ring.

It was this glamorous life-style of mine that got her in the end. Actually it wasn't the squalor that got her. It was the other things.

I remember the incident that did it. We'd come back from the cinema one night, laughing, seeing our love in each other's rain-pinkened faces, and when we came down the steps the flat was wrecked.

Every drawer had been emptied. Every cupboard turned out. Everything we owned was on the floor. With a wail, she ran to the telephone and began dialing 999. Gently I took it from her and replaced it.

Me and my colleagues don't complain about that any more than a miner would complain about getting dirt under his fingernails. Free spring-cleaning—it was almost a perk.

She made me sit down for a "serious talk." I used to call them S.T.'s, and avoid them by making a joke of them. The truth was that I was scared of a serious talk. If we had one she would leave me. We did, and she did.

She said she couldn't live like a criminal. That was when we were trying to make a life without children work. Always at the back of her mind was the suspicion that it was my life that prevented my having kids. In another job in another place, I might be happy as a father. That night brought it home to her.

We put everything back in the drawers and cupboards. The next day she went. And left her pants behind the radiator. I remembered how she used to wriggle into them and then do a neat curtsy for me.

If I took up Starburn's offer, chucked in my job with the Unit, I could pick up the telephone and be with her tomorrow. It wasn't as though I was leading a useful life. I wasn't getting far with my bank men. And Starburn had shown me the retrieval was closed down. Perhaps it was time to move on.

Except for one thing. Except for Yokel my country-boy friend with his shirt punched into his back by an assassin's spear and his blood pumping out around the rim.

I'd watched the police help the doctor get him down. They'd had a terrible job. One young officer had to leave the room with his hand over his mouth.

And all I could think was that if it had been a bayonet, you could have put two or three rounds in and it would have fallen out easily. That's the sort of expertise I've picked up over the years. I must give a talk to the Women's Institute about it sometime.

That was his life over. Perhaps mine wasn't so bad. Perhaps it wasn't even so bad alongside Starburn's. Admittedly my chicken pies came a little singed, but at least I didn't have distraught Thai wives pouncing on the guests and a crazy brother-in-law being mysterious all over the place.

No wonder Starburn had sounded touchy when he asked if I'd spoken to Kim. The driver would have told him, I suppose, and he must have wondered what she'd been saying.

Yet it was his mother who'd been unveiling the secrets on things like the sleeping arrangements. She was mortified by it. She was probably so old that she'd forgotten that the one consistent fact about sex lives is that each person thinks his is a mess and everyone else's is perfect.

In the course of tipping up a few stones and looking under them, by way of work, I'd come across a distinguished judge whose wife at forty-eight was still a virgin, one of our leading actresses who was a slave to passion until the day she married, when she froze up completely, and any number of civil servants who keep a selection of canes in the wardrobe.

Separate bedrooms didn't rate in the sex problems I'd come across.

But, if I were Starburn, I would worry about the young Thai boy. I didn't know what it was he was smoking or sniffing or swallowing with his dangerous friends, but I could see why his sister was worried.

She hadn't telephoned. I didn't think she would. Family emotions heat up quickly. Then people realize the shame of exposing their in-house failings to the world, and they drop the shutters. I wasn't sorry. I had no plans to take up a job as nanny to a teenage werewolf.

All of which got me no further forward. So I put on Count John again and decided to pay the small but sinister stack of bills I'd put behind the clock.

The Electricity Board was clearly under the impression I was paying for lighting Piccadilly Circus and my bill for the gas central heating had obviously been interchanged with Kew Gardens'.

The third was a slim brown envelope all right, but for the first time I noticed the name of a firm of estate agents in the left-hand corner.

I ripped it open. They had been instructed by a Mrs. Makins that I was entitled to remove certain souvenirs from the house she had recently vacated, and would I like to get on with it—or words to that effect.

I thought about that. I'd nothing else to do except pay bills, think about my lost women, envy Starburn. All I needed to complete my evening was to creep around a bloodstained house. Yes, I thought, I'll do that.

I trundled up in the old Morris. Liz once asked me why I had such an unimpressive car. I said I kept it in the hope that a district nurse would get in by mistake one day. With jokes like that, no wonder she left.

Sometimes my constant flippancy did upset her. She saw it as an evasion of the truth. Which is what it is.

I tried to explain it to her. All the high-risk boys do it. Divers and flyers and people who don't bother with pension agreements because they won't be around to collect always do laugh a lot. When your life is mostly spent hurtling downhill without brakes, joking is the only escape route.

There are only two types of people who don't need to joke: the very safe, and the very dull. And they are interchangeable.

Following the instructions in the letter, I picked up the key from the house next door. It was the Indian who'd been waiting outside that night.

There was whispering when he went to get the key and when he handed it over I saw small brown faces peeping at me around the door. They must wonder how they got landed in the middle of this tribe of savages.

It wasn't late but the street was wet, silent, and broken. It hadn't improved. And when I went into Neptune's Larder I could smell death there as clearly as the damp.

There was the counter where the killer must have been standing when he kicked me. There was the hole in the wall, a slot shape, where the spear had gone in. It must have taken a powerful man to drive it in that hard.

I switched on the lights, but the electricity had been turned off. Working in the dark, I took down the souvenirs he'd brought back from all over the world. There was quite a collection: a dozen or so spears, with one missing of course; some blowpipes with the curare-dark darts poking up out of a pouch; shields of animal skin; drums and carvings.

I loaded them into the back of the Morris. Some of the nearby curtains shifted. The rain had started again, turning the street into a smear of half-seen shapes and shadows.

When I went back to lock the door, I saw the letter box was jammed open. Something was stuck in it. I went around the back and tugged it loose. It was a letter that had been folded double. It was my night for the post.

I took it down to my car and examined it under the

light. It was addressed to P. Makins, Esq. Clearly I should send it on to his wife.

But you can't expect a super-sleuth to hand over something as simply as that. I did what I'd always wanted to do since I'd seen it in my Junior "Tecs" Album over thirty years ago. I held it flat against the car light.

Two, maybe three lines of typing, and a letterhead. I tried to make it out. I couldn't. It was upside down. So much for this Junior Tec. I turned it over and the black lettering showed up quite clearly against the light.

In the manner of most modern charities, it had a one-word title. The one word was WAIFS.

And again, exactly as that writer fellow said, I escalated to an even more serious crime. I interfered with the Queen's mail. I opened it.

18

The office was up one flight of stairs above a travel agent's, around the corner from Earls Court tube station.

WAIFS, it said on the door, in that sans serif lettering which usually fronts for no-nonsense, up-to-date business methods. It was the only thing that was up-to-date about the whole enterprise.

Through the door I looked into an office that was mostly designed in scarred wood on stained linoleum. Two women worked at rickety desks. Beyond them I could see rows of green filing cabinets which sagged and leaned, no two at the same angle.

I tapped the brass bell on the highly polished counter. Nothing happened. It didn't work. I gave the counter a slap with my hand which resounded like a shot throughout the quiet room.

One woman jumped and looked up. She was a young girl who was typing with two fingers.

The other woman made a slight clicking sound of disapproval at my counter slapping.

"See what the *gentleman* wants, please, Theresa."

The girl, a fat-faced little creature already flustered by this instruction, hit one last key, then bustled over to the counter. She was wearing a woolly sweater and she had another one over the back of her chair. Her mother had told her to take one off so she wouldn't feel the chill when she went out.

"What can I do for you, sir?"

"I'm trying to get in touch with a child, well more a

117

young girl really, who was helped by your organization a few months ago."

"We help lots," she said, with faded enthusiasm. "Would you have a name?"

The other woman had turned the typewriter around and was rattling away on it.

"Not so hard," I called out to her. "The last time it was used like that it wrote *Macbeth*."

She looked up with a smile, caught my eye, and immediately looked away again. She was around forty. She had a plain dress and a plain hairstyle. But in her face there was beauty and passion, now slipping slowly downhill toward indifference.

A lot of men had looked at her the way I did, and it hadn't done her much good.

"The name, sir? Would you have the name?"

"Sorry. Actually, I haven't got the name, but you shouldn't have much trouble finding her," I said. I was stalling deliberately, while I got my bearings. "It was a foreign case."

The girl, emboldened by my stupidity, pointed to a picture of a small starving African, potbellied and stick-legged. The picture was so old it could have been taken by Allan Quartermain.

"Most of our work is done overseas, so we really will have to have . . ."

"It was a girl who was brought out of East Germany eight months ago."

The girl's mouth moved soundlessly. The woman's typing ceased. She stared at me. There was no expression on her face.

"We don't know anything about that one, sir," Theresa started gabbling, her face like a great swollen plum. "Ours are all in Africa, we wouldn't know . . ."

"Mummy warned you about telling fibs, Theresa," I said, in a chiding tone.

RETRIEVAL

"I'll handle this, Theresa," said the woman, rising from her desk. She smoothed the creases over her thighs and came and faced me over the mahogany counter. "I'm Mrs. Lidgate. What was your inquiry again?"

I told her. She kept her brown eyes on me all the time. Whatever else she'd lost over the years, it wasn't her composure.

"I see," she said, as I finished. "I'm awfully sorry you've had the trouble of coming around here. If you'd only phoned . . . You see, we can't release personal details on any of our cases. I'm sure if you think about it you'll see that it is very delicate and very intimate, and we really couldn't hand out information to anyone other than those immediately concerned."

She paused. Behind her I could see that Theresa, who had been fiddling with a card index in an old shoe box, had slyly worked her way around to a door to an inner office. She'd opened it, and exactly as Mrs. Lidgate stopped speaking, her hoarse whisper carried over, "There's another man asking about that German girl."

Mrs. Lidgate closed her eyes for a second to wipe out what was happening behind her.

"This was the other man, I suppose," I said, holding the letter to Yokel down flat on the wooden top. "Let's see, that's what he was told. No information could be released . . . and all that guff."

"I'm not prepared to discuss someone else's correspondence with you, but the same holds true, of course."

"The letter was signed by a Mr. Algan. The director, I believe. Could I have a word with him?"

"Mr. Algan isn't available today, I'm afraid."

"And you can't tell me anything because . . ."

"Because this is private information to do with the emotional lives of these children."

I'd played it long enough. I'd heard Algan say. "Oh,

no." when Theresa had said someone was here, and I thought I'd seen him snooping through a crack in the door.

"It's not just emotional lives," I said to her, polite but firm. "It's real lives, too. The man who came before, the man to whom Mr. Algan wrote this letter, is dead."

"Dead? That nice West Countryman? Oh, no."

Theresa was at the office door again, calling "He's dead" to Algan or whoever behind.

"He was murdered," I went on, hearing Theresa echo my words and amplify them with terror. "And I wish to speak to Mr. Algan about it. Now."

I swung myself over the top of the counter. Mrs. Lidgate was standing there, so I lifted her by the elbows and stood her to one side. She was frozen with fear. Oddly, it made her look younger.

"Tell him I'm not . . ." Algan was saying, pushing the fat girl forward, when I walked into his office.

He was still the same scraggy crane, weary with worry.

"Is it true?" he said, abandoning resistance. He waved me to a chair across his desk and dropped back into his own seat.

"Yes," I looked around. The fat girl saw my face and nipped through the door. "He was killed, and I'm pretty sure he was killed because of this business. By the way, where's your friend Ginger Curls?"

He gave me a puzzled look.

"You know, in the hotel room. The hard man."

He flung his fingers all over. "He was no friend of mine, I can assure you. . . ."

"Can you help me? The man who was killed was a friend of mine. I want to find out why. What did he learn to make him so unpopular? What did you tell him?"

Algan sank his lined face into his hands. "Nothing. We told him nothing."

I waved the letter. "You mean that was it?"

"Yes, that's right. As you know, it was a delicate

business. I didn't like it from the start. The whole thing was . . ." he eyed me distrustfully ". . . fishy."

"So my friend came here as I did, and?"

"And Mrs. Lidgate told him what you were told. I wasn't . . . errr, available."

"Not quivering behind your desk again, Algan?"

"Don't take that tone with me. I was busy. But I did write to him, as you know, explaining that we couldn't help. And that was it."

This had me really puzzled. It didn't make sense. If Yokel left here no wiser, and the letter certainly told him nothing, why did he have to die? Algan was beginning to look almost smug.

"Okay, I'll have to sort that out later. What I want from you, Algan, is the address where the girl is now."

Panic returned. He moved his blotter, opened a drawer, shut it again, combed his thin hair with his thin fingers. "That's not possible, I'm afraid, quite out of the question. If I'd known what was involved, I'd never have . . ."

"But you did, so let me have the address or I'll find it myself."

His panic subsided. He got up and walked to the door. He opened it. "Help yourself," he said, indicating the rows of crazy, bulging filing cabinets.

At her desk, Theresa tittered. Mrs. Lidgate caught my eye quickly and looked down again.

"I don't know what my friend said to you . . ."

"His manners were a great deal better than yours."

"Right. He was a lovely chap. And I'm not, Algan, I'm a bastard. And when my friends get knocked off I get even nastier. Now, I'm having that address and I don't care if I have to bite your balls off personally to get it."

Theresa put her hand over her mouth, presumably to stop herself trying it. Mrs. Lidgate was watching without emotion. Suddenly she got up and took two steps toward us.

"This is outrageous," she said, in a voice not in the least outraged. "You cannot come into a respectable office and behave like this."

"The address," I said, my eyes six inches away from Algan's.

Quite coolly, Mrs. Lidgate smacked me across the side of the face. Her small, cool hand was surprisingly hard.

"You shouldn't bully people who can't hit back," she said, again in the most reasonable tone. "Why don't you give it to him, Mr. Algan. Surely it isn't a state secret?"

He wiped his mouth with the back of his hand to wet his fear-dried lips.

"Look, come back in an hour," he said, suddenly. He nodded at the telephone. "I'll have to speak to someone higher up. I'll have to get authority."

My eyes were on him; hers were on me.

"Surely that's reasonable enough, isn't it?" she said.

He tugged at his tie. I watched him. And I thought.

"Come back in an hour. I'll have the file out for you and Mr. Algan will have full permission to disclose it to you," she said.

I switched my gaze to her. She looked sensible and intelligent. She saw that old flicker at the back of my eyes again and this time she didn't turn away.

"Okay," I said. I pointed at Algan. "But you'd better be damn sure you have it for me."

As I left, I caught his querulous voice saying, "I knew we should never have touched it; the whole thing's been a nightmare; I don't care how much they gave us. . . ."

It's always either money or sex. In his case, it was always money.

It still wasn't eleven o'clock. I went and had a cup of tea, looked at my watch, had another, and after thirty minutes—it doesn't do to be too trusting—I went back.

"Not yet," shrieked Theresa, trying to close the door, but when I saw the smoke I was around the counter and in Algan's office in half a dozen strides. I'd been too trusting.

Algan, now in his shirt sleeves, had a metal wastebin on top of his desk and flames and smoke were gushing from it. He was poking it with a steel paper knife.

I grabbed a kettle from the top of a cabinet outside the door and tipped it into the bin. The flames died with a sizzle. Smoke wisped up. I was too late. There wasn't a scrap of white among the black char.

"You prick," I said to Algan.

He had retreated into the corner where he was breathing heavily. His eyes were huge and frightened. He held his arms up in front of his face.

"Don't you make any more trouble . . ." he began bleating, but he stopped when he saw my face. Sometimes I've got that sort of face.

I thought about trying to beat it out of him, but I couldn't raise that much anger. I was getting soft again.

I left him squeaking and hopping about his office.

At the bottom of the stairs I met Mrs. Lidgate. She was waiting for me.

"Thanks," I said. "I don't know where I'd be without you."

"Honestly," she said, "I'd no idea he would do that. The poor man is terrified, can't you see?"

"Tough."

She gave me a slip of paper with a number on it. "Ring me tonight," she said.

"Give me one reason why I should ever want to see you again?"

She held her head high. "I know where the girl lives," she said.

Then she looked up the stairs and said, "Oh, my God, whatever's happened to Mr. Algan?"

His hair and face were soaking and covered in what

looked like black confetti. He was spluttering and plucking bits out of his mouth.

"He looks as though someone's tipped a bin of wet ashes over his head," I said. Like I say, a man's entitled to his fun.

19

Whenever someone from my half of the procreating team meets someone from the other half, one immediate possibility arises. Sometimes, when the wind's in the southwest or when there's an "r" in the month or when the planets are in conjunction with a high-fiber diet, it becomes a probability.

That's what happened when Mrs. Lidgate and I laid eyes on each other. I'm not talking about romance, or even its big brother, sex. I'm simply discussing odds.

This was in my mind when I telephoned her and met her later in one of those Italian restaurants down the Fulham Road where the waiters give a high-decibel service that even caricatures their own exaggerated stereotype.

It worried me. It worried me personally, because I didn't want that sort of emotional exercise yet. Or perhaps ever. It worried me professionally: one way or the other, a wrong "yes" or a careless "no," and it could cost me the crucial information.

"Emma," she said, with a crisp handshake when she found me at the table. "And I'm sorry I hit you but I don't like physical violence."

"For someone who doesn't like it, you're pretty good at it."

She sat down opposite me and drew my attention with a sober steady look. Then she swallowed, cleared her throat, and delivered a proclamation she'd obviously been planning all day.

"Listen, errr . . ."

"Pete."

RETRIEVAL

"Pete. There's something I've got to say first. I saw you look at me in the office and perhaps you saw—or thought you saw—something in me. Perhaps you did. I don't know."

She lost herself there for a moment, then resumed in a forceful tone.

"We're both old enough and I hope wise enough to know all about that and where it might lead us. . . ."

"Hot-water bottles for one?" I suggested.

That old light flared briefly in her eyes.

"So answer me one question honestly. If that was how it turned out, tomorrow you'd get up and go, wouldn't you?"

I thought about her question. I looked at her fine sensitive face and saw the sincerity which searches for sincerity. I saw the damage, and I remembered my own.

"Yes. I'd get up and go."

She sat back and gave a little sigh. Then, with a sad-happy smile, she said, "That's a relief. And thanks for being honest. It's not you, it's just that I can't stand the knocks any more."

"Two ships that sank in the night?"

She laughed a low throaty laugh. "I think I've just been too careless in the past. Now I've decided to protect little me."

"Very sensible," I said, wondering why she suddenly seemed even more desirable. But I was relieved, too. I didn't have much experience of restraint—it was quite a novelty.

Then she became the efficient business lady, linked her face-slapping hands on the table, and asked me what it was all about. I told her a possible version. I told her that I did low-profile work for government agencies of a sensitive nature. One of them involved the German girl, and it was now essential that I find her.

"Your friend was doing the same?"

I nodded.

"I did like him," she said, sipping her wine. "He wasn't at all like you. He had a quality of innocence about him."

"And don't I?"

"You're predatory," she said. And wagging one finger at me added, "You're doing it again. Stop it. But I was so shocked when you said he was dead. He did seem a good man."

Then it was her turn to talk. She set it out clearly and with confidence, like a business report.

WAIFS had been a charity called The Smiling Piccaninny Fund. It was old-fashioned and inefficient and when it began to fail, Algan, the director, recruited her from one of the more modern firms to try to save it. So far all she'd been able to do was to rename it.

"He's not one of the world's great tycoons, but Mr. Algan is a very caring man," she said. "We were in dire straits with money and then he said he'd found a way to bridge us over into better times."

"What way was that?"

She waved away a young Italian who was dancing around our table with the black pepper. He slunk back to the kitchen where his colleagues were having opera lessons.

"Political refugees wanted to come to this country and someone wanted us—our charity and its name—to front the operation."

"Political refugees?"

"That's what he said. He was quite excited about it, you know, like a little boy."

Amateurs are always excited by danger. So are professionals. I grunted agreement and nodded her on.

"I wasn't happy about it, for obvious reasons. The whole business of international charity is a minefield of politics. You must have read about it. If you give money to help Palestinian refugees, are you really buying rifles for terrorists? It gets very complicated."

"I know."

"He rejected my doubts. He said he personally would supervise any operations to make sure there was nothing shady about them, although I thought that was simply an excuse for him to go off on an adventure."

"And did he?"

"Twice. The first time two years ago. The second time about eight months ago."

"Where to?"

She shook her head as she ate. She drained her glass. "Can we have some more wine? You're hardly drinking." I waved the bottle at the waiter. She was right. I wasn't in a drinking mood.

"He didn't say. He used to go on about it being top secret and all that nonsense. I only found out that the second one was in Germany when your pal came in and said so."

"What about the records? You must keep records of the cases you handle."

"They went into a private file that Mr. Algan kept. Our general files only had cross references to his. So we never saw any correspondence or anything."

"Did he ever mention any names?"

She leaned over the table and her brown eyes widened. "This is where I'm going to feel so silly. There was one name I heard him using on the phone. Apparently it was the man who was funding the whole business."

"Was it Starburn?"

She thought for a minute, then shook her head. "No, nothing like that at all. It was a foreign name. And when he rang it was usually an international call."

At that point she put her glass down and tilted her head on one side. It was a pretty gesture. Pretty and practiced. "Oh, God, Pete," she said. "I wish you'd stop looking at me like that."

She reached over and touched my hand.

"It's just a touch of myopia," I said. "So you can't really help me at all."

128

She held up her hands with the fingers splayed. "Wait a minute." She dug into her briefcase on the floor beside her chair. "How about these? Mr. Algan's not the only one who enjoys adventures."

I looked at the bunch of keys she was holding up.

"But he's burned all the records. It's too late."

Her head was shaking with excitement. "No, no. He burned all the reference files, the letters and everything. But I didn't see him take the card out of the personal card index."

"Personal index?"

"A simple card index, just names and addresses. Aren't I a clever girl?"

"Aren't you just. Have some more wine."

As she went to the ladies, she gave me a soft-eyed look over her shoulder and when she walked the only bit of her that wasn't moving was the tip of her nose. The waiters almost cried.

She'd told me not to look at her like that. I hadn't been. And irresistible though I am, I'm not *that* irresistible. Or perhaps I need one of those postal courses in How to Improve Your Self-Confidence.

While I thought about it, I extracted the small telephone book I'd seen in her briefcase and flicked through it. For most people that would have been impolite. For me, it was a bit of light homework.

There were plenty of names and numbers, although not one for Algan, surprisingly, and not one for Starburn. I didn't really know why I kept on trying his name. He'd lost his role in this drama days ago.

But I did find a number marked "emergencies." No names, just a number. It was the Kilburn area and the number was 5769. I'd recently taken up mnemonics, and that one was easy. Heinz Inverted. That was all I had to remember. Heinz Inverted.

I thought I'd better remember it in case I ever had an emergency.

RETRIEVAL

By the time we'd finished the meal, we'd come a long way from the sexual truce she'd called at the start. There was a lot of eye work going on and some tentative ankle rubbing. She wasn't slipping downhill to indifference any more. She was rising off the launching pad and someone was going to end up with a back full of fingernails.

"Let's look at the files first," she said, as we left. Neither of us mentioned what we were having for seconds.

She held my arm in both her hands as I drove back to the office. "What a sweet little car," she said.

"I keep it in case they ever want to do a pensioners' version of *The Italian Job*," I said.

Earls Court was raucous with light and noise, and the pavements were busy with people moving from drink to food and back again. I parked with two wheels on the pavement right outside the office entrance.

Emma opened the door from her bunch of keys and mimed excitement as she led the way up the stairs.

I followed her to Algan's office. There was no light on, which meant—don't ask me why—that we still had to whisper. We had the alternating red and blue of a neon from an Indian restaurant across the road to work by.

Significantly, she held up the key she'd shown me over the meal. Then she inserted it in the front of a long, metal, single-deck file. It opened at the third twist. There were about forty cards at the back of the drawer. They didn't appear to be sectionalized in any way. She beckoned me to go through them, but I said, "No, you."

She started from the back, flicking through them slowly with her thumb. They were names and addresses, without explanations. Three red cards, two blue, back to red again, as the light changed outside. I stood behind her to see and she shuffled her rump against me. Red, red, blue, blue, blue, red, red . . . then she held it, and the same card changed color. It was handwritten. At the top, underlined, it said "REFUGEE." Beneath that was written

"German girl, escaped Harz Mountains." Even the date was correct.

And beneath that was a name—Eva—and an address in New York. It didn't mean anything to me. I didn't know New York that well.

"She's obviously gone abroad," Emma said, holding up the card. "Do you want to make a note of it so you can check it?"

I tore a scrap of paper off a pad and dutifully wrote it down.

"You'll be able to follow that up won't you?" she said. "That's the name, I remember."

"I suppose so," I said.

She'd turned now so she was standing against me. She reached up and pulled my head down. Her open mouth worked on mine and her tongue fed off me like a frenzied hummingbird. Through half-open eyes I saw her face doing litmus changes.

Even when I took her by the shoulders and stood her off she tried to come burrowing back in at me.

"No," I said, panting, and at least that was genuine. "Tomorrow I'd go, and you'd feel terrible."

"I don't care." She wriggled to get back at me. "I don't care about that."

"No, you were right. I'd feel guilty and you'd feel used. Once you said that, I knew you were right. So no shared hot-water bottles, eh?"

She dropped her head and began to sob, a low heart-wrenching sound. I reached out a hand to console her. A second later she was strapped around my body pumping at me. More firmly this time, I detached her, and repeated what I'd said.

"All right," she said. Suddenly she gave a kindly smile. "I suppose you're right. But you can't blame me. Don't bother about running me home. I'll get a cab. And I'll need to repair the damage."

She touched her face again. I thought that made it

about time for me to kiss her respectfully on the cheek, which I did, pat her shoulder, which I did, and leave with a regretful smile, which I did.

I pattered down the stairs. I closed the door twice. Once noisily with the latch down, from the inside. The *slam-click* sound of the Yale is unmistakable. Do it wrong and everyone knows. The second time I closed the door very quietly with the latch up.

The poor old one-thousand c.c. engine almost fell apart as I revved it up, and, as much as a Minor can, roared off. I turned around the corner, stopped, and no more than one minute later I was letting myself back into the building.

I stood inside the front door. Through the frosted window at the top I could see the red and blue lights. The only sounds were the ones from outside, night noises of traffic and voices and music from a bar, all distant and dulled.

Emma's voice reached me with clarity.

"Perfectly all right . . . yes . . . he said he'd follow it up so I suppose he'll try. . . . I'm telling you, he believed me completely. . . ."

There was a pause as she listened. When she replied she sounded angry. "I've told you if it had been necessary I would have screwed him, but it wasn't necessary. It wouldn't have achieved a thing."

Another pause, then, "No, I didn't bloody chicken out. What the hell would it matter to me?"

And finally, now chastened, "Okay, I know that's what you said. Maybe it would've been safer. Look, it wasn't my fault. There's something wrong with him. Frankly I don't think he's into that stuff at all."

She listened a little longer and rang off. She was humming to herself when she came down and, from beneath the stairs, I heard her go out into the night. This time it closed correctly.

But not when I left a few minutes later.

On the way back I listened to a sex problem phone-in

on the car radio. As usual at that time of night, they were all middle-aged women, Hungarian to judge by their accents, and all complaining either that their husbands didn't do it well enough in their beds or did it too well in someone else's. They all sounded as though they had to shave twice a day.

A bit cheeky, that about me not being into that sort of stuff. I thought about asking Tamara for a reference, then canceled the idea: what would I have to do to *earn* it?

I listened for a call from Rejected Emma of Earls Court, but she didn't make it.

It was a nice try. She had me completely with the good-friends pact to start with. There's nothing like inaccessibility for stropping up desire. She'd sold me the story perfectly and her boss was right: a light garnishing of sexual flattery and bowled-over maidens would have sealed it.

Only I came over impotent. It happened when I saw the italianate writing on the card in Mr. Algan's file. Either Emma Lidgate was popping entries into her boss's private file, or he was writing entries in her telephone book. Whoever it was, it was the same writing.

What was the number again? I tried to recall it and my mind was empty. What was her emergency number?

I remembered. Heinz Inverted, 5769. My two favorite meals. How could I forget?

20

As Algan closed his office door, he found himself looking straight into my eyes. He didn't burst into song.

I spun him around with my good arm, put my right foot in the middle of his back and fired him across the room, his long, skinny frame bent over like a bow.

They say we live in a violent society, but most people have never seen violence in action. The nearest they get is waving a fist at a passing motorist or chewing out a teenage shop assistant. Real violence is strong stuff. If you're not used to it, it shakes your sanity.

Algan had never suffered anything more hostile than a nasty nip from a pet hamster. All he would need was a glimpse.

I'd left the office door unlocked the previous night. When I arrived at 7:30 A.M.—I'd guessed Algan for an early bird—I half expected to find the place crammed with bums. But that's London: leave it open and no one's interested; put three padlocks on it and they'd be geligniting the front door.

I was right about him being early. I made one telephone call, sat and watched the British workforce preparing to terrify Japan with its productivity, and then I heard him on the stairs. It wasn't even eight. That should leave plenty of time before the honest workers started arriving.

So I bounced him across the room. He hit his desk across the top of his thighs. He gave a pained grunt, twisted, and crashed into a filing cabinet.

A pretty floral cup and saucer—his badge of status—

tinkled to the floor and shattered. He sank down on top of the pieces. When he looked up he saw a raging madman coming at him.

All he could do was to claw with his fingers at his trembling mouth.

I caught him by the lapels and dragged him to his feet. I hooked one finger through the gap between his shirt collar and his scrawny neck, and ripped. Buttons flew, the shirt tore open. I put my hand through the waistband of his trousers and did the same. The zipper burst, so I tugged again and the rip followed the seam around.

All the time I was breathing like an enraged dragon and I gave him the full impact of a face twisted by crazed rage. All his features had burst open. His eyes were wide and his mouth gaping and I saw him struggling to get his breath to scream. I slapped him once across the face. His head jerked.

There was a fancy inkstand on his desk—another badge of rank—and I picked it up and emptied it over his head. Finally I jabbed him hard in the solar plexus with two stiffened fingers. I sat on the edge of the desk and watched him double up, retching.

It was a good two minutes before he could pull himself upright again, and he was quite a sight. With one hand, he instinctively hung onto the flapping rags of his trousers. His chest showed as white as chicken flesh through his torn shirt. The ink had soaked his sparse hair at the front, run down over his forehead, and was smeared across his cheek where he'd tried to rub it away from his eye.

Tremors of fear shook his body so hard you could almost hear the bones banging. He bleated, baby noises in his throat.

I didn't enjoy it. On the other hand, it didn't break my heart. He'd misled me. He'd caused me trouble. He was standing between me and the truth about Yokel.

This was the most efficient way to do it. A little humiliation goes a long way. It wasn't being cruel to be kind, but it was being cruel to avoid being absolutely savage. In my reckoning, that's generous.

This time when I slapped his face it was so gentle it was almost loving. And I smiled, to show him there was hope in the world.

"Talk," I said.

It was enough to tip him over the edge. He began to cry. His whole face shook, wet lips and blubbering eyes, and the tears ran pale blue with the ink. As a man, he was destroyed.

He talked.

Emma Lidgate was a professional liar. She'd followed the classic pattern by telling as much of the truth as possible.

It was true that the agency had got into financial difficulties, and that Algan had been offered cash if he would cover for what was initially one operation of rescuing refugees. As she said, it was two years ago.

He'd been delighted. He understood it was a case that was politically sensitive but deserving, and it fed his sense of self-importance as well as the agency's bank balance. He didn't know to what extent the agency's name had been used, if at all. He'd had no direct connection with the operation, which he understood was somewhere in the Far East.

The German one had been more delicate because the girl was being smuggled through from the East. He had to go along—and he'd been glad to—in case they had to produce a legitimate authority.

For a moment I thought I saw his eyes sideglance at the window. I went over and opened it. "Go on. Call the police."

He knew he hadn't the guts. I knew he hadn't the guts. But it's always as well to underline these things.

"You've been smuggling illegal immigrants and you're almost certainly an accessory to murder," I added. "You can shout to the cops any time you like."

He slumped to the floor, still clinging to his trousers, and started sobbing again. I almost felt sorry for him. But only almost.

I toed his ribs. "Keep talking," I said, encouragingly. "Who did you hand the German girl over to?"

"I never saw him. I went with the man who set the whole thing up. Mattorini."

"From New York?" I asked, remembering what Emma had told me.

He shook his head. "There isn't anyone in New York. That was her fabrication. She wrote the card out yesterday and put it in the file."

Mrs. Lidgate, he said, had been put into the office by Mattorini because he was afraid that Algan might crack if anyone started asking questions. It was her idea to burn the correspondence, and then to befriend me to make sure that I was convinced. She planned to offer herself as a small persuader.

"She said you'd fall for it," he said. "She said she could put you through hoops."

I was about to say I'd been through worse hoops in my time, when the telephone rang. Algan watched me without protest as I picked it up. It was my backdoor contact at British Telecom coming back with the answer to my inquiry.

"You rang with the Unit inquiry," the voice said.

"That's right."

"Would you mind repeating the number you asked me to trace?"

"Of course. It was 5769."

Surprise registered on Algan's wretched features.

"The name we have here is Mattorini. The address is 114 Broadoak Terrace, Kilburn. It appears to be a minicab office. Called Slicktrip."

"Fine. Thanks."

"Did you lose it the first time?"

"Lose what?" I was puzzled by that.

"Wasn't it you? It must have been one of your colleagues. Someone else came on with the same query a few weeks ago."

"Oh yeah, he went sick and forgot to leave his notes. Thanks anyway."

Algan was looking straight at me. Fear rose like smoke in his eyes.

"It wasn't my fault he got killed. . . ."

"Tell it straight."

He gulped and tried to smooth down his blue-dyed hair.

After Yokel had called, and Algan had sent the letter which Emma Lidgate dictated, he'd telephoned Yokel at the café. He pointed at the telephone as though hoping it might give evidence on his behalf.

"I waited till they'd all gone. I was awfully frightened. Dear Lord, I was frightened. I didn't know what was going on, and your friend seemed . . . well, a nice sort of man, and capable, too. I thought he might know what to do."

"He tried. Did you tell him where the German girl is?"

He shook his head, exaggerating the movement as proof of honesty. "I didn't know. I don't now. I only saw her when you handed her over."

"So what did you tell him?"

"I gave him the telephone number. The one you said just now. I'd been given that in case anything went wrong."

So that meant Yokel was the previous inquirer. I was still landing in his footsteps.

"Did he go?"

He held out his open palms. "Go where?"

"To the address where you find that telephone number?"

"I don't know. He thanked me for it and said he'd chase it down."

I asked him if he could remember the exact date. He was so shaken that he couldn't work it out until I'd handed him his desk diary. The leaves shook as he turned the pages. Eventually, he identified the day.

It was the day before Yokel had been killed.

Algan was watching me with a pathetic sort of affection now. It's always the same. You hand out fear, someone receives it, and a weird sort of love is born. He was the whipped puppy who wanted to follow at my heels now. He was no threat. He'd do whatever I told him. But I still had to be sure.

I knelt down beside him so I could gaze directly into his eyes. I laid my hand on his shoulder. When I spoke, it was in a pleasantly conversational manner.

"Mr. Algan," I said. "I am going now. You don't need to know where or to know what I'm going to do. You might be able to guess, I don't know. But I want to be able to believe that you won't mention this visit to anyone else, or what we've discussed. I know we've had our little misunderstandings but I feel sure I can rely on you now. Can I?"

A crippled grin lifted his lips.

"Don't you worry," he said. "You can rely on me to be discreet, young man. I won't let you down."

"No you won't, Mr. Algan. Because if anyone does know I've been here, I shall know who told them."

I leaned farther forward so that my face was within inches of his. In the sweetest of whispers, I said, "In which case, Mr. Algan, I shall come back here and I shall have to see that you have a nervous breakdown."

I left him cowering there, a blue-faced scarecrow, and his promises and assurances followed me down the stairs. I felt I could trust Algan then. He wasn't such a bad chap after all.

21

I'd never thought of a career as a minicab driver until I saw the notice in the window. Then I thought why not: it's travel and it's meeting people.

Slicktrip Minicabs was housed in a flat-fronted brick terrace. Across the road was one of those Irish pubs with posters for showbands and those adenoidal folk-singers who start every song "Come all youse gallant Irish lads." On Saturday nights they'd collect for the IRA. Out of their dole money.

The newsagents on the corner had cards in the window for old women wanting to give away unwanted kittens, and younger women who just wanted to hire them out, under more cuddly names.

A smutty-faced boy, maybe five or so, was sitting on the edge of the pavement peeing so it ran down the gutter. He was aiming with one hand and floating a matchstick in it with the other.

Broadoak Terrace wasn't in any sense a sophisticated street. A caviar salesman would have been struggling there.

As I say, I wasn't looking for work but the sign in the window of Slicktrip—"Drivers Wanted, Apply Within"— was a chance too good to miss.

I went in. It was one small room, divided by a plasterboard counter. On the customers' side was a plastic-topped bench that had been stabbed and was bleeding foam all over the floor. And a pile of magazines of photographs of gynecologists' homework.

On the other side of the counter, a young black man rocked back in a wooden chair with his feet on a low table, cleaning his teeth with a matchstick. His other hand dangled in front of a space heater.

"Morning," I said.

The free hand waved.

"I've come about the job. Drivers."

It waved again.

"Who do I talk to? Or, better still, who might talk to me?"

He turned his head and studied me without much interest. He pointed to the clock, hanging by two wires on the wall.

"Early," he said. "Too early."

"When isn't it too early?" I had my arms resting on the counter and I leaned over to try to make some sort of impact on his world.

"'Bout eleven," he said, after some thought.

"Who do I talk to then? You?"

He shook his head. "Not me. The boss."

"Who is?"

He sat up and took his feet down. I'd spoiled his rest and he wasn't troubling to conceal it from me.

"Mr. Mattorini."

"Right. Great. I'll look up Mr. Mattorini at eleven then." I gave a sudden big smile and held up my hand. "Hey, I think I know him. He's a big guy, isn't he? Fat, about seventeen stone with a black mustache and . . ."

He was shaking his head at me, sorrowfully. "Not Mr. Mattorini. He's short, tough. His hair's all crazy little curls. Sort of carroty. Like a ginger Afro."

He grinned. He was glad he'd woken up after all.

"Wrong man. I'll be back at eleven. Thanks a lot."

Of course. Ginger Curls was Algan's traveling companion on the retrieval. He'd also been there when Starburn appeared. I knew that some of Starburn's connections were not made through the local Rotary Club, and Ginger Curls must be one of them.

Quite a few of them were in the minicab business. It

was popular with your small self-employed villain. Sometimes you got into people's houses, and customers quite often told you when they were going away, how long for, and who—if anyone—was left in the house. It gave you a good reason for driving slowly around any district late at night. And no one could keep a check on how much money came in and where from.

I drove around for the best part of an hour before I could find a telephone kiosk that still had a telephone in it, then I rang Slicktrip.

My black friend answered yawning, then, "Yep?"

In a whisper, hoarse but quite clear, I said, "Tell Mr. Mattorini that the German kid has vanished."

Then I drove back to the street and parked a hundred yards away from the office.

Minutes before eleven o'clock an old Jag, rusty but still raffish, swung down and parked at an angle to the pavement. Ginger Curls got out. He was unmistakable.

I started the engine and wondered what on earth I was doing driving a Morris Minor on an occasion like this.

Less than a minute later he came hurtling out, throwing a half-smoked cigarette away as he slid into his car and set off. As I followed I saw two little boys start fighting for the cigarette.

Obviously it was a journey he'd done often. He went through the side streets without once hesitating. He slid around corners and over junctions, but he knew where he was going. He was heading south.

Two or three times I lost him and had to guess, and each time I was lucky enough to catch a sight of his Jag again in the distance. He kept to the west of Maida Vale, passed the edge of Little Venice, came out by Paddington Station, and I lost him in the traffic in Praed Street.

I drove up to the Edgware Road without seeing a sign of him. I thumped the steering wheel and cursed and swore at my stupidity in having an old maid's car. I worked my way back down Sussex Gardens. There was no trace of him.

Why should there be? By then he could have been in Guildford. Or on the way.

I tried to see if there was any logic in his route. If he'd been going to the West End, he would have either gone down the Edgware Road or crossed over it. If he'd been going more to the west he would have crossed the Harrow Road. So I reasoned he must have been going specifically across Sussex Gardens. I went back to Paddington Station and did exactly that.

Of course he could equally well have been avoiding the Edgware Road because of the traffic, and he could have headed west by turning right in the Bayswater Road.

Everyone has his own route in city driving and it's usually about as systemized as unraveling knitting.

But if you don't believe in God you've got to believe in something, and I chose this. I drove straight over Sussex Gardens, and turned into Hermon Place, and there, parked on the left-hand side in front of garage doors emblazoned with No Parking signs, was a rusty, raffish and most welcome sight: the Jag.

Only a yard beyond, up three steps, the front door of a Regency house stood open.

22

I strolled—really *strolled*—up the steps, one hand in my pocket.

Whenever you're unsure, that's the time to act with complete confidence. I don't know whether I learned that from one of our psychology talks or from *Readers' Digest*, but it's true.

Even so, I made sure it was my weak hand that was in the pocket.

I pushed the door to behind me, without closing it. I was looking down a long, dark hallway; a vase of flowers on a table, gilt-framed mirrors and some good-quality modern prints.

I edged down the hall with care. The strolling was over now. A door on the right stood half open. It looked like the sort of door that leads to an empty room. I pushed it. I was right. Briefly I saw two facing sofas, a couple of low-slung tables, a corner cupboard, and there was something about it that was different. I couldn't think what.

At the end of the hall I sensed some life. I pushed open another door and found the kitchen. But this time there was a frying pan that was still warm and the air was thick with the smell of food.

The stairs rose from the middle of the hall and I began to climb them a step at a time. I saw a finger mark on the handrail.

Instantly I knew what was wrong with this house. The whole place was newly decorated and furnished. It had the unreality of a show house in that everything was new at the

144

same time, and it had hardly been scratched by human habitation.

My steps were muffled by the unworn carpet and by the time I reached the turn in the stairs the tension was tightening me. Then I heard the voices. Just for a second I saw myself creeping up on an innocent ladies' coffee morning. Then I heard the voice of Ginger Curls, and I knew I was in the right house after all. I paused.

"So who the hell left the message for me then?" He was almost shouting.

"It certainly wasn't me," came the reply from an indignant Emma Lidgate. "There's been no trouble here. None at all."

"No, but there will be if we don't find out what's going on," he said. I heard him draw deep on a cigarette and exhale. "You botched up that cowboy last night, didn't you," he said, accusingly. "I bet it's him sniffing around."

"I didn't, I told you on the phone."

Step by step, I'd crept up to the top of that flight. The door was facing me. I saw that the room must run the width of the front of the house. I opened my mouth to let the air drift in and out, and deliberately relaxed every muscle in my body.

"That's not the way I read it." He'd raced here in panic and anger to find nothing, and so he had to have someone to blame. He'd found someone: now he needed a reason.

"How could he get to you?" Emma Lidgate said, soothingly. "He doesn't know you exist."

"That other idiot found me, didn't he? How did that happen? You tell me."

"He's not a problem any more," she said, still the woman, still trying to mollify him.

"What did Algan say to him?"

"Nothing. I told you all about that. I steered him away from Algan."

"I said at the start we shouldn't have nothing to do with

Algan. Bleedin' old woman, wringing his hands all over the place. We didn't need him anyway."

"This one thinks Eva's in America. He wrote the address down."

His anger was subsiding. He sounded more querulous when he added, "You should've knocked him off though. I wanted someone close to him. Someone who'd know what he was thinking and why he was doing it. That's two of the bleeders and it's two too many. How many more are on the way, eh?"

From the next flight up I heard the sound of a radio. It was pop music. Then the music ended and a man began talking in disc-jockey patter. Only it was in German. I was definitely in the right house.

"Listen to that," Ginger Curls said in disgust. "What a bloody row! Look, I'm going to ring Earl to see if there's been any more funny calls."

I heard him dial. The woman said nothing.

"Hello? Hello? God, he takes his bleedin' time answering, he really does. Christ, you're there. Thought you'd bloody died. Any more calls? No, I mean any more messages about Germans or anything. No. Nothing. Okay. Forget it. See you."

He rang off. "Christ, it's deafening. You get that all day long?"

Another record was coming out over the radio and now a girl's voice was singing the words, too.

"She's homesick," Emma said. "It's only natural."

"There ain't nothing natural about that," he said. "I'm going to push now. Any trouble, you bell me right away."

There was no time to go down. I had to go up, I had to go toward the German pop music and the singing. As I began to tiptoe up the next flight, the singing voice called down.

"Emma!"

I stopped dead. I was in the middle of the two of them.

"Yes?" She called from inside the room. Quickly I made the turn in the stairs and began to go up the last few steps. The door at the top was ajar. It was dark, but a reddish dark. That was where the voice was coming from.

"Can I have some coffee please? I would like coffee. Weak please. Plenty milk."

"Fine. In a minute."

There was some subdued conversation downstairs as Ginger Curls left, and I heard Emma clanking about in the kitchen below. The German girl was humming to another radio tune, breaking off occasionally to talk in German. She sounded as though she was talking to a baby.

I slipped back down the stairs. I went quietly, but quickly. Outside the kitchen door I could hear Emma humming to herself and the simmering of a kettle. Suddenly the world was full of happy, singing women.

When I heard her pour liquid into a cup, I waited for the noise to cease, then I flung the door open. She was holding a spoon. She dropped it. Before it hit the floor I had chopped the side of her neck with my hand, and I only just managed to catch her as she half-turned and crumpled toward the floor.

She'd looked vital and lovely when I'd surprised her a second before. Now age slid across her face and pulled it into lines and wrinkles. Inside her jeans and tee shirt, her body had softened and sagged, too.

I leaned her against the wall. I found a wet rag which I pushed into her mouth. Then I quickly undid her leather belt and used it to fasten her arms tightly behind her back so that the elbows were only two or three inches apart.

She'd stopped being a woman now. She was just a bundle of old washing.

And I humped her up the stairs like a bundle of washing too, lifting, dragging, and sliding her. Twice the German girl called out, but without any great alarm.

At the top of the stairs, I leaned her against the wall

147

while I got my breath back. With a heave, I hitched her strapped arms over the stair post, leaving her hanging there like a discarded puppet.

Then I walked into the room. Whatever I'd been expecting, I wasn't prepared for this.

23

I wouldn't have recognized her as the girl I'd seen in that mountain hut. But then, I doubt if her mother would've recognized her either.

At first it was difficult to see anything. As I stepped through the door I was engulfed by the darkness, the heat, and the scented air. The only light came through the drawn red curtains and it poured into the room like fire. Everything there—the walls, the carpet, the furniture, and the bed—was a bleary dark crimson.

The heat itself seemed part of the light: hot, damp, sticky. And that in turn seemed to fill the room with a heavy sweet scent.

It was a darkened, perfumed hothouse. And in the middle, banked up on a mountain of pink pillows, was the rare flower I'd come to see. And how she'd changed.

Her straight sheaf of fair hair was now a burst of golden bubbles. Her face, no longer pale and frightened, was thickly tinted.

She was wearing something silk, one of those things that was made to be ripped off by a man in a mask. She sang softly with the radio which lay somewhere in the tumble of crimson bedclothes, and as she did so, she aimlessly fluffed her curls. She was totally self-absorbed. And very happy that way.

She was a doll, a decadent doll, and the sweet scent of the room was the old stink of corruption. Once you've had it in your nostrils you never forget it.

She stopped singing when she saw me. She smiled, without fear.

"Who are you?" she asked, brightly curious.

"I'm from the agency," I said. "I've come to fill in a few details. Forms, administration, you know."

She patted the bed for me to sit down. I did. The bed sank under me, and she rolled a little toward me, and giggled.

"Eva's the name, isn't it?" I said.

"My new name for my new life," she said, stretching her arms to indicate the room.

"This is your new life?"

"Yes, yes. Isn't it gorgeous? I love red. I love luxury. I love big beds and flowers."

A bedside table was covered with flowers. That accounted for some of the scent. But most of it came from her.

"Do you have many visitors?"

She pouted. "No. Poor little Eva gets lonely."

"Ah, but you had a visit from the man who helped to rescue you. The one with the blue eyes."

"Him?" She laughed at the back of her throat. "He wanted me to go with him. He said he would save me from this. Save me! From this! Who wants to be saved from paradise?"

"Why would he want to do that?"

"Who knows?" She picked up a pack of cigarettes and took one out. "Who cares? Light me please."

I found the lighter down among the bedclothes by the cigarettes. It was gold, smaller than a house brick but heavier.

"Thank you," she said. When she blew out the smoke, it looked like a sunset cloud against the red window. "Where is Emma? Why is she so long?"

"She'd had a phone call. She'll be up in a minute," I said, then, "How old are you, Eva?"

"Why do you want to know that? I can be ten years old or I can be a hundred? Which do you like best?"

The brown eyes in which I'd seen puppy fear were

now mocking me. She was more child than woman, but a child who'd seen too much too soon.

From outside the door I heard a moan. Quickly, and raising my voice, I asked, "And who pays for all this luxury, Eva?"

Instantly she was suspicious. "You must know that. You are from the agency."

"Mr. Starburn maybe?"

She was sitting up now, with a defensive air. "He has been very kind to me. He got me out of that ugly, gray country. Perhaps he pays for these things. Perhaps he does not. I do not know. I am a refugee. Where is Emma? I want my coffee. I do not like these questions."

Time was running out. Now I'd found her I didn't really know what I wanted to ask her. I sat forward and grabbed her wrist.

"Why were you brought here, Eva? Why are you being hidden away? Who's paying for it all? What's so special about you?"

"Look at me," she said, giving her big-girl laugh again. "Can't you see what's special about me?"

I heard another moan from outside. I tried it tough for my last go.

"Save that bullshit for the sailors," I began. "I've seen plenty of two-quid whores in my time and there's nothing different about you—"

"Help!"

Emma's shout drowned my voice and the still-murmuring radio. The girl's eyes widened and she began backing up the pillows and telling me to get away. Emma shouted again and again. There was nothing left for me to do. I went.

Emma was still hanging off the baluster post. Somehow she'd spat out the rag and was struggling to pull herself upright to shout.

"Unfasten me," she said, trying to command me with her eyes. She had guts, I'd got to give her that.

RETRIEVAL

"I'll leave that to your little playmate," I said.

I didn't rush. Whatever the urgency had been, it had gone now. It would take Eva a few minutes to get Emma free. They wouldn't be ringing the police. And Ginger Curls or Mattorini or whatever his name was would have to do his high-speed trek across town again. So I walked out as casually as I'd walked in.

A traffic warden, a thin-faced man, was standing next to my Minor with his pad in his hand.

"I'm sorry," I said. "A bit of an emergency."

"I've heard that a few times," he said. "But I'll let you off this time. Now move it."

As he strolled on to his next epic battle, I stood for a moment and breathed in the clean, cold air. But the stench of that room stayed with me.

I went back to my little gray home underground. I listened to Mr. Jelly tinkling at the piano and telling me all about Buddy Bolden while I boiled some kippers in a sealed bag. Fish are supposed to be good for the brain but they didn't do a lot for mine.

I'd retraced Yokel's steps. I'd found the girl. That room was where the retrieval ended. But I was no wiser.

I didn't know why anyone would want to import an underage tart, when it's one of the few areas of British society where we're completely self-sufficient. There had been a moment when I'd wondered if Starburn . . . It passed quickly. Starburn was never a boy for the women. He was too interested in power.

Perhaps he was building up a team of hookers: a bit of entrepreneurial work in the sex industry. Or perhaps he was aiding his Marxist chums to travel and see the world.

I didn't know, and I had no means of finding out. I had no questions left to ask, and no one to answer them. I'd followed Yokel's footsteps and they'd brought me back to the edge of his grave. But I still didn't know why he'd died.

24

"Oh, Pete, you're even worse than Kit. You never give the boy a minute's peace."

I'd taken an apple out of the fruit bowl and was giving Luke catching practice while Jenny slaved over hot stoves. It was a good twenty minutes since he finished rugby: we didn't want him to get out of condition, did we?

"He's got to work at it if he's going to play for England, haven't you Luke?" I said. I flipped the apple high into the air. "Let your hands give, that's right, cushion it when it lands. Well held."

"Play for England at what precisely?" Jenny asked.

"Everything. Ready, Luke? A right-hander."

I tossed it down near his right foot. He hit it with the end of his fingers and it rolled away under the kitchen cupboard. "Well he's not to do that, even if we do grow our own apples," she said, not altogether joking. "Put it back in the bowl, Luke."

I exchanged boring-women glances with Luke and left him to retrieve it.

I'd been glad to get away from London for the weekend. The meeting with the German girl had left me feeling tainted, and I'm not normally noted for my daintiness. But it was more than that. I felt as though I'd seen the answer and failed to recognize it. I was conscious of my own stupidity.

For once I was glad that Kit wasn't there. Much as I liked him, there were always sparks running between him and Jenny which altered the balance between the three of us. It was nice to have Jenny as little sister for a while.

She'd been with me to the Sunday morning game, covering her eyes every time Luke was tackled; now we were looking forward to an old-fashioned lunch and maybe a walk over the Ashdown Forest.

I needed a heavy overdose of normality to get the Yokel business out of my bloodstream. It was over now. I didn't believe in vain regrets.

"He looks like you, you know," Jenny said, doing something female with a pan.

"Who does?" Luke and I both pretended we didn't know. Me out of pride, him from shame, I should think.

"You know very well," she said, giving me the old sideways look. "Luke. Everyone mentions it."

"You reckon?" I was absurdly pleased, of course, but embarrassed too. "I thought perhaps he looked a bit like Kit."

She froze that conversation with one glance. And she got her own back by reviving the old, but never quite dead, discussion over why I didn't get married. She said Tamara was enchanting. I said Tamara was enchanting. She said I was taking advantage of the poor girl. I said I was hoping to once I'd got my strength up.

"But you will marry someone one day, won't you?" she asked.

"How can I? It's not fair when I'm in the bang-bang business, is it?"

"Well, leave."

Luke was across the kitchen table from me. I signaled him to do some arm wrestling.

"Not so easy, is it?" I said to her.

"Why not? Come on, tell me why not?"

I had a feeling I was substituting for someone else in this conversation, but I didn't mind.

"It's the old adrenaline. Once you're used to that you can't drop down a couple of gears so easily."

My knuckles were almost touching the table. Luke was

154

standing up to put pressure on me. Miraculously, my arm slowly raised and crashed his down.

"Wow, you nearly had me there. Again." I angled my arm so that his could reach. Gradually mine subsided under his relentless power.

Jenny, who'd been quiet for a moment, continued, "That's what Kit always says."

As Luke's cheers died at his victory, I quietly replied, "But I thought he was out now."

Jenny looked flustered. We were on dangerous ground again. She passed out some warm plates from the top of the oven.

"Carve this and make yourself useful," she said, sliding a trussed joint in front of me. "I meant in whatever it is he's doing now."

"Well if he really was organizing security for some fat, old Ay-rab it would involve about as much risk as cleaning windows and light removals. He's still with the Unit, isn't he?"

"Unfair question," she said.

"Unfair question," I agreed. "But does this mean the big romance is back on again?"

"Don't be silly," she said, in a nasty voice. I was greatly encouraged by that. It usually means I'm getting near the truth. "There's his job and there's Luke to consider and anyway I like being independent. And that'll be Kit on the phone now."

Luke had rushed to answer. I could hear him telling Kit about the morning's game. Then he called me.

"Kit," I said. "I've noticed something else wrong with the countryside. Would you believe it, they've got their sweet chestnuts chucked all over the ground beneath the trees, instead of in paper bags at the greengrocers."

"Very amusing," he said. Sometimes I think Kit might be getting sick of my running joke. "Young Luke played rather well, I gather."

"Yeah. But his hand-off's still risky."

155

"We'll have to work on that. By the way, any news on that other business?"

"The country lad who got into trouble? No. I think it's all over."

That was twice Kit had tried to check me out on it. I didn't like it.

"Absolutely. Sleeping dogs, eh?"

"We've had fried dogs and broken-necked dogs so why not sleeping ones."

"What?" He sounded angry. Then he quietened himself, chatted for a while, and went.

My annoyance with him must have been showing, because Jenny went into a long defense of Kit's principles over coffee in the kitchen.

"Where he's different from you, Pete, is that he's a patriot and you're a cynic. You'd do any job if it was exciting enough and the money was right."

"Yeah, he's a patriot all right. He's fighting to defend his fifty acres of Surrey or whatever it is he's got. It's difficult for me to get that excited about four square yards of subterranean Wandsworth."

"Don't you come the class warrior on me, Pete," she said. "I come from the same home, remember?"

"Maybe, but by the time you were born we were living in luxury. We had a shoe to take turns with on Sundays."

"Why do you do it then?"

I'd never talked about it. Not seriously anyway. I'd hardly ever thought about it in any conscious way. But after the business with Yokel, I'd had to try to understand the geography of the terrain which I worked. I wasn't sure I could any more.

"Do you remember when me and Starburn used to peep at the Kray twins in the pub?"

"You were always in trouble for that." Luke snuggled up to her. She drew him closer with one arm and listened.

"I knew then, even when I was a kid, that I was seeing the reality of power. It doesn't matter about the cops and the CID and the magistrates and the judges, that's all so much window dressing. The reality is the Krays walking into your house with pickaxe handles in their hands. That's power."

"They locked them up though, didn't they?"

"Sure, but that doesn't mean there aren't plenty more around. Anyway, that's not the point. If you get someone who won't play to the rules, who ignores what's fair and all that, who simply won't accept the law, the only justice that's left in the end is who's got the biggest punch."

"That's a terribly cynical way of looking at things, Pete."

"It's true though. Locally it was the Krays, internationally it's terrorism. If some of the boys from Belfast stand half-a-dozen innocent people against the wall and say we shoot them unless, what do you do? Dial 999? Ask Lord Denning to discuss it? Get the archbishops to say it's wicked? Doesn't work. The only thing you can do then is to pay me to swing through the bloody window with my black balaclava on and get shooting. And afterwards some limp-wristed MP will have the nerve to ask if I gave them a fair chance."

Jenny had abandoned her argument. She grinned at me over her coffee cup and said, "British sense of fair play."

I shook my head. "Never. It's shame. They're ashamed that they have to employ rough boys like me to stop the wolves eating their babies."

Little Luke was gazing up at me. "Did you really swing through windows to get terrorists, Uncle Pete?"

"Not me," I said. "Although I did swing through a few to get air hostesses."

"Go on," Jenny said. "Behind all the jokes you're just as much a patriot as Kit."

"The difference is that Kit was very put out that no one asked him to die for his country. He would've liked that."

I was almost sorry I'd said it when I saw Luke's solemn

eyes fixed on mine, "Wouldn't you die for your country, Uncle Pete?"

"I've got a better idea than that, Luke" I told him. "My idea is that the other fellow ought to die for *his* country." I thought that was enough of my country, right or wrong, but almost always wrong. We went for our walk.

When we got back, Jenny made us crumpets and we ate them around the fire, licking the butter off our fingers. Then we let Luke roast us some chestnuts in the fire.

I really did feel like a part of Kit's England then. I wouldn't have been surprised if Margaret Rutherford and Wilfred Hyde-White had walked through the door.

Then the telephone went and life stopped being like a quiet day at the Ealing studios.

It was Tamara. We began with a lot of silliness about how one of her banking friends had promised to buy her a diamond as big as the Ritz. I said I didn't know they could read. She said, read what? I promised her a rhinestone as big as the Cavendish Guest House.

"*Quelle* cheapie!" she whooped. "Just for that you only get to make love to me five times tonight."

"There's always a snag in everything," I said. Maybe I was going to die for my country after all.

Then she told me why she'd telephoned. Miller had been looking for me. "You know," she said. "That sweetie from Tracy's club." I knew which sweetie she meant.

He was the sweetie in the heavy coat. The one with a face like a half-demolished factory. The one who knew most of the staff of Dartmoor by their first names. And the one who I hoped was going to set me up in the banking business.

I rang the club.

"Pete," he said. "You ain't been in for a while?"

"Been busy," I said. "Thought I'd better ring in case there was any chance of that job cropping up. You've got to be quick with all this unemployment about."

He laughed like someone breaking glass. It wasn't

about that, he said. It was something else. A little problem. He sounded so friendly I began to feel nervous. Arousing any emotion in Miller was a dangerous game.

"I'll be honest with you, Pete, you being a mate an' that. Saw an old pal of mine today. Mattorini. Sounds like an Italian, but he's a Cockney Londoner like us."

"I know him," I said, trying to keep it casual. "Ginger."

"That's him." Miller sounded delighted. "Well, he was telling me he's been made unemployed, as you might say. There he was, earning an honest crust, and some nosey parker came along and messed it up for him."

"Go on." That was all I was prepared to say until I'd seen where this was going.

"Yeah. S'right, I'm telling you, Pete. Job around Sussex Gardens way. Paddington. Haven't you been having a look at something up that way?"

"Now you mention it, I have," I said. I didn't want to lose Miller, so I added, "I think I saw your pal over that way. 'Course I didn't know he was a friend of yours."

"No, you wouldn't, would you? Were you representing any other business interest over there, Pete? Just between the two of us."

"No. Just a little free-lance venture. A minor inquiry."

"I see." There was a silence. A long silence. I could hear him breathing. I was meant to hear him breathing. "It's like this, Pete. You being a pal, another pal like, I can tell you. I've got a little interest in a property around there myself. I was hoping to keep it quiet like. Everyone gets in on the act, it pushes the price up, don't you reckon."

"I know what you mean, Mr. Miller."

"'Course you do, you're a sensible young man, Pete. I don't suppose you'll be going round that way again?"

"I shouldn't think so."

"'Course not. I was saying to Big John, I said to him, it's a good job, it's a pal like Pete because we can explain it to him without any misunderstandings nor nothing."

"Right."

Then he gave a huge roar of laughter. "What a relief, eh, Pete!"

"Yeah."

"I says to Big John, I says, last thing we want to see is old Pete in casualty with his brains in bits."

Before I went back to town I had a look at the base of Luke's fort. I thought it might be a bit loose. Afterwards he said it was much lighter.

It was exactly one Browning nine-millimeter pistol lighter. And my pocket was one Browning heavier.

People were beginning to crowd in on me. Suddenly I felt as though I'd walked into a party where they all knew each other except me. So I thought I'd better take a friend. And the Browning was a friend. My best friend.

25

As I got into my car, the leaves, newly laundered and starched, crackled under my feet.

Back in Wandsworth, where it had been raining, the leaves were a soft porridge in the gutters.

I'd been thinking all the way back. Not that I needed to. All my instincts fizzed with expectation.

If it was big enough to interest Gus Miller, then it was big. Miller was into everything, which was why I was trying to get close to him. He had a hand in the action-man stuff, banks and wages heists, and also the long-term investments like clubs and gambling. If there was a road lamp lifted south of the river, he'd know about it.

And he wanted me out. Well. If I was drawing up a list of the men I'd most like to upset in London, Gus Miller wouldn't be in the first five million. On the other hand, in a list of people you'd least want sticking pins in your model, he'd be on everyone's short list.

The logic of what had happened had more gaps than facts. He knew the ginger-haired Mattorini. In Germany, Mattorini had taken delivery of the girl and he was watching her here. Mattorini knew Algan and it was through Algan and WAIFS that Yokel had found his way to the girl. Signing checks and smiling his saintly smile above it all was Starburn.

Now there was Miller. And me.

There was no pattern. That didn't bother me. I felt something much more important. I felt the rhythm of events begin to accelerate.

I'd thought it was cold and finished, but now I could

161

hear the music I'd heard so often before, the tunes of death and danger, and my heart sang.

Everything had come alive again. Including me.

In Wandsworth I did well to park within forty yards of my door, on the opposite side of the narrow street. I hauled myself out and hung between door and roof, inspecting the street scenery.

When I first moved in, I did this several times during the first few days, sometimes for up to an hour at a time. I knew this street the way babies know their mothers' faces. And there was something wrong.

It was quiet. The rain had stopped some time ago. The light from the ungainly street lamps caught the damp patches on the pavement and the tops of the cars.

A hundred yards away on West Hill, commuters were humming homeward. But here all was dark and peaceful—two long terraces of what the Edwardians called artisans' dwellings, and inside them two long terraces of parked cars.

Within this simple geometry, there was almost no movement. At the far end, several hundred yards away, a man loitered while his dog snouted in the wet leaves. Two Sikhs passed me with courteous tilting of turbanned heads.

There was nothing to worry about. Everything was normal. My imagination was overheated. I'd go in and telephone Tamara and we'd . . . Then I saw it again. A flash, light on metal, in the dark of the doorway next to mine.

It could be anything. It could be a steel crowbar or a collecting tin for distressed gentlefolk. It could be a charm bracelet or the barrel of a gun. It could be something to cut Christmas cakes with. Or throats. All I knew was that in this street where I knew the sights and sounds, this one was new and nonresident.

I'd been holding the Browning in my pocket—if I'd let it go it would've dragged my coat off my shoulder. Now I slipped it out and held it by my leg. I slammed the car door and set off across the road whistling. The sound echoed weakly in the damp night. The forty yards was short-range for a gun but long-distance for a pair of legs.

All my antennae were twitching at the doorway, still black and blank, when a car came zipping around the corner with lights flashing and horn sounding, and stopped so sharply that it nearly stood on its end. I scuttled between the parked cars and had the Browning up and aimed when I heard Tamara's voice.

"Darling, wherever have you been? You take so long to get anywhere in that silly little car of yours that I've been ringing every two seconds and I've been positively wriggling to see you. *Quelle* abstinence, you've no idea, positively *pas idée* . . . so I'll park and . . ."

I was at the driver's window with my gun hand hidden from Tamara, toward the doorway. I was still watching it as I spoke.

"Go. Sorry, sugar, but just go. Now."

"Don't be silly, Angel Face, I've only just this minute arrived. . . . Oh!"

I risked a quick look. In the pale moon of her face, her eyes looked huge. "Oh, Peter, you've got another woman in there, haven't you?"

Even as she spoke her eyes topped up with tears.

"That's really awfully horrid of you. Is she one of those common girls? I'll bet she is. And you'll catch something awful, like Toby did from that typist. Well, I don't see why she should steal my jollies like this. . . ."

The door banged against my legs as she began to get out.

Hastily I crammed her back in and slammed the door. "Oh, no you don't." Then I used the voice we were taught for emergencies. It comes like a high bark from the back of the throat, and it's all teeth and no lips. "Beat it. Piss off. Now!"

I screamed the last word and stood back.

"Oh, horrid man!" she wailed. With a crash of gears, her little sports car went howling down the deserted street.

I breathed out. There was still no movement in the doorway. If he was going to take me, he'd had plenty of chances.

I went down the steps, opened my front door and went in. I left the door open. I put the pistol on the table. I put Jelly Roll on the stereo.

I poured myself a Scotch you could have drowned six kittens in, and sat down.

The woman who walked hesitantly into the room, stopped and regarded me with some distaste. She was as elegant and expensive as the diamonds at her throat.

They catch the light just as well as crowbars, guns, and knives. And they're just as lethal.

"Do you always throw your women aside with such brutality?" she asked.

"Not usually," I said. "But there's a bit of a glut this year, Mrs. Starburn."

26

There's a quality you only find in people who've been stripped of their humanity.

You see it in Jews who survived the death camps. You sometimes see it in the refugees from the torturers' régimes you get in places like Cambodia.

Afterwards, their backs are always a bit straighter and their chins a little higher. It's dignity, but it's a dignity that's seen the futility of pride.

She had that. I've seen it before, and I know you never get that unseen strength without terrible suffering.

She sat on a dining chair, her hands loosely clasped in her lap. She wore a simple black dress with a ballet-style top that made her look even more slender.

It struck me that she wasn't like a small member of my race so much as a perfect specimen of a quite different and much more exquisite species. In my little underground cavern, I felt as lovely as a warthog beside her.

I'd sat her down and made some coffee and she'd begun to tell me what had brought her here, apart from her fondness for stately English homes. Her brother, Lee, had gone. I said her husband was a very influential man and could easily have him traced. She said, without emotion, that her husband didn't care. The police? She almost smiled. It was far too delicate for the police.

"My husband says you are very clever," she said. "He also says you are a man of principle."

"And I thought he was bright," I said. "It just shows how wrong you can be."

RETRIEVAL

All she had to do was to cast her eyes down to her hands to make me feel cheap and flippant.

"Look," I said. "I don't find missing persons. I usually help persons to go missing."

That's a device of people in the predatory professions. Doctors, lawyers, killers, they all get you expecting the worst so anything better than that seems like a miracle.

She simply lifted her eyes and said, "Do not try to shock me."

And I looked back into them and knew that my bad days had been birthday treats alongside hers.

"Tell me," I said.

"Things have not been very good. Lee has been very unhappy. Things with him and my husband have not been happy. Do you know a man with an Italian name?"

"Mattorini," I suggested. "Red hair?"

"That is him. He works for my husband. Yesterday Walter had a big row with him. He called him to the flat and there was a lot of shouting. Walter was very angry.

"The man with red hair had done his job badly. Walter accused him of this and he also accused him of selling him out. Tricking Walter behind his back, I think he meant. Like a traitor. Walter said he would kill him if he found it really was true."

"Did he mean it?"

I filled up her mug of coffee. It looked like a cauldron in her hands.

She nodded. "Call me Kim. That is the name I use."

She said that as though it was a hat she'd recently bought and didn't dislike too much.

"Did he mean it?" she repeated. "You are a friend of my husband. Surely you know the answer to that. Of course he meant it."

"How did you hear all this? Listening at keyholes?"

I was trying to dent her composure a little. I needn't have bothered.

"I tried not to hear. I went into my bedroom. But you

could hear their voices all over the flat, they were shouting so loud. Lee was listening. He heard things I did not hear."

She dampened her lips on the coffee without taking any in. I thought of what the old blind woman had said about her having her own room.

"And?"

"Lee followed the red-haired man out. I followed to see he didn't get into any trouble. I couldn't hear everything. It was in the street, you see. The red-haired man gave Lee a letter. He said it was one he was supposed to deliver to my husband but he was damned if he would hand it over now. 'It'll be more use to you, Chinky,' he said. Some of Walter's friends spoke of us like that. It means nothing."

She shrugged.

"What did Lee say?" I asked.

With an effort, she began again. "Lee kept asking the red-haired man where he would find him.

"Find who?"

Imperceptibly, her shoulders rose and dropped. "Someone," she said.

In the light of one reading lamp, her face was cream and her eyes wet slate and I knew that her sort of truth was not the sort I would understand. I was on the wrong side of her eyes for that.

"Then he went missing. A bag has gone. Many of his clothes. He loves his clothes, Lee. He was such a beautiful baby when he was little."

For the first time since she came in, she smiled.

"What does your husband say?"

"I told him. He says he will come back when he needs money."

"That seems a bit heartless. How did they get on together?"

She wrapped her thin fingers around the clumsy mug. I heard her hold her breath a couple of times as she was about to begin, then think better of it.

"They used to get on fine," she said. "Now, not so fine."

The telephone rang. She looked down at her hands again. She had that knack of making herself almost invisible. I never know whether it's humility or good manners.

It was Tamara. She was crying. She started off about what a beast I was and she should have known better than to tangle with such an obvious rotter, and so on. I interrupted her. I told her I had someone with me in the flat. It was work. It was very important.

"You're not really a burglar, are you?" she said, much mollified.

"Only for fun," I said. And I did tell her I was sorry I'd had to be so rude, and I'd ring her the following day. With lots of splashy kissing sounds and mild whooping, she went. I was glad I'd spoken to her.

"You are forgiven?" said Kim, when I put the phone down. "Does she love you a lot?"

"Twice a week," I said. "And how about Starburn? Does he love you a lot?"

In a quiet tone, she replied, "People get married for many reasons. Sometimes it is love, and then that goes away and leaves them very lonely. Sometimes it is for sex, and that is also very lonely. We live together. We speak. We do not fight. Many people cannot say as much."

"I see," I said. It wasn't strictly true. It wasn't even loosely true. For every sentence she uttered another five were being smuggled past me.

For something to do, I dropped to my knees and turned the gas fire up. I stayed there, looking into the pink glow. All I could see of her were her legs and shoes, formally side by side, as though for a school photograph.

"Tell me," I said, "did the red-haired guy tell Lee where to find this . . . this someone?"

She nodded. "But he wouldn't tell me."

"What about the letter? Did you see it?"

She shook her head. "But he did read it out to me."

At last. I was beginning to wonder if she was helping me or obstructing me.

"Can you remember any of it?"

She took a deep breath. Her close-cropped head sat even higher as she straightened her back. But her voice was firm and clear.

"It was an obscene letter. Perhaps some people would call it a love letter. It was about the things they had done to each other in bed. It praised his virility and strength. There was a lot about the size of his sexual parts. I remember one phrase. It said, 'You ride me like a stallion.' It was that sort of letter. Full of men's foolishness about themselves."

"But this was from a woman?"

"From his lover. But they were the sort of stories men like to hear about themselves."

She recited it as though it had been a telephone directory. A crude sexual letter from her husband's lover must have caused her great anguish, but she contained it without apparent effort.

I found myself admiring her. She was quite a woman.

"And the letter was for your husband? Starburn?"

"Yes," she said. "For my husband."

She kept her eyes on mine. She knew I was testing her, and she wasn't afraid.

"Didn't you find that hurtful? That another woman was writing to your husband in those terms?"

She tilted her head toward the telephone. "Did you not hurt that woman tonight? We all get hurt. Sometimes it is the only way we can be sure we are still alive."

"What was Lee's reaction? That must be pretty awful for a boy of his age, to read a letter like that to his sister's husband. How old is he by the way?"

"He is sixteen, but of course he looks younger."

"Is that why he went off in a rage? Has he gone looking for the woman to revenge his sister? Oriental honor, and all that."

"Perhaps."

"And perhaps he feels the jealousy you won't allow yourself."

"Perhaps, also."

I looked at her and wondered. Was this simply the famous Eastern inscrutability which concealed a writhing snake pit of emotions? Was she going to pounce on her rival in an alley one dark night and slit her lovely throat? I could have studied that face for a century and still not be any nearer knowing.

"Let me get this right, Kim," I said. The light from the gas fire turned her skin a warm sienna color. "You don't want me to find the woman. You don't want evidence for a divorce. You don't want information you can use against your husband."

"That is right."

"You just want me to find Lee and bring him back to big sister."

She heard the irony in my voice as doubt. Suddenly the emotions did begin to break and run over her face. Her lips parted and trembled. Tears swelled in her dark eyes.

"Please. I beg you. Please find Lee. He will be killed, I know he will. Find him and I will keep him safe. Please," she said again. "Please."

As I sat looking up at her, she took a small handkerchief from a pocket and touched the corners of her eyes.

It was odd. Brothers and sisters, I know about that. It's a lateral love. It doesn't have the crazy passion of sexual love, or the knotted history of parent-children love. It's an uncomplicated affection, friendship with a bit of depth.

What it doesn't produce is despair, and that's what I saw in her eyes.

I rose and stood over her. "You love your brother far more than you love your husband."

"I love my husband as much as he loves me."

"Don't talk in Chinese riddles, please."

She snuffled, and dabbed her nose with the hankie. "I

am sorry." Then she looked up at me and, to my utter astonishment, asked, "Do you know Sheffield?"

I said I did. I didn't know what else to say. Then I waited as she fussed with the handkerchief.

"Lee's father was an English sailor. He met my mother and fell in love with her and used to visit her often. They called him Wayne. That is a film star's name, isn't it? He looked like a film star. She used to tell him that. She used to say he looked like someone from Hollywood, and he would laugh and make her say it again. He liked the way she said it—"Horrywood." It is a hard word for us to say. He was tall, very, very tall, and had fair hair, soft, fair hair."

As she told the story, she relaxed her rigid pose. Her shoulders had softened, her back rounded. She had become more feminine. Her eyes were fixed in the white-pink square of the fire. She didn't know I was there any more.

"When she found out she was having his baby, she was afraid to tell him in case he would not come again. But she tried to be brave. She did tell him. She was also afraid he would tell her to get rid of the baby, and she did not want to. She wanted to have Wayne's baby. But he did not say that. He was happy. He kept on coming, and still he asked for her. He said he would take her to his home in Sheffield. He showed her a photograph of his house. He said she would be the most beautiful girl in his city and everyone would envy him. She dreamed of his Sheffield. To her it was like a vision, a vision of paradise."

In the silence, there was only the hiss of the gas fire. Slowly her shoulders pulled back, and her chin rose.

"And Sheffield is not paradise, is it?" she said. She spoke directly to me.

"Not total paradise," I said. "Did your mother ever get there?"

"No. This story has a sad ending. He stopped coming. She never saw him again. He was a sailor; he must have been killed. Because he did love her."

171

"Yes, of course. And then you were left with Lee to bring up and care for?"

She nodded. "It wasn't easy, me and the baby." Suddenly she snapped out of her dream mood. "That was after our mother died. Then I had to look after my brother."

"No," I said. "Your son. He is your son."

Gently I reached forward and took her hand. I raised it and brushed her silken cheek with my knuckles. I could feel her shaking. I thought of her sitting in those bars in Patpong, watching for her Wayne from Sheffield to come and rescue her.

In that part of the world, little girls have only one use. They are brought down from the villages and sold into the sex industry.

She sat there, demure as a curate's wife. It was impossible to imagine the fleets of sailors and regiments of soldiers, the Aussie globe-trotters, the oilmen, the Japanese salesmen, who'd pounded out their own peace on her.

I wondered if Wayne ever had meant to take her home. More likely it was a good story to tell his mates back on board. Maybe he'd moved on, or maybe he'd had to find another bar girl when it became too embarrassing.

And, out of all the lies she'd heard, why did she choose to believe his? That wasn't so surprising. Everyone keeps a dream of paradise, even if it's only Sheffield.

"Why do you have to pretend he's your brother?" I asked her. That did puzzle me. Then an idea struck me. "Hang on. Let's think. . . . Starburn didn't want a wife with an illegitimate child, but he didn't mind one with a kid brother, right?"

She nodded. "He had to have both of us. He could not have the one he wanted without the other one. This way would look best for the public, he said."

I could see that. Starburn had to be conscious of his public front.

The last thing she said stayed with me all night. I promised to look for Lee. I drove her up to Putney High

Street to find a taxi. We were quiet, but there was an intimacy between us now. As she turned to leave, I remembered another thing that had been puzzling me. Why did Lee use that old red-light phrase, "Wanna buy my sister?"

She shook her head at my innocence.

"Even in Bangkok," she said, "boys do not like to sell their mother's bodies."

Then she laid her cool lips briefly on my cheek, and went.

27

London taxi drivers are about as sensitive to quality as to the average cobblestone, but this one called her Madame— even when he knew she wasn't a Jap tourist he could take home via Glasgow.

She was one of those women who was a lady in any language. I watched her fingers wriggle good-bye in the rear window of the cab and I could imagine how she must feel.

She'd hauled herself and her baby son out of a Bangkok gutter. She'd come halfway around the world to a safe haven. Now the only person who meant anything to her, her son, was threatening to pull the roof in by defending her honor. As Barbara Cartland would have understood it, she'd lost all claim to any honor around about the time she got her second teeth. But there's more to being a lady than keeping your knees together, and she had it.

I looked at my watch. It was after eleven. If I was going to get eight hours sleep to keep my skin young and fresh, I'd have to get moving. I'd also have to get a new skin.

I drove up to Putney Station and waited outside a pay phone while a barrel-shaped girl in a yellow waterproof explained to her mother that she'd missed the last train to Guildford, but she was staying with her friend, Monica. All the time she was squeezing Monica's hand. It was a hell of a name for a six-foot man with a Mexican mustache.

Bangkok's not the only city with gutters, and people sometimes fight to get in them, as well as out.

I dialed the number. Heinz Inverted, 5769.

"Slicktrip Minicabs," yawned a bored voice. It sounded nasal. It had to, with a nose flattened like that.

RETRIEVAL

I borrowed Kit's my-good-man accent to ask how long they'd be open. Ginger assured me he'd be there till two.

Closing time is a good time to travel across London. All the drunks make themselves inconspicuous by driving at ten miles an hour with two wheels on the pavement, leaving the center of the road clear for sober speed-kings with their Morris Minors. In less than thirty minutes, I was in Broadoak Terrace.

There was one streetlamp at the far end which the vandals had either overlooked or were saving for the regional stone-throwing finals. Beneath it, two recent clients of the Irish pub were trying to bring their faces into contact with each other's fists. Without any success.

Apart from that, it was deserted. The only light was the pale square that was the window of Slicktrip Taxis. And inside I could see my old friend Ginger glancing at the pages of a magazine and scraping inside his ear with a matchstick. Around here that made him the man who has everything.

In the violence business, shock is worth a lot more than muscle. And when you're left with one-and-a-half arms, you get to be very sharp at forward planning.

I parked past the office, and walked quietly back. Half-asleep, Ginger had his chin on one hand and the magazine flat on the desk. In the corner, a paraffin heater gulped quietly. Ginger yawned, not so quietly. Otherwise, all was silence.

I went through the door screaming as loud as I could. All I saw was his face wide open with amazement as I bore down on him. One leap took me over the counter. I hooked my arm around his neck and swung him backwards on his chair. His knees were trapped under the wooden desk. The chair swayed on its back legs. His spine, the pivot for this demonstration of leverage, creaked.

"One thing, Ginger, and make it quick. Where'd you send Lee?"

He gargled at me. I couldn't hear a word. Just in case

he was gargling lies, I tightened my arm. I could feel it nip his throat. His face was blue.

I allowed his clawing fingers to loosen my arm a fraction.

"You know where he's—"

"Aha. No fairy tales please, Ginger."

This time I swung some real weight on him. He bent bowlike over the chair and I could hear his spinal discs pinging like popcorn.

When I let him go this time, he was croaking for mercy. "You know," he said. "I meant it, soldier. Hermon Square. Twelve Hermon Square. You was there yourself."

Now that was a surprise.

I stood up and watched Ginger as he swore softly and massaged his throat. Then he tried to straighten his back and flinched as the ripped muscles moved.

"You bastard," he said. He sounded like a punctured bellows.

"So," I said, pleasantly enough. "Lee's going to visit little Eva."

In his eyes, I could see the reckoning beginning. He thought I should have known that. Now he was wondering what I did know, and what I didn't. So, for that matter, was everyone else in the room.

"Eva's in her little love nest," I went on. "Loyal employee Ginger feeds the info to Gus Miller who black-mails Starburn."

Moaning, Ginger tried to rub his spine with his right hand. Then he sipped from a cup of cold coffee after stirring it with a blue plastic spoon. But his eyes never left me.

"He's not going to pay on that," I said. He still looked at me and went on rubbing his back.

"He's a big name, all that, but he's not the first to have a bit on the side."

Mysteriously, a twist of a smile touched his upper lip.

"You can't work it on his wife," I went on. "She doesn't give a damn. He could have a harem for all she'd care. And the great British public, well, they'd be amazed if he wasn't knocking something off. Things have changed since Profumo resigned from Parliament after they caught him out."

I knew from his face I'd gone wrong. Somehow I'd put all the pieces together and got the wrong picture. He was laughing at me. Whatever ascendancy I'd had was destroyed.

He'd got a half-broken back and a stretched neck but he was winning again now.

"You're going blind," he jeered. "You're like a bloody bull in a china shop. You don't even know what the game is, do you?"

For a moment I was tempted to knit my fingers into his thick hair and bounce his face on the desk. But that time had gone. I'd have to beat him around that room all night to get any more out of him.

"I'll tell you one thing," I said, leaning over him. "You've gone and set that young Thai kid loose and you don't know where he's going to stop, do you?"

He wasn't one of our great actors. I saw the shadow float up on his face.

"Whatever the setup is," I went on, chancing my arm now, "whatever the setup is, Ginger, it'll all be in bits and pieces when he's finished."

"He won't do anything stupid," he said, but sullenness had replaced his certainty.

"You don't know that," I said. I was trying to read his reactions and to guess what had happened at the same time. I'd got it wrong before. This looked more promising.

"You've got him rampaging around and if he's been on anything really heavy . . ."

"He's been speedballing, that's all," he snarled.

"Oh that's great!" I'd got him running now. "Out of his skull, he'll be. If he messes this up, you'll have Gus Miller and Big John after you, as well as Starburn."

I let that one work on him for a minute. I was still thrashing about, but I knew I'd hit somewhere near center.

RETRIEVAL

The heater burped neatly in the corner. Ginger picked at the corner of the magazine. A soft-porn model smiled up at him over her melon buttocks.

He grabbed the telephone. Without even looking at me, he dialed. I could hear it ringing. The heater gulped again. His breathing, already ragged, quickened. Now he did look up at me. It was still ringing. No one was answering.

"Bloody 'ell," he said.

He replaced it slowly. I walked to the door. I said one word to him before I left.

"Emigrate," I said.

I took the route I did the day I followed his Jag. This time I knew where I was going. There was no point in rushing.

When he'd been kicked around by Starburn, Ginger couldn't resist the one touch of petty malice. He'd let Lee in, a hot-headed amateur among the cold-blooded pros. By now he would have raised such a row the house would be empty and the German and her nursemaid, Emma Lidgate, would be holed up somewhere else. But I still had to go and see.

I wasn't going to get my eight hours. My complexion was already at risk.

28

In the soft glow of the moonlight, Hermon Square was like a drained swimming pool.

The smart, cream fronts of the houses were flat enough for the walls and, standing on the pavement looking up at a naked half-moon in a clear black sky, I felt as though I was at the bottom of a tank.

There were still some spaces among the residents' parking places. Those who'd staked their careers on laughing at the right people's jokes were still out doing that, in the right places no doubt. Those who'd pinned everything on a clear head and a sound digestion were in bed.

And the door of Number Twelve, just like last time, was ajar.

There was no light to be seen in the house. I pushed the door farther open and moved inside. The only light was the wash from the moonlight behind me. Here and there it gleamed on the new paintwork.

Slowly, silently, breathing softly, I moved up the first flight of stairs. At the turn in the stairs I could see more moonlight. It was filtering through the half-open door to the room where I'd heard Emma and Ginger talking. I opened the door fully. Shadows and moonlight filled the long room. Through two casement windows I could see the white cliffs of the other houses. No one breathed. No one moved. It was dead with emptiness.

Again the moonlight followed me up the stairs. Again I lost it on the turn. But this time, beneath the closed door of the German girl's room was a rose-red strip of light.

RETRIEVAL

The sweet rotting smell was there in the air again. But this time there was no music, no girl's voice to sing.

The brass doorknob was cold in my hand. I opened it quickly. The scented heat, hotter even than before, hit me like a punch.

It was the same heat and the same smell, only this time a bedside lamp with a shade the shape and color of a rose spilled crimsons and scarlets all over the room.

Only now the room was upside down. Cupboards and drawers hung forlornly open. Clothes—silk, fancy, fluffy—were strewn around. The pink pillows and crimson sheets were heaped on the floor. The place had been ransacked. You could see the rage with which it had been done. Even the ornaments from the bedside table had been scattered with the sweep of an angry hand.

The gold lighter, the one she'd asked me to use when she was doing her bad Dietrich impersonation, was on the floor, too. It was only a few inches from her hand. But she wouldn't be using it. And she wouldn't be asking anyone else to either.

Little Eva sprawled pink and soft, a broken doll among her broken toys.

The slip of silk she'd been wearing had been ripped right down the middle. Not all my predictions work out so accurately. It was still draped over her outflung arms but it left her body naked so that I could clearly see the knife which was stuck between her ribs, about third and fourth, left-hand side. I touched her wrist. She was warm. She'd only been dead for minutes. The blood was welling around the blade and creeping down her chest and stomach. It was dark red. Her favorite color.

Only she wasn't a "her" any more. For all the bubbly blonde hair and the black fringe of lashes around glazed, brown eyes, it was the body of a male.

Not what you'd expect to see in a rugby shower, but indisputably male.

A single sheet of paper lay as though it had been

thrown on the corpse. I picked it up. I only had to read a few words to see what it was: "You ride me like a stallion. . . ."

I suppose it was a love letter, of sorts.

I'd always admired Starburn for having the wit to let fools like me waste their breath and money chasing women while he hunted success.

And all the time he'd had a sleazy love life tucked away. He'd certainly been discreet about it. There'd never been a hint of anything suspect about his private life. I wondered if Kim knew her rival was a teenage boy in silk and paint. I wondered if she'd care.

Another dagger stabbed at the dark. This time it was the telephone. It rang sharp and fierce, an electronic toll for a very contemporary death.

I found it in the room downstairs. It was a fake antique, on a low table by the casement window. In the square below a taxi's diesel drummed and I could see a woman in a fur climbing out.

I picked up the earpiece.

"Eva?"

I said nothing.

"Eva?"

The silence was a neutral zone between us. I wasn't going into it.

Then he said, "Emma, is that you?" He waited a few more seconds, then spat an obscenity into the mouthpiece before putting it down.

It wasn't often Starburn sounded that agitated.

I hung up the receiver and stood by the window for a moment, thinking. Down below, the woman's escort was slurring his thanks to the driver so effusively you'd think the man had carried him home on his back. Drunks are always so depressingly democratic.

Of course she knew. It suddenly struck me. "Men's foolishness about themselves," she'd said. She'd know the letter was from a man to a man.

181

She must have known. Starburn must have kept his playboys for years. This love nest, newly set up and furnished with Emma as resident nanny, wasn't a novice's style.

It was easy to see why Lee would be enraged to see her humiliated by this treatment. And if Ginger had got him speedballing—a mix of cocaine and barbiturates that gives a hit like frenzy—and shown him the poem for provocation, too, it was a miracle he wasn't sitting on top of St. Paul's throwing pieces of Eva to the crowd.

But what had he been searching for? He hadn't tipped the drawers and cupboards out in fury. He—someone—had been hunting for something. Then it struck me that perhaps it wasn't Lee who'd killed the girl-boy.

It was a classic blackmail setup—maybe Miller had killed Eva accidentally when gathering his evidence. Maybe Starburn himself had had her killed when she became an embarrassment.

Or maybe Mrs. Starburn was jealous as any other jealous wife but a better actress than most.

I picked up the telephone again. I dialed her private number, the direct line to her bedroom. Did jealous wives have separate bedrooms? Perhaps that's what made them jealous?

It rang. She'd be sitting there laughing at my stupidity.

It went on ringing. She'd be lying on the floor with a knife in her ribs.

I couldn't tell the villains from the victims any more.

Then I heard her fluting voice, but she was talking on an answering machine, saying that Mrs. Kim Starburn was not available at the minute. . . .

"Hello?"

It was Kim, interrupting her own recording. For once she didn't hit the consonants cleanly, and I remembered how her Sheffield sailor laughed at the way she said "Horrywood."

I asked her if she was all right. With a slight hesitation, she said she was.

"Have you heard from Lee?"

"No."

"Do you know where he is?"

"No."

"Is it difficult to talk?"

"Yes."

"But the phone's okay?"

"Oh, yes, quite safe."

"You think someone may be listening to your end of the conversation."

"That is possible."

"But you can listen to me?"

"Yes."

"Fine. Things are getting tricky. I don't think you're safe there. I want you to get out. Can you grab a clean pair of undies and get ready to run?"

"A clean pair . . . oh, yes, I suppose so."

"Right. Now Lee is pretty sure to ring you on this line, isn't he?"

"I think so."

"Leave a message on your answering machine for him telling him where he can find you."

"Is he in danger?" A tremble touched her words.

"Yes. Lots."

I gave her my sister's telephone number and told her to put that on the machine.

"But, Pete, anyone will be able to pick it up!"

"If it's in Thai?"

I told her I'd pick her up in an hour. I told her to wait a hundred yards away from the house so I didn't have to meet Starburn. Whatever was going on, he was still an old friend and she was still his wife. Then I told her everything was going to be all right.

I hooked the earpiece back on its stand and put it back on the table.

RETRIEVAL

I'd made a few decisions there. I'd enjoyed it, too. Ever since the start of this business, I'd been trailing in the wake of events, half a mile and two days behind the action. Now I felt as though I was getting up there with the front runners. It was my turn to make a few moves.

Feeling fairly pleased with myself, I set off down the stairs.

When I heard the pat of a foot behind me, I remembered how I'd hidden higher up the stairs. And when I spun around I just had time to see an expressionless, pale circle of a face.

Time split into milliseconds. I found myself hoping that Lee had heard my conversation with Kim, and I still had time to realize it wouldn't mean anything to him if he had.

All the time I saw the truncheon shape in his hand rising and falling. By then I was hopelessly off-balance. I held my good arm up to protect my head, which left me no means of hanging on to the rail.

So I was in the middle of the stairs, twisted around and swaying like a drunk when he hit me. The stairs and the ceiling came up at me in turn, like a domestic kaleidoscope.

Then the blood red and the rose red of the boy-girl's room flooded up from behind my eyes, and I was trying to wash it away under a cool and beautiful waterfall, but it wouldn't go.

29

The water was cool because it came from the cold tap and it was being poured over my head from a blue-and-white jug by the quivering hand of a young cop.

"He's coming around, sergeant," he said, full of excitement. He could only have been on the force about twenty minutes to be that keen.

I squinted up at him and the neon striplight behind his head.

Blinking, I struggled into a sitting position. I'd been slumped on a kitchen chair with my head hanging over the back while they doused me.

I was in the kitchen of the house in Hermon Square. I was at a four-seater pine table. On it was a split chair leg marked with a dark bloodstain.

The teeny cop had stepped back now. Behind him, leaning against the wall was an old sergeant. He looked as though he was due to retire in twenty minutes. That's how interested he looked.

Opposite me was Ironside, Holmes and Marlowe all rolled into one six-foot, skinny frame. He wore a cheap brown leather jacket and a cheap brown mustache he'd grown to try to look older. He had one eyebrow jacked up in disbelief and his top lip curled in readiness with contempt. He'd seen it all. Kids trespassing on railway lines, half-wits stealing lead from church roofs. He was CID and he was all ready to be unimpressed.

"All right, lover," he said, "let's have it."

I asked him to ring the Unit number.

He didn't move. "Look, lover, let's get this straight

from the start, shall we? I don't care if you are a friend of the Chief Constable. I don't care if you're the bloody Chief Constable himself. Don't piss me around telling me who to telephone. Get talking and then we can all get home."

He was going to be difficult. My head felt like a split log and I wasn't at all sure I had the patience for him. I saw a kitchen clock over his head. It was one in the morning. Kim would be waiting.

"It might save time if you rang that number," I said, drawing on my thin reserves of sweet reason.

I signaled for a tea towel hanging by the basin. The young constable looked at the detective, got his nod, and passed it to me.

He put his elbows on the table and leaned toward me.

"All I want to hear from you, lover, is where your pal's gone, his name, your name, and what happened."

I dabbed the cloth into the jug of water and touched my head. Even through the cloth I could feel the tender swelling. I looked at it. It was soaked with blood.

He was about to explode with impatience when another CID man pushed his face around the door.

"Party next door says a middle-aged woman, smart type, moved in six months or so ago with a young foreign girl. Girl was a bit of a tart, they reckon. Hardly ever went out. The woman had nothing to do with anyone."

The detective never took his eyes off me.

"Very few visitors. A feller who came in a Jag, smashed nose, red hair, very distinctive, and a man who came at night, they reckon in a Rolls-Royce. They never got a look at him. Party heard some screaming up here earlier tonight, about eleven she thinks, but thought they were up to fun and games."

"Fun and games?" He was still staring at me. "Was that it, lover?"

"Oh yeah, there's some cash around, too. She reckons the house went for two hundred grand plus, and it was furnished from top to bottom—carpets, antiques, the lot."

RETRIEVAL

The detective rubbed his knuckles along his mustache to see if it had grown in the last two minutes.

"Will you please ring that number," I said. He ignored me.

"Lover's not the sugar daddy, is he? He's more cycle clips than Rolls-Royces. So what were you, lover? You were the big butch boy, were you, and your little pal upstairs was the one with the frock and the pink undies. Or did you take turns at being Milly, Molly, Mandy? And what about your pal who left early? What was he? Animal, vegetable, or bloody mineral?"

He slapped the table with his hand and looked away. "You make me sick, you perverts."

The sergeant tapped a rolled-up cigarette over the basin. "I think you've got it wrong," he said. "He's a hard bugger, is this one."

"Hard?" The detective went for a full lip curl. "I've seen harder bloody ballet dancers. Come on, lover, you lost your rag because your friend borrowed your lipstick. . . ."

He knuckled his mustache again. It had been a long day. I'd been knocked out. I'd crashed downstairs. I'd been unconscious for God knows how long. I'd still got a lot to do and here I was being questioned as a criminal pervert in a sleazy sex murder.

"Don't you think you'd better take it back?" I said.

"What?" he asked, surprised.

"The mustache. Before the joke-shop closes."

The young cop gasped, the sergeant choked on his cigarette, and the detective's jaw nearly hit his knees. Before he could decide what to throw at me, the door opened again and the other plainclothesman called to him. Reluctantly, and promising me plenty of attention when he got back, he went outside.

I was kept there another twenty minutes.

The sergeant gave me a glass of water. "You shouldn't have said that to him," he chuckled. "His face, though!"

RETRIEVAL

The teeny cop peeped outside and I heard him whisper to the sergeant, "And he's got his hair in ribbons!"

The detective opened the door once and asked me again for the Unit number. I heard his raised voice insisting, "I'm not telling him go without authority from my own force."

Then there was some more whispering and the sergeant opened the door, winked at me, and said, "On your way, Riley."

The Chimp was waiting in the hall. He was still wearing a bandanna over his shoulder-length hair. I should have known it was him from what the young constable had said.

We walked past the stony-faced detective and out into the square. It was clean and cold. We didn't begin to talk until we were well clear of the house. Even then there wasn't much to say.

"Thanks," I began.

"Not my decision. The Unit said to pull you out."

"Very embarrassing for them, I suppose," I said.

"I suppose," he said.

"Were you on a watch here?"

"Questions?" he said.

"Did you see him leave?" I asked.

Instantly he asked, "Who?"

And I thought, I don't seem to know very much about anything but if, just for once, I know something that someone else doesn't, I might keep it to myself.

"Shan't tell," I said, in my best baby voice.

It didn't annoy him. It didn't amuse him.

"Ring the Unit," he said. "They want you to check in immediately."

He loped back to the house and up the steps.

The Unit would want to speak to me. I'd ignored my instructions to leave this business alone. I'd blundered into a murder without any authority. And I'd had to be hauled

188

out by backstage string-pulling. By now I must be one place ahead of Martin Bormann on their wanted list.

So I hopped in the old Minor and drove down to Starburn's place on the north bank of the river.

If Bormann can get away with it, why not me?

30

It wasn't until we were crossing Blackfriars Bridge that there was enough light in the car for her to see where my hair was matted with blood.

She stifled a shriek. "What happened?" she asked.

"Your brother, I'm afraid," I replied. Then corrected myself. "Your son."

"Lee? Why did he hit you? Is he all right?"

"He didn't explain why. Or maybe I was too unconscious to hear him. No, he hit me because he thought I was after him. He was right, too, I was. But then, so is half of London."

I wondered if that was a good time to tell her that her son was a murderer. I decided to let it wait.

I'd made that decision about once every ten seconds since I picked her up. She was waiting in the doorway of a boarded-up shop on the old dock road that led down to Starburn's riverside palace.

She was wearing one of those oversized sweaters so that she looked like a delicate flower inside a very large pot. She had a soft leather grip bag with her which she held on her lap next to me.

By then I was beginning to feel worn and old. My head hurt like hell. Nothing was quite what it seemed any more. Girls were turning into boys and Thai teenagers were rampaging through the city with knives and the Chimp had suddenly walked into my life again. The day had already been running for about two weeks and showed no sign of ending.

Then Kim slipped into the seat next to me. Her

smooth face was creamy and shadowless in the light from the streetlamps and she offered a small smile as a child offers a present.

Already living was beginning to look better than the alternative.

She told me she had no problem in getting away. At the best of times, Starburn had little interest in her. Now he was too preoccupied with all that was happening. Kim seemed quite happy to think she was being taken to my sister's. Then she noticed my head.

"Is he safe?" she repeated.

"At the moment, I think so," I said. "But he's in a lot of trouble. He found the someone, the person who wrote the letter."

I sneaked a quick look at her to see if she knew. She caught my glance and smiled.

"The boy?" she said, quite calmly.

I remembered what she'd said about men's foolishness. She'd always known. In a way, she'd tried to tell me.

"You knew, didn't you?"

"Yes, of course. Walter always liked boys."

"Never women?"

She stared straight ahead. "Never," she said.

"Then it strikes me that perhaps Lee wasn't just defending your honor."

"No. It was his own honor. He was a very jealous boy. He knew that Walter lost interest in his boys once they began to grow up. It started to happen to Lee. He tried to disguise it, but it was no good."

"So that's what he meant about being too old."

She nodded.

"He must have been scared, too. What was going to happen to him once Starburn lost interest? You, too, for that matter?"

"He worried more about me. He is a lovely boy, Pete; he really is. When he met Walter in Bangkok and Walter wanted to bring him home, he told him he had to bring me, too."

"You can't have one without the other."

She smiled at the memory. "That is true. When he thought about it Walter was quite happy with the arrangement. It made a romantic story for the newspapers. How the great benefactor fell in love and brought his bride home, and adopted her brother. But in private Lee was the bride, of course. It was all right until Lee's voice started to go. Then he found some notes from a German boy."

She looked out of the side window at the black slabs of sleeping London slipping past.

"Do you know Patpong?" she asked.

Patpong is the neon-lit strip in Bangkok where you can buy sex in every shape, style, and size. For ten quid there, you can get the equivalent erotic content of a hundred British honeymoons. I'd been there on R. and R. I told her.

"I used to go to a place there," I went on, "where the girls all wore white robes and sat on benches behind a two-way mirror. They looked like a church choir."

Her eyes were fixed on the empty road ahead.

"Each girl had a number pinned on her robe and you told the madame the number you wanted. We used to call it the Thailand takeout. When I was there the going rate for a girl was about three hundred bahts."

The car was a confessional now. Outside, litter turned in the wind in cold streets. I knew what she was going to say before she began talking.

"I was number 23," she said, in a quiet conversational tone. "I was lucky. Often I would get four or even five hundred bahts. I was pretty to Western eyes."

"I suppose Starburn was a way of escape?"

"Yes. At first I was so happy because I saw that Lee might get the chance of a new life. I didn't think I would, too."

"Was Starburn kind to you?"

"He was fair. He told me the truth. That is more than most men do."

I knew she must be thinking of her dream of Sheffield so I changed the subject.

"Where will he hide?" I said. "Gerard Street?"

"Please?"

"That's where all the Chinese live, and Westerners always say . . ."

"I know. That we all look the same. We are not Chinese, but I know what you mean. We say the same about people from the West. Long noses, we call you."

We both laughed at our mutual ignorance. It was as near as we could decently get to admitting that we might have had sex together, and did not even know.

To her I would have been just another long-nosed soldier. To me she would have been just another slant-eyed whore.

"Let me tell you more," she said. She'd sunk down into the seat and stretched out. She was the only girl I'd seen who could stretch out in that car. Beside her I felt huge and clumsy.

"My mother sold me to a man when I was ten. I was lucky. It was better than being a peasant in the fields. It did not seem an awful life to me. It was the only one I had ever known. I was frightened of getting older because then the girls were sent down to the docks where the men were like beasts and there was not much money. But again I was lucky. I looked young."

We were out of the city now. We passed trim privet and closed curtains. I sensed the thin-lipped reticence of the suburbs.

"Didn't you mind Lee living like that?"

"Going with men?" She laughed. "Why? I used to go with men. How can I make you understand? Life is very cheap out there. If a human being dies it is no different from a fly dying. So what does it matter what people do with their bodies? I have seen them do everything. I have

193

done everything myself. I am not ashamed of that. If you were born there you would think the same. Sex with men, sex with women, with animals and instruments, after a while none of it matters. It is the end of another day, and you are still alive. That is all that matters. No, I did not mind for Lee. I did not expect him to be a priest."

In the darkness, her voice sang like a flute. Suddenly I wished the sleeping people on either side of us could hear what she said. They were the people who complained about nudity on television and then tried to ginger up their stale sex lives by groping their neighbors at the Christmas parties. A lesson in fundamental morality from a Bangkok whore might do them a world of good.

We were the last honest people alive, the warriors and the whores.

Civilized society shunned us both. They were like Rosemary, hating the touch of Yokel's bloodstained hands. Civilized society deplores violence . . . until they hear a floorboard squeak in the night or they think the Russians are coming to get them, and then they shout good and loud for someone like me.

It was the same for the whores. Civilized society deplores them, too.

Except when they're away on a business trip and come crawling home on their fat little bellies, full of guilt and dirty dreams.

For the truth is that they can't fight and they can't do the other thing either and they have to pay us to do it for them.

After that attack of high-principled honesty I had no choice. I had to tell her about Lee stabbing the German. She didn't cry. She wrapped her arms around herself and rocked. I'd seen that before. It was peasant grief, a private grief that doesn't need mourners.

I left her to it and concentrated on my driving. We buzzed down the empty bypass at Sevenoaks and turned off along the back roads toward Crowborough. All that was left of the sweet chestnuts now were patches where they'd been smeared into the road.

After a while, she stopped rocking.

"Can you help him?" she asked.

"I can try."

"The police will want him?"

"Among others. It's the others we have to watch."

Suddenly she began rooting into her bag. She said she'd forgotten, we'd been so busy talking. Walter had been on the telephone lots of times. For one call, just before she left, he'd retreated into his bedroom.

She'd listened in, thinking it was the police, but hadn't been able to understand it.

"So," she said, grinning with delight, her grief on one side now, "I do this. I have seen Walter do it hundreds of times."

She was holding up a tape cassette. She'd made it from the central console in the living room.

I slipped it into the cassette player and listened. It wasn't the police. I immediately recognized the style of talking: laconic, oblique, anonymous.

Starburn was talking to the Unit. And the man he was talking to was one of the deskmen, young Oxbridge graduates who roll up every year with their Russian dictionaries under one arm and Le Carré under the other.

Although—as I'd said to Kit more than once—a certificate in heterosexuality might be of more value.

I listened. And I realized why the young Thai was the most sought-after man in London that night.

". . . and you can't find them?" Starburn said. That was how it began: the earlier part was missing.

"Our representative on the spot says that neither he nor the authorities can find any photographs like the ones you mentioned."

"Christ! That's bad. I don't want them floating about."

"It's certainly not desirable."

195

"Too bloody right it's not. It's got to be Lee who's got them."

"If he killed the German . . ."

"It was him all right, I keep telling you. He brought that knife back from Bangkok. I know it just from your description."

I had to give it to Starburn. He didn't apologize and he didn't defer.

"What's your response going to be if you are blackmailed?"

Starburn gave a big bark of a laugh. "Lee won't do that. You don't know him. He don't want cash, I'd give him that anyway. He's a passionate kid, that one. He'll want revenge."

"To disgrace you in public, you mean?"

"Yeah, that class of work."

"And how will you respond to that?"

"I'll have to do a bit of arm-twisting, won't I? I can see that the newspapers don't touch it. It's not the sort of thing the radio or TV would do, so I reckon he's up the creek with it. He can send copies of the pictures around to individuals, I suppose, but there's only one whose opinion bothers me and she'll never see them."

He was still full of bounce, but the college boy soon blew up his theory.

"That won't hold. Even if you can stop the papers here, the ones on the Continent and in America would eat it up. Then they'd have to follow over here."

Even with the car engine buzzing away and the noise of the tape, I could hear Starburn suck in his breath.

"All right, it's down to you then. That's what you bleedin' fascist spooks are for, isn't it? Security of the state and all that. Is Pete in on this?"

In a stiff voice, the desk man said, "I can't divulge details like that, I'm afraid."

"No, all right then. He was nosing around before,

that's all. And a little birdie tells me that Gus Miller's got a sniff of it. He isn't working with your lot, is he?"

"I don't think we know a Mr. Miller."

Starburn laughed. "Go on. You'd employ Jack the Bleedin' Ripper if it suited you."

"I don't think we know a Mr. Ripper either. And to be quite candid with you, sir, I don't think you're in a position to be flippant. You've made yourself very vulnerable. A lot of people could put those photographs to use."

Good for him. He'd given Starburn a sharp tap on the nose. But the old crook came back as fast as a rattlesnake.

"Maybe that's right, young feller, I'm not saying it's not. And if this bursts open there'll be my guts all over the pavement. But if someone else gets hold of those pictures, someone a bit brighter than a runaway Thai kid, they could lean on me something rotten. And you'd never know, would you? And no one else would either. They could push me into all sorts of things, and you know I've got a lot of influence in industrial relations in this country. So you'd better get up off your arse and get looking, son, or we're all in *shtuck*."

There was a click as his telephone went down.

"So Lee's got some naughty photos," I said. "He could do some damage with those."

"What did Walter mean by what he said at the end?" Kim asked. "Does it mean it's very important?"

Very important. I thought about that. There'd certainly be people at the Russian Embassy who'd like to have those pictures. At the American Embassy, too. Any villain, from your corner-shop blackmailer upwards, could find a use for them. In the offices of the British security agencies, they'd be having nervous breakdowns all over the carpet. Porn pictures of a leading left-wing MP and industrial militant was the espionage equivalent of the crown jewels.

"Yes," I said. "It's important."

The light was on outside Jenny's. She came to the door

when she heard the car. She had hot soup ready for us. I left the two of them drinking coffee at the kitchen table while Kim advised her how to recognize high-quality batik.

If the world's going to end, you wouldn't want to be wearing the wrong sort of batik, would you?

31

One second after my clothes hit the floor, I hit the mattress.

It was four o'clock in the morning when I got back to Wandsworth and I was so whacked that one of the burlier members of the local brownie pack could probably have taken me without much effort.

I dreamed. It was one of those "nearly" dreams where whatever you want is always just beyond your fingertips. I was chasing Starburn through Sheffield when we came to a square where a girls' choir all in white were singing. Each girl had a face like Liz, but when I bent to kiss them, each one turned into Lee.

For two days I did nothing, with contemplative intensity.

I dozed in front of the gas fire. I practiced my washing-up. I built myself up with nourishing foods like chicken pies and Cornish pastries and alphabet spaghetti to help me with my reading. Next I'm going to do number spaghetti for my sums.

I did exercises for my weak arm. When I was in hospital after being shot up, I couldn't move a finger. My first efforts were with a matchbox. So I was pleased to be able to do some restricted movements with a light dumbell.

Even so, I decided to restrict it to light work—like slipping down ladies' underwear. Then I remembered Liz and was sad, and thought of Tamara and almost rang her: but in my mind I could only see that straight-backed survivor from the sexual holocausts of Bangkok.

In case it got to be a habit, I rationed myself to no

more than ten playings a day of the Kid Ory trombone break on "Sidewalk Blues."

I sent a card to my Auntie Norah for her eighty-first birthday. The first from me since about her fifty-eighth.

The farthest I got was the launderette, spiritual home of the spouseless.

When I was washing my Morris in the street—in the hope that it would go faster, cleaner—the woman from the flat upstairs stopped to tell me a man had been looking for me. I asked if he had a bandanna and immediately felt foolish, like a *Treasure Island* character forever on the lookout for a seafaring man with one leg. Anyway, the man she described was too tall for the Chimp.

"Your lady friend hasn't been around for a while," she added smugly. "It's been nice and quiet."

"She can't get away," I said. "The convent has got her on night duty."

I carried out the only two rituals I have left from my army days. I cleaned my shoes. Both pairs. I did them bullshit-style: wax, water, polish; wax, water, polish. It isn't pride, it's therapy.

And I took apart my Browning Hi-power on the kitchen table and cleaned it. That isn't pride, that's love.

They're standard issue to army officers because they're easy to work.

I knew an officer in the signals—a fighting crew second only to the Royal Corps of Commissionaires—who'd only fired his once in anger. It was when the storeroom key was lost. He remembered seeing gangsters shoot doors open in films and thought he'd do the same.

"Stand back, chaps," he said, and fired. The bullet ricocheted off the brass plate and he shot himself in the foot.

I cleaned it up with Rangoon oil, did the barrel with rod and brush, and put it together again. I weighed it in my hand. It was cold, black, and heavy, and it had the one indispensable quality I look for in a gun: people who'd been shot by it didn't get up again.

All I was doing, really, was passing time. I'd known that joyous ache in my bones too often to mistake the coming storm for a change in the weather.

Two or three times a day I spoke to Kim.

"Has he phoned?" we'd both ask. Kim had recorded both telephone numbers for him, safely camouflaged in Thai.

She took Luke out for walks and talked with Jenny, and, to my delight, told me how she loved them both.

On the second day, early in the afternoon, she told me that Kit had walked in unexpectedly.

A bit indignantly, she insisted that he hadn't asked her anything about why she was there. He was charming, she said. Even so, I couldn't be sure how much he knew or why he was there.

"If Lee rings, don't let him come to the house," I told her.

"Where shall I tell him to go?"

She didn't know that part of the country at all. I didn't know it much better. Then I remembered the Winnie the Pooh map Jenny kept on the pinboard.

It didn't mean much to me. When other kids were listening to stories about Pooh-sticks, I was sharpening up my shop-lifting techniques in Woolworth's.

But Kit and I had kept the map on the wall for finding good training runs for Luke. There was one we'd marked with a ball-point ring, I remembered. It was the place where we'd met Blanchland. On the map it was Gill's Lap, between Chuck Hatch and King's Standing. In the books, it was the Enchanted Place.

Kim found it. Carefully she repeated the instructions on how to get there.

Lee would be coming by car, she said. He'd taken Walter's blue-and-silver Panther.

"When he phones, give him instructions to go there.

Give me ninety minutes clearance. I can get there in that time. And tell him to bring the pictures. And don't say a word of this to Kit."

"I won't, of course, Pete, but you're wrong, he's very—"

"Charming, you already said. But don't tell him anything."

The next time I telephoned, Kit himself answered.

"We want you to be the first to know," he said. "Diana has okayed a divorce. Jenny and I are getting married."

"Oh, God, so it's Waterloo after all," I said in mock-misery.

"Well, I asked about your old school but all the juvenile prisons are overcrowded," he said.

"Hey, don't start getting witty," I said. "That's great news, Kit. For Luke and everyone. You're the only fellow I ever knew who was nearly good enough for our kid."

"We've got a bottle of bubbly on ice and it won't be opened until you get here."

"And Luke really is . . ."

Quietly, he replied, "Of course, Peter."

He was so excited he nearly said "yes."

And I was, too. It was what I'd always wanted. A full-time chap for Jenny and a proper home life for Luke. I thought I could chance leaving the telephone for five minutes while I nipped around the corner to get a bottle of champagne to take down with me, whenever I went.

I was whistling when I slipped on my jacket and whistling when I opened the door. I was still whistling when Big John's knuckles grated on my teeth.

By the time I'd shaken the fireworks out of my head, I was back inside the flat. The door was closed. Ginger had my jacket pulled down to my elbows behind me. My good arm was as immobile as the weak one.

In front of me Big John Dodd held up his famous flat knuckles. I'd been so busy thinking of the Chimp that I hadn't thought he might have been looking for me.

He was watching me without any pleasure.

"Get to it John!" Ginger urged him over my shoulder.

He ignored him. "This is business, Pete." It wasn't far off from an apology.

"Let me work him over," Ginger demanded.

John kept his eyes on mine. "He'd stuff you with both his hands behind his back, Ginge," he said. Then to me he said, "Mr. Miller isn't pleased, Pete. He says to ask you who you're working for."

Behind me, Ginger snickered. "Whoever it is don't pay much or he wouldn't live in this soddin' dump."

"I'm an eccentric millionaire," I said. "The last of the amateur baddies."

"Who is it, Pete? Who is your boss?"

"Who's yours, John? Miller? Who's his? Starburn? Who's working for who and who's against who? Tell me, John. I don't know."

He shook his head. "And you're going to say you don't know about any photographs or any Chinky boy?"

"And you're going to say this hurts you more than it hurts me, aren't you?"

This time he grinned when he shook his head. "Not soddin' likely," he said, and he hit me. Then I knew how he'd got flat knuckles.

His fists flew at me in flocks, four or five hammering in at my stomach and ribs, and then three or four more at my face. He worked in spurts. He'd half turn away, then move back in with both his big hands going. Then he'd take a couple of steps and come around at a different angle. When I began to sink, he worked like boxers do on a punchball, drumming his fists downward.

By then my faculties for appreciation were dimming. Pain's like humor; you can only take so much. The first punch is the one that hurts most, just like the first joke makes you laugh the most. After a dozen or so it's just another punch or just another joke, and the law of diminishing returns sets in.

RETRIEVAL

He didn't really try to get anything out of me. You don't do that with fists. He was teaching me not to be a naughty boy.

When the telephone rang he was breathing heavily with the effort. So was I. I could hear the blood and spittle bubbling in my nose and mouth. Although it was like seeing underwater, I could still see: mostly his hands, red as a butcher's, and his serious craftsman's attention to his job.

He dropped his hands when the telephone rang.

Ginger must have released my jacket because I crashed face down on the floor.

"Leave it," I heard John say.

"What if it's the Chinky?" Ginger said.

Neither of them were very interested in me.

"Yeah," John said, thoughtfully. "Yeah, it might be. I'll take it."

He walked across to the telephone and I watched him pick it up. Ginger trailed behind him.

That was all the time I needed to climb to my feet, wrench open the door, and start swinging myself up the steps to the pavement.

For a late November afternoon, it looked dazzlingly bright. There was shouting everywhere. From behind me in the flat and from in front of me here. I could see the woman schoolteacher from upstairs, her mouth wide open, backing away.

None of that mattered. As I hauled myself up the steps, I saw in outline a drawing of great clarity and beautiful simplicity. It showed that a man at the top of a flight of eight stone steps has his feet on the same level as the face of a man coming up behind him.

I spun around. I grabbed the rail for balance. I jabbed out my leg like a man kick-starting a motorbike. My heel hit Big John half-an-inch under the right eye. I felt it give, like a rotten floorboard.

One of his hands, still red from his afternoon's work,

rose and touched the spot. He straightened. Slowly he
wheeled around, as though he intended going back inside.

Finally he crashed face down and lay still at the bottom
of the steps.

My heels hit just beneath his shoulder blades and the
wind went out of him like a burst bag.

I leaned against the wall and looked at him. There
wasn't much left, and what there was wouldn't cause any
problems.

I didn't even bother to move when Ginger burst out of
the door, scrambled up the steps with fingers and toes, and
went clattering away down the street. He was only ever a
walk-on part, even in his own life.

"Sorry, John," I said. "It's just business."

He didn't seem interested.

32

But Gus Miller did half an hour later when I walked through the door of Tracy's with Big John over my shoulder and dropped him on the cribbage table.

Cards scattered. The cribbage board landed on the floor and spilled its match markers.

Miller was on his feet in a second. He shot around the back of his chair, pointed at the vast frame loosely hanging face-downward over the table, and said, "Christ, who's that?"

"Big John," I said, between gasps. "I've brought back your garbage, Miller."

When he saw me, astonishment broke up his face: his jaw gaped, his eyebrows flew up, his eyes widened. I knew why. I'd seen myself in the car mirror. My face looked like a raw hamburger.

"Don't worry," I said. "We've just been doing a bit of light knuckle-flattening. He came second."

For all the pain, I'd got another shot of adrenaline to fire me up again. Ask any psychologist—if you take a hammering and lose, you're down, but you can lift yourself from a beating if you win.

When I jumped on him and saw Ginger run for it, a surge of triumph put the heart back into me. I dragged John up the steps by his collar. Somehow—it wasn't easy—I heaved him into the passenger seat. By this time, the headmistress was watching me out of her ground-floor window. All I feared was the police coming around the corner before I got away. They didn't, and I still had time to pick up the Browning and drink two pints of cold tap water.

RETRIEVAL

I willed myself to concentrate on the drive across South London. Twice my sagging passenger fell across me and had to be toppled back. At a traffic light in Clapham, a young black idling at the guardrail saw the pair of us and reeled back with his hand over his mouth.

At Tracy's, I ran the car up on the pavement outside the front door. I had to conserve this last flood of strength. I didn't think it would last long.

All I wanted to do was to nail Miller and find out which end he was playing from.

It was late afternoon now and the club was almost empty. Apart from Miller and his cribbage partner, the other heavy coat, there were a couple of drunks at the bar and four youngsters playing pool. The drunks sobered up and the pool players stopped playing when I delivered my parcel.

"You bleedin' killed him," Miller gasped, awestricken.

The pool players began to move toward the door. Miller's pal tried to edge around behind me. I froze him with a glance.

"He's not dead," I said. "I just bent him a bit."

"Why d'you bring him here?" Miller asked. Slowly the shrewdness was returning to his face.

"I thought you might like to see what happened to him."

There was a sudden scuttering at the door. I looked over my shoulder. The pool players had gone.

"I don't get you, Pete," Miller said, affable in a white-faced sort of way.

"You sent him. I returned him."

I gave him a stony stare.

"Pete!" Miller stood there, his coat hanging open and his hands widespread as he declared his innocence. "On my mother's and father's lives, God bless 'em, I ain't had nothing to do with it. Honest."

I slapped John's foot. It flapped. "He said you wanted to know where the Thai boy was and what had happened to the pictures. He said you were angry I hadn't taken your warning. He's your boy, Miller. What's left of him."

"No, Pete, you got it all wrong. . . ."

Focusing was a problem. Miller's figure faded into a mist then came up again, leering sincerity at me. My legs were trembling.

"You warned me off, Miller. You'd been tipped off by Ginger Mattorini."

"Granted, I'd heard a little dicky bird," he said, by now positively avuncular. "And I was hoping to turn it to my advantage, I'll give you that. When I decked you, I was asking you to step aside and let the dog see the rabbit, that's all."

"Oh, no, Miller, you waved Big John at me."

"'Course I did, son. I knew you'd seen him and I knew you were impressed. I thought it wouldn't do any harm to throw him in as a persuader."

"So you sent him around."

"No, that's what I keep trying to tell you. John didn't work for me. He was too big-time. Very expensive boy, Big John."

"So why was he with Ginger then?"

"Ginger'd string along with anyone for a few quid. He was about as exclusive as Nell Gwyn, eh?" He cackled and tried to pass the laugh on to me. It died on the floor somewhere between us.

I couldn't think. He could be telling the truth. It would be out of character, but he could be. And he'd probably say that anyway with a bloodstained monster lurching around in front of him.

I gave up the mental struggle. The trembling in my legs was beginning to hit my arms. My brain was swaying.

I flapped one arm at him.

"Don't get under my feet, Miller," I said. I headed for the door. I was rocking now. The room tilted and I saw that Miller and his friend were working their way along the walls, also toward the door.

208

RETRIEVAL

"You don't look too good, Pete," Miller said. "You sit down for a minute and I'll get you a drink."

They were doing what we military strategists call a pincer movement. I tried to speed up my walk but the two of them had met at the door and turned to face me.

I looked back. The two men at the bar suddenly turned their backs on me. Head down, the barman busily polished glasses.

Then the U.S. cavalry came skipping through the door in a knitted dress that had more holes than wool.

"Yummy! All my favorite people here together," whooped Tamara. Then she saw my face. "Oh, my poor love, what have you been doing."

She pushed through Miller and his friend and took me by the arm.

"Excuse me, sweeties, but I simply must get him home and we'll have to have drinkie-poos another time."

Whatever they started now would have to include her. They exchanged glances and nods. It wasn't worth it.

"That's what we was just saying," Miller said, taking my other arm and helping me through the door. "Get yourself home and get to bed, Pete lad, I said. But he would drop his friend John off here first. Anyway darlin', you get him home and in bed and don't you go dancing around in your frilly nighties, eh?"

"You see," she told me, in the car, "it's always the same when you socialize with the working class. They take advantage."

33

Tamara took me back to her house in Flood Street. She said she'd be worried if she left me in my own place.

I'd never been there before. Through the haze of pain, I glimpsed a long drawing room with a white baby grand that looked unfinished without Noël Coward. Then I lost my feet in a shag-piled bedroom carpet and finally sank into a bed as wide and warm as a merry widow.

Tamara had been threatening me with doctors but, after some opposition from me, settled for a friend of hers called Sammy Dalrymple who was a medical student.

Sammy turned out to be one of her lissom female friends, but she seemed to know her way around a tenderized carcass.

"Dozens of contusions and lacerations," she reported to Tamara at the bedside afterward. "But, apart from one rib, I don't think there's anything actually broken. I think we ought to run him to hospital for an X-ray though."

"He won't," Tamara said. "Will you?"

I shook my head and immediately wished I hadn't. My brain had shattered into a dozen pieces.

"What have you been doing?" asked Sammy.

I pointed at Tamara. "She's a tiger," I mumbled.

When I woke up again, it was noon the following day. Tamara brought me a strong coffee and a croissant.

"How's my little hero?" she asked.

"I feel as though I've rolled down Everest," I said.

"And what," she said, holding up my Browning in its waist holster, "is this for?"

"Careful. You'll soak everything. Those water pistols
are so dangerous."

She rolled up her eyes. "*Quelle* silliness. Oh, Pete,
darling, whatever are you mixed up in?"

That sounded a profitless line of inquiry, so I let it go.

"And how dare you lie in my bed and shout out the
name of that dreadfully common little union person?" she
said.

I couldn't think who she meant.

"That horrid Starburn man," she explained. "You kept
on calling out 'Starburn sent him!'—I assumed that was
who you meant. There can't be two like him."

If I hadn't been afraid of the pain, I would have smiled.
Starburn didn't have a big following in fashionable Chelsea.

As my head began to clear, I was able to understand
what had happened. It had been Tamara who'd telephoned
when Big John and Ginger were working me over. He'd
said "hello," then put the receiver down, so she'd driven
straight over to see what was the matter.

Our teacher friend upstairs had called to her and said
there'd been a dreadful scene. I'd come home with some
friends, all of us drunk, and there'd been a fight. I'd gone off
in my car with one of them. When the woman described
him, Tamara thought it was John, and she also thought
she'd recognized his voice from the one word on the
telephone.

At Tracy's, she'd realized what was going on and had
extricated me as quickly as she could.

"There," she said, all fluttery with delight at her
success. "I'm quite G.O.O.B., too, aren't I?"

"Keep everything very simple, there's a good girl," I
groaned. "What's G.O.O.B. mean?"

"Good Out Of Bed, silly. I'm terribly G.I.B., but you
know that anyway. Perhaps I'd better come in and curl up
with you now you're feeling better. Sammy said there was
only one bit of you that wasn't damaged and I said it was the
only bit that seemed to do any work. . . ."

I stayed in bed all day, rested and molested in turn.

Big John had done a good job on me. Looking at the result, you could almost hear his instructions, "Work him over but don't break anything." He was very well-disciplined with those fists of his. On the other hand, I had the edge when it came to footwork.

It had to be Starburn. I was reluctant to think my old friend would send a hood out for me. I was even more reluctant to think that Miller might tell the truth. But it made sense.

If Miller had sent him, he couldn't have cared if he'd snapped off my limbs and fed them to the ducks. And John could have speared Yokel. He was strong enough. He was certainly mean enough.

All along it had been Starburn trying to save his reputation. He'd tried to buy me out of the game, now he was trying to beat me out of it.

But he couldn't bring himself to have me killed, like Yokel. It all squared off neatly.

I must have willed it to happen. As I lay thinking about him, the LBC newsreader on the bedside radio mentioned Starburn's name. I turned it up.

". . . denied the reports in the newspapers. Mr. Starburn said his wife and her brother had gone away for a short break and he had no intention of exposing them to this type of personal publicity. There was no possibility of his marriage breaking up."

Then came Starburn's voice, aglow with confidence and vivacity. "It's typical of the capitalist media, when there are millions of honest workingmen on the dole, to try to discredit one of the few politicians who's forthright enough to stand up for them. And these sorts of squalid gutter tactics show how low the so-called free press is prepared to sink."

He was sincere all right, but he seemed to believe his sincerity absolved him from all normal human responsibilities.

212

RETRIEVAL

While I administered some Caledonian medicine to myself, single-malt whisky, taken orally, Tamara waltzed off to ring in to my answering machine.

When she came back she was crying. She sat on the edge of the bed and tears hung in her eyes.

"What's wrong?" I asked, reaching out for her hand. She let me take it, without joining in much herself.

"Oh, Pete," she said. "You've got another woman."

"Another woman?"

"Yes, don't pretend, that's horrid. I heard her on your answering machine just now. She sounds foreign, Japanese or something."

She gave a great gulping sob. The tears swelled over the eyelids and wobbled down her cheeks.

"What did she say? I've got to know what she said."

I was crushing her hand. She winced, but she saw the urgency in my face.

"She said she wants you desperately. There were quite a few messages. She'd obviously been ringing a lot. Oh, Pete, is she pestering you?"

"What else? What else did she say? Did she mention anyone called Lee?"

Tamara's eyes widened. "Yes, she did. She said Lee had phoned and it was all arranged, everything you'd suggested."

"What? Where? Did she give a time?"

She wiped the tears off her face and stopped crying. "She said midnight at the Enchanted Place. Oh, Pete, you're not going to meet her for jollies, are you?"

I said I wasn't. I said it was work, an important job I had to finish. I swung my legs out of bed. I had plenty of time. All the same, I was in poor shape and I wanted to get moving.

"Oh dear." Tamara was standing watching me.

"What's the matter? Hey, Tamara, look, you've been marvelous, you really have."

RETRIEVAL

"You've been a brick, Angela," she said in her best upper-class accent.

"I don't mean it like that; you know I don't. As soon as I've finished I'll take you for the best dinner in London."

"It's the Big L, isn't it?"

"What? What do you mean, the Big L . . . oh, I see."

"It's that foreign girl, isn't it? It's the Big L and you're going to want to marry her and live in Reigate. Oh, *quelle* agony."

The thought that she could be right was more scaring than anything John's fists had done to me. I hadn't thought about love for many years. My experience of it had been limited and entirely disastrous.

The idea of it now was like most adults feel about getting mumps: that they're far too old for it, it will be very undignified, and possibly crippling.

By the time I'd got dressed and had something to eat, Tamara had recovered.

She snuggled up against my chest as I was going. "It's marvelous news really," she said. "You'll be hopeless at being faithful, and anyway all those funny little Eastern people are useless at jollies so you'll want to come to see me at least 2.3 times a week. . . ."

34

This time I did get my bottle of champagne—and without running into any fists.

I headed down through Crystal Palace to avoid the rush-hour traffic. So, too, did half-a-million other drivers, so I had time to sit and marvel at the way Tamara's treatment—drawn equally from the *British Manual of Nursing* and the *Kama Sutra*—had at least half-restored me.

She'd cried when I left, but I knew she didn't feel too badly about it. She was convinced I'd be back. She said we had so little in common it was a miracle we weren't married already. This was getting dangerous—the girl was taking my lines.

"And you'll find anyone else awfully bland after me," she said.

As I left, she was thumbing through an address book that would have made Errol Flynn's look like the property of a recluse. Today's women.

It was an odd mission I was going on: to celebrate with one friend who was marrying my sister, and to search for the killer of my other friend. We'd come a long way since Yokel and I refused a lift in Kit's truck in the Black Mountains.

At Jenny's the celebrations were delayed while she examined my face. It had improved so much I'd almost forgotten about it. But there was still enough puffiness and bruising to upset Jenny.

"Whatever have you been doing?" she asked.

Kit coughed and fussed with a champagne cork.

RETRIEVAL

The atmosphere was one of affectionate embarrassment. All the years of secrecy and discretion couldn't be cast aside instantly.

"You did suspect, didn't you?" Jenny asked. She was so happy she couldn't stop talking about it.

"He was number one suspect, a cad like him," I said, "despite all your denials."

"But you weren't sure?" Kit asked.

"No." I looked nervously at Luke who was wandering around dazed by the revelation. I whispered to Kit, "Don't you remember? You told me you couldn't have kids."

Kit reddened. "I seem to remember something of the sort."

"Why?" I asked.

"It wouldn't have been the thing to let a woman take the blame," he said, amid much spluttering and coughing. "Even Diana."

"Isn't it great, Luke?" I said, kneeling down to give him a hug. He couldn't speak for happiness.

"I'll tell you something. I was thinking of taking you to the dads' department in Selfridges, but they wouldn't have had one as good as this, would they?"

He shook his head.

"But, I'll tell you something. He was a rotten uncle. So I'll take over the uncle duties full-time now, eh?"

It was a pleasant little wallow in domestic emotions—something of a break for a fellow like me—and then I looked up and saw something which stopped my heart.

On the pinboard was the Winnie the Pooh map. My small pencil mark next to the Enchanted Place had been replaced by a thick red ring. Alongside it was written the one word: midnight.

You could have read it from the other side of the road.

"Where's Kim?"

"Upstairs," said Jenny. "She wanted to keep out of the way. She said it was a family affair. You know, she's an awfully nice girl. . . ."

She was sitting on the bed in a dark-blue terry cloth robe that I'd left there.

I sat down beside her and got her to tell me the whole story.

Lee had rung from a coin box in central London. He was frightened and he had no money. He'd been sleeping in his car. She had told him carefully where we were to meet, and he'd now so lost his nerve that he'd be glad of any help I could give him.

She suggested midnight because she thought it would be safer to meet in the dark, and also to give me plenty of time to get down here.

I saw there was no point in telling her she shouldn't have written it up on the map on the pinboard. It could have been worse. She could've put it in the *Standard*.

"Can you help Lee?" she asked.

I nodded. "If he gives me the pictures, I can get Starburn to cooperate. He's going to be on a murder charge; there's no doubt about that, but if he gives himself and the pictures up I might be able to make it a bit easier for him. That's all I can promise."

"If he doesn't?"

"If he doesn't, he'll be killed."

Her round head bobbed. That was what she'd expected.

She rose slowly, her head down, and unfastened the belt of the robe. It fell open. She stood there for a moment, as though expecting help. Then she opened it fully and shook it off her arms at the back. Only then did she raise her face and let me see her eyes.

She was perfect. A cream-colored miniature of delicate detail.

I had to reach hard for my next breath.

I didn't move. I didn't speak. I couldn't do either.

She realized and smiled. Then she stepped forward and touched me and said, "You like?" in exactly the same way as the bar girls in Patpong.

I looked into her eyes and saw neither love nor lust. She was simply paying a debt with the only currency she had.

Confusion came into her face.

"Don't you want me?" she said.

I was pretty close to being dumbfounded. I put my hands on her shoulders in an asexual sort of way.

"Look," I said, wondering what I was going to say next. "Is this all?"

She frowned and looked down. "Isn't it all right?" she asked.

"Oh yes, fine, I mean wonderful. But are you just doing this as . . . well, a favor . . . because . . ."

In my bumbling she had seen the truth. She sat down, but made no attempt to cover herself.

"What else can I do? You have been very kind and this is the only way I can thank you. This is all there is, my body. You are welcome to use it."

"Yes, but, like that, without . . ."

She kept her gaze down. "Without anything. I am sorry. That is all I have left."

Slowly she did lift her eyes. "Sometimes a man would sit looking at me and wonder whether to have me or another bottle of Tiger beer. Often they would have the beer."

Pitifully, I tried to swerve the conversation. "Yeah, I know, but what you've been in the past doesn't change . . ."

"It changes everything. I have learned that sex is nothing and my body is nothing and it doesn't matter what people do to it. Love? Yes, there is love of my child. That is all."

"Have you forgotten Wayne and Sheffield?"

"There was no Wayne," she said. "I got the name from the film star, John Wayne."

"But what about Sheffield? And your dream?"

She shrugged. "Some customer must have mentioned

Sheffield. That is all. You don't understand. How can you? I didn't have a dream so I had to invent one. Everyone has to have a dream."

"So who was Lee's father?"

She picked up the terry cloth robe and began to put it on. She was too naked now, in every sense.

"His father?" she repeated wearily. "Every man was his father. Sometimes I would have twenty or thirty men a day. It could have been any of them. It could have been you, couldn't it? We all look the same."

I left her sitting there. There was no more to say. The truth is strong stuff and you don't want to overdose on it.

I told Jenny and Kit I had to go back to London.

"Really?" Kit said. "I was hoping you might stay overnight."

I tried to read his face but there was nothing there.

As I was getting in the car, I heard Kim's voice calling me. She was at an upstairs window.

"Look after Lee please," was all she said.

35

By day it belongs to the picnickers and pony riders and families in rubber boots and lone men with Labradors. But at night the Ashdown Forest is handed back to the old gods.

I'd whiled away an hour or more in a pub and dawdled up the road through Hartfield and Chuck Hatch and past the sign warning motorists against deer, sheep, and horses. But it was still half an hour short of midnight when I pulled off the road at Gill's Lap and got out.

It was an enchanted place, but not in any way I'd imagine A. A. Milne would write about it.

From the top of the slope, the only signs of humanity at night were the far lights of a distant village. I was in the middle of a clearing ringed by a ten-foot fence of dagger-sharp gorse bushes. The hillside sloped away in patches of bracken and heather, with clusters of trees here and there, and vanished into a valley that was lost in the moonlight.

I realized I was standing under the five pines where Blanchland had briefed us that day on the retrieval. This was where it had begun. This was where it would finish.

A clear moon lit the plateau where I stood and the hillside below, but you could still have hidden a regiment there for six months.

It wasn't a comfortable thought. I had to stand out in the open to encourage Lee to come to me. I wasn't the hunter at all. I was the tethered goat, and I didn't know how many tigers were going to turn up.

To pass the time, I walked around, the moorland grass springing under my feet. A wind got up. It hummed in the heather and the bracken. In the silence, it sounded like the earth breathing.

When I first saw him he was near the bottom of the valley. He must have parked on the other side of the forest and walked across.

Although he was hurrying—he stooped once or twice to pull himself up the gradient on the heather—I found myself urging him on as though it was some sort of race. And I stepped out of the five trees so he could see me clearly, and see that I was alone.

You couldn't have shouted there any more than you could in church. I tried calling out his name, but it was whipped away on the wind. He didn't look up. But he kept on coming.

When the hill began to level out, he stood upright and looked around. All I could see was a diminutive figure in a short jacket and jeans. I called his name again. This time he did hear. He raised one hand and began to jog toward me. He had a packet in the other. I went to meet him.

"Hold it!"

I hadn't got three paces when a voice—a voice I knew and in the trained, imperative tone I also knew—stopped both of us.

Twenty yards away to my left, a figure had stepped out of the gorse. He was a short, stocky man and his long hair only lifted around his neck because it was held down by a bandanna above his ears.

It was the Chimp. At his hip he had the Mossberg. It was trained on Lee. The three of us formed a triangle, each roughly twenty yards apart.

"I'm sorry, Lee," I called over to him. "I didn't know."

The Chimp ignored me. He almost always did.

"Bring the photographs here," he said. He motioned with the barrel of the shotgun.

The Thai boy said nothing. He was in the bent-knee position he'd held since the Chimp surprised us.

I could see the tension in his pose.

RETRIEVAL

"Take it to him," I urged him. "Hand it over, Lee."

An age passed. The wind stiffened. A scarf of a cloud hazed the moon. The yellow tips of the gorse were the only color in the whole valley.

Then the Chimp made his mistake. He got impatient and moved forward. Even as he did it I was wrenching my Browning out of its waist holster, but I knew I was going to be too late.

Lee spun and ran for it. His legs kicked up sideways to clear the tangle of the bracken and he doubled up to make himself a smaller target, but none of that mattered now.

The boom from the Mossberg blasted him in the back and flung him forward, arms and legs out like a star. The crack of my pistol was a fraction behind it, but it was still too late.

Lee went down with a high, final yowl. The Chimp gave a beast's grunt as the shotgun was kicked out of his hands by the bullet which hit his elbow. He was going to dive for the Mossberg when he saw the look on my face and the steadiness of the pistol in my hand. Then he cursed and grabbed his elbow with his left hand.

I walked past him without a word. Behind me, on the road, I heard a car draw up, but I wasn't interested in that now.

When I reached Lee I turned him over. My stomach turned to lead and the night cold suddenly ran into my veins. It was Kim.

She was still alive. But I could see from the blood that was pumping out between the fingers she had clasped over her breast that she wouldn't be for long.

I knelt down beside her. I touched her cold face with one finger. I didn't speak. They don't make words for times like that.

I remembered her words. At night and at a distance, I hadn't recognized her. They did all look the same. She'd banked on it. She'd survived starvation and brothels to be gunned down beneath the moon at an English beauty spot.

RETRIEVAL

"I thought you might betray him," she said, her voice no more than a sigh now. "So I came in his place."

"Sshhh," I said, touching her face again.

"But you didn't," she said. "Not you."

"No. Not me."

"Try to help him. Please."

She didn't die. One minute she was alive. The next she was dead. She simply moved from one state to the other.

And all I could think was that if I'd made love to her earlier she might have trusted me more and let her son come.

I picked up a large brown envelope she'd dropped as she fell. I could see the word "Eva" handwritten on the front. As I walked back up the hill I saw Kit was standing with the Chimp.

"Give them to me please, Peter," he said, as I got near. He held out his hand.

"It's the girl," I said. "She's dead."

"I know." Kit nodded toward a black sedan parked farther up the hill. "Lee's in there. She met him in the village. We missed her but picked him up okay."

I turned to the Chimp. He was still holding his elbow. The sleeve of his anorak was dark with blood.

"You bastard," I said, calmly. "You didn't have to shoot her."

"That's your judgment," he said, without concern.

"He was right," Kit said. "We couldn't risk losing her. Not with those photographs. Let me have them please, Peter."

"Was this your operation, Kit?" I asked. "From the start?"

"It was," he said.

His face was strained. Three hours earlier he'd asked me to be best man at his wedding. Even his sense of propriety must be sagging under this pressure.

"We used to think we were the elite, didn't we? The best soldiers in the world. Now the best funnies."

Neither of them spoke.

"So we end up shooting up a load of Germans and risking our lives to drag a little painted poofter back for an old London queen. Is that the great battle for democracy? Is that all there is to it, Kit?"

He pushed his hair back. "You know there's more to it than that. We couldn't leave the boy in the East. The Russians would have had complete control over one of the most important figures in British politics. You know how much influence he's got in industry. God knows what they would have had him doing. And he did ask us to get the . . . to get the boy out."

The Chimp was looking bored. He went and picked up his shotgun, cursing as his injured arm moved.

"What about Yokel?"

Kit raised his voice in self-justification. "He was warned off enough times, God knows. He shouldn't have blabbed like that. Then to start playing at amateur detectives on top of everything else . . . dammit, Peter!"

"So this ape killed him?"

The Chimp never even looked up at me, although he heard me well enough. Only actions interested him.

Two men who'd got out of the car earlier walked back with the girl's body. It only took one of them to carry her, although the other must have gone to help him. I could have told them that, I thought. She was so delicate, so lovely.

"And then I wouldn't be warned off, Kit? That must have been very irritating for you."

He ignored the irony. "You were a problem, certainly."

"So Big John came to call. A thug, a criminal . . . these are our new colleagues-in-arms, eh?"

He shifted from one foot to the other. "We have to use whatever raw material there is. Starburn wanted him to go much further. But I insisted that he mustn't do any real damage."

"So honest men die and others are beaten up to keep a
xual pervert safe?"

"To keep the country safe."

"That's the joke of it, isn't it? Starburn's a revolutionary,
Marxist who'd tear down every institution you believe in,
d he'd start with outfits like ours."

He breathed in and gave a long sigh. "A revolutionary
an essential part of the fabric of democracy. And if he's a
volutionary who's under control, so much the better."

"Because he gives the illusion of freedom to the poor
ols who put crosses on ballot papers?"

"We'll talk about it later," he said. "Right now I want
ose photographs."

He held out his hand again.

"No, you can't have them."

He brought up his other hand. It held a Browning,
o. He felt the same way as I did about the officers' gun.

"Give it to me, Peter. It's your duty to your country."

"I prefer my duty to me."

"Enough people have died. Hand it over."

"No, enough haven't. Not yet. One more. Just one
ore."

He pulled back the slide. He thought I was talking
out myself.

"Don't make me, Peter. You know I will if I have to."

I nodded. "I know you will. That's what's really so
rrible about it."

"I will do my duty. We both took the oath of allegiance.
oesn't that mean anything to you?"

He'd hoped it wouldn't come to this, but all the time
'd known it would. He'd wanted to do it by beating my
ill down with his own. He'd failed. Now it was the gun. In
e end, after all the talking and all the voting and all the
erished processes of civilization, it always comes down to
man with a gun.

I pointed to my Morris Minor.

"I'm going now. I'm going to get in my car and drive

back to London. You've got a good two hundred yards in which to shoot me. You used to be pretty good, Kit. You can't miss."

I set off.

When I'd gone a few strides I heard the Chimp's voice, low but clear. "You don't have any choice, boss. Shoot"

I called back without turning my head, "And when you've done it, work out what you're going to tell Jenny and Luke. Because this time you daren't tell them the truth, however honorable you reckon you are."

I walked on. The men in the black sedan, which now presumably housed Kim's body, too, switched on their headlights. They shone directly across my path. They must have wanted to give him an even clearer target.

I walked through their beam like someone crossing a stream. The Morris was only thirty yards on the other side. I was in darkness now, but there was nothing to stop Kit running over to get a clear shot.

The car lights went off. Again there was nothing between us except an open stretch of moorland.

At the car door, I stopped. I looked around. It had been a long walk. They were both standing there as I had left them. I waved once, then struggled into the car. She started the second time. I drove off without rush. They were still standing there, in the moonlight, when the road dropped down and I lost sight of them.

In the end he was a better man than he was a soldier. I was glad about that. And not just because it kept me alive.

I switched on the car radio. I wanted noise. There's no silence quite as sinister as the silence you're not being shot in.

36

I didn't go straight to Starburn's. Instead, I went home.

I rearranged the heftier bits of furniture behind the door and slept sitting up in a chair, with my Browning on my knee.

I needn't have bothered. No one came. And no one was waiting the next morning when I drove down to the offices of the Royal National Institute for the Blind in Great Portland Street.

I had an interesting chat with a woman in their research department and an hour later I came out with the photographs in one of their envelopes. I drove east.

The door which led to the lift at Starburn's was open. All I had to do was walk in and press the button. There wasn't any muscle around at all.

I knew why when I saw Starburn standing by the window of his vast sitting room.

"Pete!" he roared, ablaze with bonhomie. "I've had your chief spook on half the night saying you were on your way. Gawd, they're a real panicky lot, aren't they?"

"Right now they are."

He held his arms up as though he was being attacked, then gave another blast of laughter. "They say I've got to beware of you. You're after my blood, that's what they reckon. Know what I told 'em, Pete?"

I did, but I still said "no."

"I told 'em Pete's my oldest mate, we go back a long way, and if the day ever comes I have to defend myself against him I'll jack it in, the bloody lot. Right?"

He was so confident he could turn me with the power

of his tongue. And it was hard not to respond to him. But I didn't.

"Where's your old lady?"

He looked surprised. "In her room. Down there." He indicated down the corridor. "Why?"

"I want a word with her. Okay?"

In his mood of trust and friendship, he couldn't say no. He waved me on the way.

"Second door down on the left," he said.

I knocked and went in. It was a big room, oddly furnished. The bed and bedside cabinets were as expensive and luxurious as the furniture in my room the night I'd stayed here. But there was a dining table and two chairs and an armchair that were all old, cheap, and battered. I realized they must have been relics from her earlier life.

She was sitting at the table, her head cocked.

"It's Pete again, ma," I said.

"Peter!" she said, holding her arms out for a kiss, "Back again, eh? What a treat."

She switched off the radio she'd been listening to, and dropped her voice to a whisper.

"You know she's gone, don't you. That Chinky. And her brother, the funny one."

"So I heard."

"Well, it didn't work. Stands to reason, don't it? He'll get a really nice girl now, you'll see. Someone who'll give him a bit of love."

"And you'll be a granny?"

She put a hand to her mouth to suppress her delight. "Don't get me going on that again. If wishes were horses . . ."

"Ma, there's something I wanted to ask you. If you heard something about Walter, a rumor like, but it's true as well, and it was something really awful wicked, would you believe it?"

"Like what?" She looked worried.

"Oh, I don't know. Say like if he was a rapist or something like that."

"Well, I wouldn't believe it, would I? Rubbish like that." She was scolding me for having even suggested it.

"No, but if it was proved. If there was evidence."

Her face set. "I still wouldn't."

"What if it was something like murder, or him being a sexual pervert, or something awful like that."

"What're you saying, Pete? It don't matter anyway. I wouldn't listen to it, I wouldn't believe it, and if I did then I'd know he had a good reason for anything he done. He could shoot the Queen and I'd still love him."

"I thought so."

"'Ere, he's not in trouble, is he?"

I knew that would be her reaction. There wasn't any point in leaving her distressed.

"No, no, don't worry about that. It's just that someone's making up a lot of wicked lies about Walter and I wanted you to be prepared for them."

She relaxed. "Thank goodness for that. I wondered what you was on about. Let 'em come to me. I'll tell them. He's been an angel to me, that boy has."

When I went back to the big room, Starburn was on the balcony. The black curls of his hair were lifting in a steady breeze downriver. The Thames was gray-brown, wide, and lifeless.

"You know she's dead?" I said, joining him.

"So your bosses said." He gave me an appraising look. "I was sorry. Really I was. She was a good girl."

"But you don't like girls, do you?"

He had both hands on the rail and he was watching a tourist boat puttering up the river. "I could stand here all day and watch them. Fascinating. Girls?" He grinned at me over his shoulder. "No, not for me, Pete, you know that."

"But little boys?"

He glanced at me again. Then he began to chuckle. It was a happy laugh, a happy, evil laugh.

"'Course I do, Pete. Always have. 'Course, it's n[ot]
approved of by this sick, bigoted society we live in toda[y].
No one minds VD running rife and little bits of girls havir[g]
abortions by the dozen and adultery and porn and all tha[t].
But if your fancy happens to be a beautiful boy—and h[e]
fancies you back—it's not allowed."

He turned and balanced on the rail. From where I w[as]
I could lean forward and push him over. I could. But most [of]
I couldn't.

"So where's the justice in that?" he asked, spreadir[g]
his innocent hands open. "One sort of love is as good [as]
another, isn't it? Where does it say your sort's better tha[n]
mine? Where's it say that? All them Romans and Gree[ks]
liked it that way and they started civilization off, did[n't]
they?"

"If you're so proud of your sexual preferences why a[re]
you so furtive about it? Frightened of what the voters mig[ht]
think?"

Oddly perhaps, I didn't really think that. He had a so[rt]
of integrity—distorted, maybe—that didn't need approva[l].
He was a strong man, Starburn. He always had been. [I]
wanted to hear what he'd say. I wanted to know I was righ[t].

"Me? You know better than that, Pete. Come on! [I]
don't give a toss what the great British public think. N[ot]
about me anyway. All right, so I don't get elected again. S[o]
what? I got power and I got cash through all my union ti[es]
and businesses."

I held up the packet with the photographs in.

"So no one could have blackmailed you with this l[ot]
anyway?"

Again he laughed, again it was a rich victory roll [of]
laughter.

I thought I'd let him have that one.

"No, that's it," he said, his whole body shaking wi[th]
laughter. "They can print them on the front page of the S[un]
for all I care."

"So what was it all about?"

230

"Security, that's what your lot call it. They wouldn't have it when I told them I didn't care. They said they couldn't risk it. Man in public office makes himself vulnerable. Turned them white overnight, that did."

I thought of Yokel speared, and the boy-girl knifed, and of Kim who died for her son, and that was the only real love in the whole damned business. A mother's love for her son. There was a son's love for his mother, too.

"But you wouldn't want her to know?" I tilted my head toward his mother's room.

He was still smiling. The whole thing amused him enormously. They'd all died trying to save him from something he didn't fear anyway. He'd always been impregnable.

"She never will."

"Someone could tell her."

"Go ahead. Tell her. She'll laugh in your face."

"Not if I proved it."

"Seeing's believing, and she can't see. That's the only way you'd ever convince her. I know you've got the photographs there. Go on in and give them to her."

As I stepped toward him, he pretended to fing an arm up to defend himself. "Help, he's going to push me off," he said. Then he gave me a playful punch in the chest.

I held the envelope up so he could see the lettering. RNIB.

"I know that lot," he said, puzzled. "That's the blind organization. I give them a quid or two."

"That's why I was late," I explained. "I called in there this morning and saw this woman in their research department. You been there, Starburn? You ought to go. Wonderful place. They're spending your money well."

"What's this spiel all about, Pete?" For the first time his rock-solid confidence began to flake.

"They've got some great equipment for blind people. New stuff, coming in all the time. From Japan and all over. Have you heard of photo-Braille?"

He shook his head. A darkness had come into his eyes.

"Shove an ordinary picture into it and it reproduces it for blind people."

"Rubbish! How can you have pictures for blind people?"

"They see with these," I wriggled my fingers at him. "Your old lady is brilliant at Braille. She told me so herself. She's so quick-minded, that's what does it. Anyway, where was I? Oh yeah. It's the same as Braille. It builds up a black-and-white picture with thousands of tiny dots and blind people can see the picture by running their fingers over it."

"It can't work," he said, quietly. "It can't."

"It did."

He pushed past me into the room and set off toward the corridor. Then he stopped.

I followed him back onto the balcony.

"Go on," I said, pleasantly. "Go in and ask her. She's very upset at the moment, though. She was crying."

He turned around slowly. Shaking his head from side to side, he said, "I don't believe you, Pete. You wouldn't."

I pulled the pictures out of the envelope. The greatest single invention for the benefit of blackmailers has been the time switch on cameras. In bedrooms all over the world, people who should know better set the camera up on the dressing table and run around to get in a suitable erotic pose for it.

I fanned them out for him. I wanted him to remember exactly how explicit they were. The two of them were naked. All the bits and pieces were shown, and in operation, too. Apart from that, they were mostly mouths and splayed legs.

"It took her a minute to pick you out," I went on. "'Course, she's only been blind three years and you're a very distinctive-looking feller. She thought little Eva was a girl at first because of that picture—there, that one of her in a wig. But not when I gave her this one."

I tapped another of them.

Starburn was transfixed. He stared at the photographs. He saw himself smirking with lascivious heat.

Finally, after a long silence, he said, "What do you want? Money?"

"No. What I want is this. This is your spear through the heart. Your bullet in the back."

He nodded. He could see that was reasonable.

"You always did beat me, you bastard," he said. "She took it bad?" His eyes went to the corridor.

"I think it's going to kill her," I said, quietly. "Unless it kills you first."

"Do you think she could live with it? If no one else ever knew?"

"Ask her," I said. It was so finely balanced now that I dared hardly trust myself to breathe.

He shook his head. "I can't face her, Pete. She'd never understand. Do you think she could manage?"

I held his pleading gaze for second after long second. The more it hurt, the more he'd believe it in the end.

"Yes," I said, eventually. "If someone cleaned up after you."

"Will you?" he asked. "For old times' sake."

I said nothing.

"Do it," he said. "Just bloody do it!"

He always had style and he always had courage, and never more than at that moment. Two-handed, he vaulted up, so that for a second he balanced with one foot on the top of the railing. I saw him look down, smile briefly, then stand up. For a timeless second, he wavered, with a wild swinging of his arms.

Then he just walked off into space. He went without a cry.

I walked over to the rail and looked down. Some workmen were hurrying over from a building site. One of them was pointing at a low crane he must have hit before bouncing off into the water. Then they were pointing into the lifeless water of the river.

One of them lay down on the concrete wharf and reached out. Another ran back into a works shed and came back a minute later with a pole.

When they got him out they laid the body on the wharf and waited for the police. He was dead. I could see that from the balcony.

"What's all the commotion?"

It was Mrs. Starburn. What were tiny squeaks of alarm to me were much more to her.

As a reflex, I quickly began to pick up the photographs and shuffle them together before putting them away.

"What are you doing? Walter? Pete?"

"It's only some old photographs, Mrs. S.," I said.

"What of, Pete?"

"Your Walter mostly," I said.

"I'd give anything to be able to sit down and have a good old rummage through some photos," she said. "That's one thing I do miss."

"There's some things they can't crack, even in this age of miracles."

Those were the exact words the woman at the RNIB had used when she told me there was no Braille equivalent for photographs.

"I suppose so," she said. Then she moved toward the window. "Whatever is going on down there?"

"I think it's an accident," I said.

A police car had drawn up at the wharf now and the two cops were looking up at the balcony.

"Oh dear. Poor sod."

"Poor sod," I repeated.